Myst DB.

MW01614098

Submission to Murder

by R. J. Loring

This book is a work of fiction. Names, characters, places, and incidents are the product of the author's imagination or are used fictitiously. Any resemblance to actual events, locals, or persons, living or dead, is coincidental.

First Edition 2012
ISBN-13: 978-1478308966
ISBN-10: 1478308966

Always for Ann

1

Her head felt heavy, and her vision was blurred. She attempted to move her arms and legs, but they wouldn't respond. Her throat was dry; her jaw ached. A few minutes passed—or was it a few hours?—before she tried to move again. Nothing registered correctly.

Then the clouds began to lift. She felt cool air waft over her bare bottom: someone had stripped off her clothes. She tried to move once more but was still unable. Her long, lean body was bent forward from the waist. Her wrists and ankles were bound to the legs of an antique whipping horse.

Standing before her was a shadowy figure. She tried hard to focus her eyes, but whatever drug the intruder had forced upon her made doing so extremely difficult. Finally, she was able to make out the trespasser's form: the ominous figure was wearing an executioner's mask and garb.

She wanted to speak, but speech was impossible: the pain she felt in her jaw was from a ball gag in her mouth. Frantically, she began fighting against her bonds. But it was useless. She knew no one escaped the grasp of the whipping horse once they were secured. All she could do was await the sting of the lash.

The figure in black reached for a flogger on the wall. Moving slowly behind her, the Executioner raised the cat-o'-nine-tails. It landed across her exposed buttocks. She shrieked. She heard the Executioner count, "One."

The whip came down again. She howled. By the third stroke, she was crying. The fourth initiated inarticulate pleas for mercy, but the beating continued.
Six...seven...eight.... She fought against her restraints, but they wouldn't give way. Nine...ten...eleven.... She began to bite down hard on her gag, but nothing eased the pain. Her muscles were tense, her eyelids shut tight, and her long blonde hair cut through the air as her head heaved violently. Each new stroke was more painful than the last. She didn't know how much more she could endure. Then the assault ended.

Tears stained her cheeks. Her eyes were red and swollen. Her nose ran profusely, and her throat was raw. She wasn't sure for how long the beating had gone on. The pain was excruciating. She tried to catch her breath and determine where the Executioner had gone. But the agony she was in prevented her from concentrating. Then, a sound.

Standing motionlessly behind her, the black-clad figure surveyed the victim. She winced as the fiend ran a bare hand across her welted bottom. Then her tormentor appeared before her. Balanced on one knee, the Executioner unbridled her mouth. The corners of her lips burned where the gag's leather strips had cut her. She gingerly moved her mouth. She was trying to extend her jaw when her head was yanked backward by the hair. She found herself staring deep into her captor's eyes. They were lifeless, like those of a shark about to attack. The silence terrified her. Then she heard a clock chime. It was midnight. As the sound of the final chime faded away, she gathered her courage and spoke.

"Who are you?" she gasped. "Why are you doing this?"

"You never said the safe word."

From behind the Executioner's back came a hand brandishing a knife. She felt a scrape across her outstretched neck. Blood sprayed across the room. Her eyes rolled backward in her head. The figure in black released her hair and watched her head go limp.

"Happy New Year. Welcome to 2012, you whore."

2

It looked as if all hell had broken loose. Two patrol cars blocked off either end of West Ninety-first Street. Their pulsating red lights splashed across the brownstones. It looked like the block was on fire. Yellow crime scene tape sectioned off one residence in the center of the street. While crime scene investigators and uniformed officers hustled about, I leaned against one of the police cruisers and watched the carefully choreographed chaos that inevitably accompanies a murder scene. Three years earlier, I would have been directing the chaos. This morning I was just a spectator. My name is Jerry Gold, and I had been a New York City Police Department homicide detective.

It was four a.m., and a cold morning wind was hitting me head-on. Something big was going down, but I wasn't told what. And even if I had been, I wouldn't have given a damn. My days of giving a damn were long over. If it weren't for the phone call, I would have been anywhere else but here.

I was blowing into my hands and cursing the cold when a squad car maneuvered through the barricades and parked nearby. Emerging from the backseat was a well-dressed man: thirty, brown hair, brown eyes, just over six feet tall and about a hundred eighty pounds. I knew because the guy was my twin brother, Ron. As he approached I noticed that his long, black overcoat was open, exposing a black tuxedo. As always, his wardrobe was immaculate.

"Happy New Year," he said, approaching me.

I nodded. Ron took a minute to look disapprovingly at the way I was dressed: old jeans, dirty white Reeboks, a worn-through New York Giants football jersey, and my drab green army jacket stared him in the face. "Been to a formal New Years party?" he asked.

"Not as formal as yours."

"New Years at the Met."

"Let the good times roll."

"The Metropolitan Museum of Art had its New Year's Eve gala. Emily and I always go."

"How is Emily?"

"Good. Bet you're wondering—"

"—why you asked me to come?" I said, finishing his sentence. He nodded. I used to think finishing each other's sentences was something all brothers could do. Ever since I can remember, Ron and I have done it. Maybe it's because we know each other so well. Or maybe it's just a twin thing. Either way we can do it.

"About two this morning I got a call from an old friend of ours on the job in the Homicide Division."

"I have no old friends on the job."

"You have no friends, period," he needled. "Anyway, this friend requested we talk to his associate."

"My talking days are over. It's taken every day of the past three years to get it through my head that this part of my life is over. Why bring me down here now?"

"It must be important for them to get up the nerve to call us. All we have to do is listen, Jerry. If we don't like what we hear, we're free to leave."

It amazed me how Ron could still care after all the department had put him—put us—through. But Ron was always the caring one. After college, when I told him I was joining the police academy, he joined also. Ron wanted to make a difference. I wanted the excitement. Ron wanted to change the world. I just wanted to survive it.

Seeing him at this crime scene brought back unwelcome emotions. Ron and I had been partners—two of the youngest detectives in the history of the Homicide Division. We were two of the best, taught by the best. Then came the case that changed it all. In a matter of weeks we went from outstanding to unwanted and unemployed. Now, at thirty, as I stood, freezing, on the street, I was somehow wanted again.

"Who—"

"—asked us here?" Ron motioned toward a man stepping out of the back of a black town car. The man was in his early fifties, on the tall side, with graying hair. He wore a suit and long black overcoat. He was Deputy Chief Thomas Flaherty—Captain Flaherty when we had worked for him. A no-nonsense cop who said it like it was. He didn't kiss ass or want his ass kissed. Our mentor, he was an old-fashioned detective who ate, slept, and breathed the job. He was the best and he taught Ron and me to be the best.

Flaherty met us halfway. He offered Ron his hand. Ron accepted it. He didn't extend the same courtesy to me. He knew I wouldn't accept it. The tension from our last meeting hung in the air.

"Take you long to get here?" Flaherty asked, breaking the silence.

"Three years," I replied.

"You don't look any worse for it."

"Look closer."

Flaherty turned his attention to Ron. "You've done well since you left. I hear you're a lawyer."

Ron nodded.

"He the reason?" Flaherty asked, looking in my direction. "I figured *you'd* be in prison or dead by now."

"Sorry to disappoint you."

"You'd be better off dead. Working as an investigator for Wall Street. A waste of your gifts."

"Not your concern, Flaherty."

"It is my concern. I made you and your brother the best damned detectives this city ever saw. I taught you everything you needed to know. You learned fast—except for how to play the game."

"On the streets there is no game," I spat out.

"There's always a game," he replied. "If you're fortunate enough to get old on this job, you learn that."

"What I learned was you earned your promotion from our work on the Madam Murders. Then when it came time to stand up for us, you were nowhere to be found."

"I was there. You wouldn't listen. I warned you when you caught that case that it was high profile. You weren't ready for the politics that come with that kind of situation."

"Dr. John P. Evanston was a sociopath who tortured and murdered his victims. Five women in less than six months, all tortured, their throats cut. Ron and I caught the bastard. What was the brass's gripe?"

"You still don't get it. They needed a suspect, a perp. When you identified Evanston, you solved their problem. When you started having second thoughts, your own problems began."

"They were valid concerns," Ron said. "We knew Dr. Evanston would be attending a Christmas party at the Water Club. We went to get him for questioning. The lieutenant intercepted our call and sent half the squad. By the time we made our way into the hall, Evanston was out on a ledge overlooking the East River."

"I agree that Evanston should have been persuaded back inside, but the lieutenant was in command of the site. It was his call."

"It was *our* case. It was *our* call," I insisted. "The lieutenant went through the motions. He never intended for Evanston to see the inside of a cell. He pressed the situation until the perp had no choice but to jump."

"And that's where it should have ended. Evanston jumped to his death to avoid arrest, and the current dragged his body out to sea. End of story."

"The brass used us to hunt a man they didn't want to try or convict. They wanted Evanston dead—'end of story.'"

"But you agreed that Evanston was the man," Flaherty went on. "He fit the FBI profile. You found a scalpel with his prints at one of the murder sites. Why couldn't you leave it at that? He deserved to be in hell."

"Hell's too good for him. That didn't give the department the right to use us to send him there," I said. "We were cops, not vigilantes."

"Whatever you were, you didn't need to become crusaders. You never should have leaked the story to the press. Once you did, it was out of my hands. I couldn't protect you."

"We never leaked anything," I fired back. "You let those downtown bureaucrats rob me of the only thing that ever mattered to me."

"It's over, Jerry. Stop reliving it," Ron said softly. "I have." He turned to the chief. "You asked us down here. We're here. Who do you want us to meet?"

"I don't give a rat's ass. I'm out of here," I said, turning to leave as Flaherty moved toward the open door of the town car.

"Jerry, you're here already. A few more minutes won't kill you."

I watched as my brother followed Flaherty.

"Come on, where else are you going at this hour—to visit a friend?"

I reluctantly acquiesced and followed Ron to the town car. In the backseat was a man in his late forties—dark hair, well groomed. He was of average height and weight, but those were the only average things about him. He was dressed in a hand-tailored Armani suit and overcoat— impeccably dressed for early in the morning. Hell, he was impeccably dressed for anytime. He was reading what looked like our personnel files. When he realized we were watching, he put them aside and got out of the car. Standing in the cold night he looked as if he owned the city.

"Jerry and Ron Gold, this is Deputy Police Commissioner Edward Sanchez," Flaherty said.

I recognized the name. Edward Sanchez had come to

12

New York via the LAPD, where he had been promoted to chief of detectives after the riots. The NYPD, fearing similar racial unrest—and wishing to showcase its own supposed racial diversity—persuaded him to move east. At forty-eight, Sanchez knew his way around a squad room; he also knew his way around city hall. A deputy police commissioner appointed directly by the mayor, his next stop, according to the press, was the police commissioner's office—and then anywhere he wanted to go.

Sanchez extended his hand. "Good to meet you, Ron, Jerry—or is it Jerry and Ron?"

"You were correct the first time," Ron replied, shaking his hands. I kept my hands in my pockets.

"Do you mind if we keep this informal?" Sanchez asked smoothly, as if we were friends. "We have a serious situation here you may be able to help us with. Not to imply that we can't handle it—"

"—but you probably can't," I interrupted.

Sanchez was taken aback. He was not a man accustomed to interruptions. After he saw I was unconcerned with what he was accustomed to, he regained his composure and continued. "Not that the NYPD can't handle it, but there are times it's prudent to engage outside consultants."

"And what times might they be?" Ron asked.

"Times when they can't figure out what the hell is going on," I said. "Look, it's cold out here and I haven't had my coffee, so why don't we just cut the bull and get to the point."

Sanchez was losing patience, although he tried not to show it. But to the trained eye there is always a tell, a sign that gives it away. An involuntary twitch of the cheek, a turn of the head—with Sanchez it was a slight droop of his right eyelid. He was funneling his rage through his eyeball. It was his portal of release for all the energy that builds up in a man like him. Normally, a torrent of fury would have ensued. But he needed us. So, he curbed his anger and tried an unheard-of tactic for a politician. The truth. He looked up at the brownstone, then back in our direction. Letting out a deep sigh, Sanchez watched as his breath dissipated into the cold. Then, with a conciliatory smile, he said, "You're right. We don't know what the hell is going on. But you might. The woman murdered in the brownstone is—*was*—Diane Westlake."

He said the name as if we should have recognized it. It meant nothing to me. I looked at Ron. It meant nothing to him, either.

"We believe she ran an escort service catering to an exclusive clientele."

"How exclusive?" I asked.

"Extremely. Her clients consisted of the very wealthy," Sanchez replied.

"How was she killed?" Ron inquired.

"That's why you're here." Sanchez took a pause. "The MO is similar to that of the Madam Murders."

"She the first?" I asked, suddenly interested.

"No," Flaherty answered. "Another woman, Susan Atwell, two weeks ago."

"This situation jibes with your unique talents. No one was or is as familiar with the Madam case as the two of you," Sanchez said. "Your input is needed."

"We lost our jobs because of our input. What makes you think you're going to like what we find this time?" I asked.

"His body was never recovered," Sanchez said. "I want to be certain whether this is the work of Evanston or—"

"—or a copycat," Ron anticipated.

Sanchez nodded. He motioned to Flaherty, who went to the back of the town car and returned carrying two leather packages. He tossed them at us. They were holstered guns. Not the water pistol 9-millimeter Berettas the force is presently using, but stainless-steel Colt 45 accurized semiautomatics with custom sights and grips. They held fourteen in the clip and one in the chamber.

Attached to the holsters were gold detective's shields. One had my old shield number: 2358. This is a Hallmark moment. I wonder if they make a card for it.

"You'll both be reinstated to your original rank and report directly to Deputy Chief Flaherty," Sanchez said. "Are we in agreement?"

"What guarantee do we have we won't get used again?"

"You have my word," Sanchez added.

"Got anything more tangible?"

Sanchez ignored the comment, but his eyelid didn't.

"Could I have a minute? I'd like to talk Jerry." Ron and I stepped away.

"Something bugging you?"

"What they're asking us to do is dangerous, Jerry."

"So?"

"We're not kids anymore," Ron said, looking away.

"So?"

"I have a new life. I have Emily."

"So?"

"So if something should happen to me...I don't want to leave Emily. Before, the only one I would have left behind was you, and sometimes that was more of a comfort than a fear. What about you? Aren't you worried about Cindy?"

"There is no Cindy. We split a week ago."

"Two months: a new record. You go through women like-"

"-like nothing. Let's stick to the case. And that's all this is: another case."

Ron removed his gun from its holster. "It's been a long time since I had to use one of these. It's a large responsibility to take on."

"You handled it before. Nothing's changed."

"Everything has changed. I'm not on the streets anymore. I don't have the feel for what's out there. I don't have the edge, the sixth sense anymore."

"Brother, once you have the sense it never goes away. You just stopped listening to it."

"Either way, it's a mistake to think I can return to that world. Understand?"

"Better than Sanchez will." I looked him in the eye. "As much as I might want back on the job," I conceded, "I won't go back without my partner. Are you sure?"

Ron nodded.

We made our way back to where Sanchez and Flaherty were standing. I told Sanchez our decision. Flaherty understood. Sanchez didn't.

"I was led to believe you were men of integrity," Sanchez said flatly.

"We are," Ron said, stiffening.

"Then how can you stand by while innocent lives are taken? This madman has killed two women in as many weeks, and you just want to walk away."

"Calm down, Ace," I said. "You have the entire NYPD at your disposal. What difference can two retired detectives

16

make?"

"A big difference. I need to stop this maniac. I don't know if he is the Madam Murderer or a copycat, but what I do know is that more innocent women are going to die if we don't get to him fast. Women that could have been saved. Women that you could have saved."

"We're not in the saving business anymore," I replied. "Your people took care of that."

"These women have families—people who depend on them, care for them. How would you like to face the next victim's family knowing you could have prevented the loss of their loved one?"

"Don't make this our problem."

"He already has, Jerry," Ron admitted.

"Ron, you don't have to justify yourself to him."

"I'm not. But I don't want to have to justify myself to the family of any future victim either. Think of all the families that could be hurt. If we can help but do nothing-I couldn't live with that. I don't see where we have a choice," Ron said after a beat. "We have to do it."

"You're doing the right thing," Sanchez said, shaking Ron's hand. "What about you, Jerry?"

"My partner's in then I'm in."

"Good," Sanchez said. "Flaherty will give you the particulars. Look over the crime scene and get a preliminary report to me by nine a.m."

"We need time to get organized," Ron protested.

"Ten a.m."

Ron agreed.

"One more matter: no one talks to the press other than Flaherty and our PR people. I don't want this investigation compromised or played out in the papers, understand?"

I understood what Sanchez was alluding to. I didn't take the bait. Sanchez turned toward the car and motioned with his hand. A uniformed officer ran over and opened his door. I watched as Sanchez's car shot from the curb, like a Champagne cork shooting from a bottle disappearing into the night.

The new year was only three hours old and already I had the feeling I was going to miss 2011.

3

Standing in front of the brownstone, I felt like an intruder poised to invade the privacy of the late Diane Westlake. Inside her house, Ron and I would rummage through her drawers, her files, and the most intimate aspects of her life. What personal items did she leave lying around thinking she would be right back—a diary, the laundry, e-mails open on her computer? It's as if she would be victimized all over again.

There are two steadfast rules at a crime scene: #1, look, don't touch; and #2, if you feel the need to touch, refer back to rule #1. For those of us who don't always adhere to rules there are latex gloves. Flaherty carefully pushed Westlake's front door open with a gloved hand; it hadn't been dusted for prints. The door showed no signs of forced entry. The inside of her townhouse had marble floors and lavish, rose-colored paper on the walls. This place had to be worth a fortune, even by New York City standards.

We stepped into a large hallway. To our left, French doors led to an elegant parlor, behind which was the dining area. Further down the hallway was the kitchen and pantry. In front of us was a long staircase with a carved wood banister.

Uniformed police were everywhere. I turned to Flaherty, annoyed. "This place is a zoo."

"Like it sure is, man." The voice came from the staircase. Coming down the stairs was Bruce "The Goose" Everett, MD, the county medical examiner. Goose was the closest thing to a hippie in the department. He did his autopsies to the music of the Grateful Dead, and the way he spoke confirmed that the seventies had been good to him. He was an undisputed genius in his field and could complete an autopsy faster than shit through a goose."

"Goose, how the hell are you?" I called out.

Since last we met, Goose had packed about fifty pounds onto his five-foot-seven-inch frame. Other than that, not much else about him had changed. He was still wearing his long blonde hair pulled back in a ponytail, and on his nose were his signature: wire-rim glasses.

Goose pushed his glasses up on the bridge of his nose and looked at me; a glimmer of recognition appeared.

"Gold?"

"In the flesh."

"Like, wow, man, what's it been—how many years?" He shook my hand hard.

"A while," I replied as he reached over and embraced Ron. Another Hallmark moment.

"You both look the same, man."

"We're twins," I reminded him.

"No.... I meant you don't look any older," getting the joke after the words were out of his mouth.

"Neither do you," Ron interceded, making the peace sign with his fingers.

"There's a positive thought. Thanks, man. What are you guys doing here?"

"That's Detective Guys to you," I said, clipping my badge to my coat lapel.

"Cool. Like how long you been back?"

"Too long," Flaherty sniped.

"About an hour," I replied, ignoring him.

"And already pissing the chief off. It's like you never left, man."

"Whaddya got for us, Goose?"

"Like nothing you haven't seen before," he said evenly, climbing back up the stairs with us in tow. "The victim, Diane Westlake. Female Caucasian. Approximately twenty-nine years old. Tortured and killed."

"That's all you have?" Ron questioned.

"You know the drill, man. Until I complete the autopsy..."

"Off the record, Goose, what do you think?"

"The lady was stripped, her body stretched across an—"

"—an antique whipping horse?" I interrupted. Goose nodded his assent. "Her limbs bound?"

He nodded again. "Just like three years ago."

"We figured that," Ron replied. "This victim have a ball gag in her mouth, too?"

"Yeah, and she'd been beaten severely," he added.

As we got to the top of the stairs, I asked Goose if he had any extra gloves. He reached into his coat pocket and tossed each of us a pair. As we put them on, I noticed that the stairs continued upward from the second floor. I was curious about what the upper level housed but opted to stay with the group. There we saw seven rooms hugging the second-floor hallway, and one at its far end. Elaborately designed light fixtures resembling gaslight sconces decorated the walls.

"This is some setup, huh guys? Wait till you get a load of this," Goose laughed, pointing to the room at the head of the hall.

It was decorated like a schoolroom, blackboard and all. Another room was furnished with oversize baby furniture—an adult nursery—and another like a doctor's examination room. All had the unmistakable tracings of powder: they had been dusted for prints.

"Man, it's like Mayflower Madam decorated this place."

"I have a feeling the corpse isn't the only thing that's going to stink," I said. "Flaherty, who caught the case?"

Flaherty hesitated, then said, "Greeley."

"Lieutenant Walter Greeley?" Ron was incredulous. "That can't be."

"He was ancient when *we* worked with him. Doesn't the department force you to retire once you've reached your second century on the job?" I quipped.

Flaherty answered, "I know you got history with this guy."

"*Got* history? This guy *is* history."

"It's his case. Deal with him."

"I'd rather kiss a snake."

I could see a twitch developing in Flaherty's right eye. Flaherty wasn't particularly fond of Greeley either. But Greeley was the father-in-law of Lieutenant Governor

Patrick Denton, and as long as his daughter kept screwing the Lieutenant Governor, her father could keep screwing the force.

"Greeley is part of the team," Flaherty said through clenched teeth.

"Not my team," I snapped.

"This is a murder investigation; you and Greeley will handle yourselves professionally. By the book."

"The man's illiterate; he's never read the book—or any book, for that matter."

"Regardless, you work with him and report to me."

"Make sure you tell that to the fossil. We report to you."

Flaherty grunted his assent and pushed ahead of us, continuing down the hall.

"Greeley still gets to you?" Ron laughed.

"Not really."

"Come again?"

"I don't lose any sleep over him. But if I heard Greeley was about to eat his gun, I'd offer to mustard the muzzle."

"Like are you ready man?" Goose asked as we entered the room at the end of the hall. "Dudes, let me introduce you to Diane Westlake."

4

The room looked like a medieval dungeon. Shackles hung from the ceiling. Suspended along the walls were whips, paddles, and other instruments of pain. In the middle of the room was the most frightening of all: the whipping post. In the back of the room was the victim, draped over a whipping horse. On the floor beside her was an empty black body bag, unzipped, waiting patiently for its soon-to-be tenant.

The crime scene unit was dressed in their dark blue jackets with "NYPD" lettered across the back in bright yellow. They were methodically going through the room, dusting for prints and taking photos.

I stopped a few feet away from the corpse as Ron meticulously circled the scene. Even in death, you could see Diane Westlake had been a beautiful woman. Now her face was pasty white; the ends of her long blonde hair were resting in her own blood. Moving around her I could see she was completely exposed, her most intimate parts on display. The smell of freshly spilled blood permeated the air.

"I hope Ms. Westlake wasn't a modest woman," a cop next to Ron joked. He was in his twenties and didn't look old enough to shave, let alone be a detective. The badge on his lapel said otherwise.

"This is how the body was found?" Ron asked.

"Yes," said the detective.

"Who's heading up the crime scene unit?" I asked.

"Mitch Palmieri. He's finishing up on the third floor. My name's Wilkins. Dave Wilkins."

"Ron and Jerry Gold," Ron said, extending a hand.

He looked at Ron, then me, then Ron again, but said nothing. "I'm working the case with Lieutenant Greeley."

"My condolences," I said.

"Where is Greeley?" Flaherty inquired.

"With Palmieri."

"How much time you got on the job, kid?" I asked.

"About three years"

"How long in homicide?"

"Six months."

"Before that what did you do—traffic?"

"Narcotics."

"Not a lot of time in on homicide."

"I'm no virgin to the streets, if that's what you're asking."

"You have people canvassing the neighborhood?"

He nodded, then informed me it was slow going at five a.m. because the investigators were reluctant to wake the neighbors.

25

"Hey, I don't get to sleep, nobody sleeps. Get your guys moving now." Wilkins looked at Flaherty for approval.

"Don't look at him. I gave you the order. Look at me."

Wilkins turned to me, then to Flaherty, uncertain how to respond. Flaherty nodded for Wilkins to go.

"I'll be back," Wilkins said, heading for the door.

"We'll be here." Turning back toward the corpse, I noticed Ron was rubbing a foreign substance between his thumb and forefinger. "What've you got?"

"I'm not sure," he said, moving closer to Goose and me. "Goose, you're going to run cavity checks back at the morgue, right?"

"Standard procedure. You think she was raped?"

"Three years ago the second victim was raped. What was the time of death?"

"Right after he slit her throat," I said, kneeling down in front of the body.

"I was asking Goose."

"She's, like, showing early signs of rigor mortis. Considering the cool temperature in here and the victim's core temp, I'd say she was snuffed about four hours ago."

"That would make the time of death somewhere around midnight," Ron said to me. "Hell of a way to end a year."

"Hell of a way to start one," I replied.

"Judging from the thin striped markings, I'd say she was, like, whipped with a flogger. One was found hanging on the wall over there. It has traces of blood. The lab will confirm if it's from our lady here."

"Abrasions around her wrist and ankles," I said. "Must've fought like hell."

"She wasn't whipped to death, was she, doctor?" asked Wilkins, who had returned.

26

"No. The whipping must've hurt like hell, but it didn't kill her. Cause of death was, like, probably circulatory volume depletion, secondary to massive hemorrhaging from the inflicted knife wound."

"Come again?" Wilkins said.

"She's exsanguinous."

"Again in English, doc."

"She bled to death, kid," I said. "Haven't handled any slashings?"

"Not many," Wilkins admitted.

"Take notes then, kid, you're about to watch a pro at work," I said knelling down to get a closer look at the victim's throat. I took a pen from my pocket and gingerly moved her blood-soaked hair to one side. "The murderer is most likely right-handed."

"Or ambidextrous," Ron added.

"Or ambidextrous," I concurred.

"Although I would consider it highly unlikely."

"Are you going to bust my chops?"

"Sorry, most likely right-handed."

I could tell Wilkins was about to ask how we knew. "Keep listening, kid, we're not through yet. The initial blade puncture appears just below the left earlobe, correct?"

"Appears to be," Ron said, kneeling next to me. "And the wound gathered depth as the blade traveled obliquely under the ramus of her mandible—

"—through the tracheal cartilage, well to the other side. The murderer probably severed the carotid arteries bilaterally when her throat was cut," I said. "Do we still have it or what?"

"Don't pat yourself on the back just yet. It could have cut the jugular vein," Wilkins added in an attempt to save

27

face.

"Highly improbable," Ron responded, pointing to the blood on the floor. "That splattering is definitely the result of severing one or both carotid arteries."

"How can you be certain?"

"The heart *pumps* blood out through the carotid like water through a garden hose. That would explain the spray of blood around her. If the jugular vein had been severed, the blood would have gathered in a pool below her."

"Pretty good for two dudes who haven't seen a corpse in years," Goose said.

"Some things you don't forget."

Goose nodded. "The laceration found on the victim's throat appears to be consistent with our man's style. Like with our first corpse, he used a serious blade, like a surgical implement."

"Similar to this?" Wilkins displayed a plastic evidence bag containing a blood-drenched scalpel.

"That would do it, man."

"This knife is on its way to the lab," Wilkins said.

"Make sure they not only type the blood, have the lab spend the extra bucks and run a DNA check ," I said.

"That's standard operating procedure today. Besides, Palmieri knows his job," Flaherty said. "You just worry about yours."

Before I could respond, Goose called out, "Take a look at this, guys."

Ron and I moved closer. Goose pointed to a small mark burned or branded into the victim's right thigh.

"Hey, like, is this déjà vu or what?"

5

I left the brownstone feeling the chill of the morning air. Or was it the sights inside that gave me the chill? Ron joined me on the stoop. A pack of reporters were assembling on the sidewalk, waiting for the signal to lunge forward and annoy us with their questions. I never could decipher exactly what the signal was, but all the reporters knew it instinctively, like sharks that know when to start their feeding frenzy.

"What time do you have?" I asked, taking a cigar from my pocket.

"Six o'clock." Ron licked his right index finger and held it to the wind. "You want the temperature?"

"Some things should remain a mystery."

We cut through the crowd of reporters and leaned against a new Mercedes parked at the curb. I cut the tip of

29

my cigar and lit it.

Feeling the cold, Ron pulled up the collar of his coat. "She seemed younger than the others."

"Just as dead."

Wilkins joined us.

"You have anyone taking the plate numbers off these cars?" I asked, tapping the Mercedes under me.

"A Mercedes on West End Avenue. How suspicious," Wilkins said sardonically. "They'll get to it. What's our next move?"

"Coffee," Ron and I answered together.

"First we get Jerry his coffee," Ron elaborated.

"Have to have my morning java," I said, smiling.

"Then over to the safe house and check out the previous murder book," Ron continued.

"Couldn't have said it better myself. I also want to see—"

"—Palmieri's crime unit report."

I nodded.

"The preliminary should be available by noon," Wilkins said.

"That should cover it. Let's get moving," I said.

"No car," Ron replied.

"No car could be a problem." Then Flaherty appeared on the stoop. "Problem solved."

Unfortunately, the press saw him first, and the feeding frenzy began.

"Deputy Chief!" one reporter yelled as he pushed his way forward. "Has the victim been identified?"

"The victim's identity is being withheld until the family can be notified."

"Any suspects?"

"No comment at this time," Flaherty said quickly,

acknowledging another reporter.

"Is this killing mob-related?"

"No comment."

"Mob?" another reporter interjected. "What leads you to believe this might have been a mob-related hit?"

"No comment."

"He really is very masterful with the press," Ron smirked.

"No comment," I said, making my way to Flaherty. I asked for his car keys. He passed them to me and pointed to an unmarked car at the curb.

"You going to the safe house?" he asked.

I nodded and flipped the keys to Ron as I made my way back through the crowd.

Reaching for the passenger side door, a voice from the past caught my attention.

"Excuse me, Deputy Chief Flaherty," a female voice said. "Have you obtained any evidence that leads you to believe this murder might be connected to the Atwell murder a few weeks ago?"

The voice sounded calm and collected. Unlike the other reporters, whose questions were quick and strained, the quality of her voice demanded an answer. Flaherty looked through the crowd. Standing in the second row was the stunning Nicole Horn. She stood only five-foot-two, with long, dark hair, and she was dressed in tight blue jeans, black knee-high boots, and a fur-trimmed leather waist-length coat. I'm against animals being murdered for fur. But if these animal knew they would be clinging to her body, they would have died happy.

She was holding a microphone that flaunted the call letters of New York's premier news station, WZAD. Nicole

Horn was New York's premier news personality, who, it was rumored, might one day be in line to replace Barbara Walters. Her cameraman was recording the entire moment for posterity and the eleven o'clock news.

"Well, sir, is there a connection?" she pressed.

"Any conclusions along those lines would be premature."

"But the NYPD is not ruling out a possible connection?"

"This is an active murder investigation, Ms. Horn. We haven't ruled out anything," Flaherty said cantankerously. "However, we presently believe a connection is unlikely."

"How unlikely?" she probed, not letting Flaherty off the hook.

"Ms. Horn, you got your answer. That's all for now. We will keep the press informed as the investigation progresses."

Flaherty turned and made his way back into the brownstone. The sharks tried to follow but the patrolmen guarding the door wouldn't allow anyone to pass. The good old beat cop: the NYPD's equivalent of shark repellent.

"She's as beautiful as ever," Ron said, leaning against the car. "I can't believe you let her go."

"I never had her."

"Never had her? Have you dropped acid up there with Goose? In all the years I've known you, the time you were with Nikki was the only time I was jealous. The two of you were perfect together."

"That was a long time ago. Shut up and get in the car."

Ron got behind the wheel. As he started the engine, a fragrance I hadn't smelled in years flooded the car. There was no need to turn around. The scent of Joy perfume could only belong to one person. Then I heard the voice of the woman I had once loved.

"Jerry?" the voice questioned softly. This was not the same voice that had grilled Flaherty earlier. It was a kinder, gentler voice. A voice I could never forget.

"Hello, Nicole," I said coldly.

"Nicole?" she grinned awkwardly, "So formal? You used to call me Nikki."

I said nothing. An uncomfortable silence hung between us. She looked at me as I looked at the dashboard. Then she leaned down. "It's been a long time. How have you been?"

How have I been? How have I been? I stared incredulously. I didn't know how to answer that question while a flood of emotions coursed through me. I chose to say nothing.

We had met five years ago. Nikki was a recent graduate of the Columbia School of Journalism and was working as a news writer for a local station. We had both attended a conference whose purpose was to bring the police and media together. It worked. One look at her and I was hooked. We were inseparable. If we weren't working, we were making love. If we were working, we were in touch constantly. Hearing her sweet voice helped me get through some tough days.

But that was then. Now I wanted to tell her how much I loathed what she had done—what she had become. But I didn't have to. She must have seen it in my eyes when I turned to face her. She reached out to touch my shoulder. I averted her hand.

She quickly drew back, and inhaled deeply. She wasn't visibly shaken, but I knew I had hurt her. Good. Not good. Damn. Why did I have to run into her?

"You never returned my calls," she said, regaining her composure.

"We said what we had to say."

"You said what *you* had to say. You wouldn't listen to me. For God's sake, Jerry, haven't you punished me enough?"

I just listened.

"Damn you, talk to me!" She slammed her hand down hard on the roof of the car.

"What's there left to say, Nikki?"

"You are acting like a petulant child. I may have made a mistake...."

"Me too. I trusted the woman I loved."

"Get over it. We were both adults. We knew what we were doing."

"What we said in bed was never intended for publication."

"That's unfair! What I did, I did for you. I loved you."

"Not as much as your job."

"What about *your* job? I never stood in the way of that."

"You helped me lose it."

Nikki stared deep into my eyes, then moved away from the car.

"I'm sorry I've taken up your time, Detective Gold."

I saw tears. Nikki turned away from the car. When she faced me again, the tears were gone, but the hurt that had engendered them remained.

"I was the best you ever had," she said. "You'll come around."

"Will I?"

"You're a cop. I'm a reporter. You're going to need me, and I still need you."

Nikki turned and left. I wanted to grab her, but something held me back. As I watched her leave, Ron put the car in gear and slowly pulled away from the curb.

"Couldn't help hearing...."

"And?"

"And sometimes, Jerry, you can be a real bastard."

"Product of my environment."

He made a right onto Broadway, and we continued to the safe house in silence. Next stop The Twilight Zone.

6

The safe house was on the top floor of an office building at 396 Fifth Avenue, in Midtown. We stopped for coffee and donuts, but we still arrived in record time.

"You think that Evanston is responsible?" Ron asked as he headed for the building.

"Don't know. I was leaning more toward a copycat until Goose showed us the mark on her thigh. Westlake had the same small uppercase *R* branded into her thigh as all the other victims."

"Then you think he's back from the grave?"

"Could be."

"Jerry, this isn't a Stephen King novel. Drowned corpses don't resurface years later."

"Maybe it's an obsessive compulsive corpse."

"Maybe it's a copycat."

"Or maybe a copycat. Except the mark was never leaked to the press. No one on the entire investigating team ever knew about the mark. How would a copycat know about it?" I asked.

"I don't know. What I do know is dead men stay dead."

"Hard to argue with that. But they never did find the body."

"So?"

"So remember the Alcott case?" I continued.

"Alcott... The cat burglar?"

"It took two years to catch him. In between his fifth and last theft, he was nailed for drug possession and got two years. He wasn't nabbed for the burglaries until he was released from prison and picked up where he'd left off."

"And your point is?"

"Maybe Evanston survived. Maybe he was arrested and convicted for something else and was just released from prison, and he decided to begin a new reign of terror and—"

"—and stay tuned for more of our exciting show after these commercial messages," Ron chimed in.

"Think about it before you discount it."

"OK, Jerry. Let's see. Dr. Evanston survives the freezing East River current. But he washes up on shore and is saved from a watery grave by cops who arrest him for...what? Fishing without a license? He pleads guilty, serves three years, and comes back to New York City—where he nearly got caught once already—to start again. Is that your theory?"

"What part don't you buy?" I asked.

"The part after 'let's see.'"

We entered the safe house lobby and headed toward the three elevator bays to our left. The concierge's station to our right was abandoned. Ron pressed the call button for the elevator. As I waited, I gave the joint a once over. "No guard on duty?"

"Seems like anybody can walk right in."

"Anybody just did," I said. Out of the corner of my eye, I saw something move. Instinctively I went for my Colt as I heard someone shout "gun!" I turned and collided with a female officer—and a hot-looking one at that. I was off balance, and she was able to use her body to pin me against the wall.

"What the..."

"Good detecting. You found the guard," Ron laughed.

"Easy, mister," the tall, dark, blue-eyed woman called out. "Easy."

"I'm easy," I assured her, "But I'm not cheap."

"You can release him, Officer MacDonald," Ron said, looking at her name tag above her badge. We were told to report here." Ron held out his shield for her to read. "How about easing up on my partner."

"Honey, you can stay just like you are for as long as you like," I said, smiling.

She looked from me to my brother. "You must be Jerry and Ron Gold," she said, stepping back.

"In the flesh, babe."

"I've heard about you." Her meaning was ambiguous. She straightened her uniform.

"Let me help you with that," I offered. She pushed my hands away. Less ambiguous.

"I'm Jeanne MacDonald," she said.

"MacDonald... I thought I detected a wee bit of an Irish brogue."

Ron rolled his eyes.

"I'm a trained detective. I'm paid to notice these things."

"Then you're overpaid, detective. I'm Scottish. My name is spelled M-a-c. If I were Irish, it would be spelled M-c." She pointed to her nametag.

"Scottish would have been my second guess."

"Good for you, Dick Tracy," Ron said. "Jeanne, your accent isn't that pronounced."

"I moved here in my teens," she replied while unlocking the elevator doors. As she entered the elevator, I admired her perfectly shaped backside, which was attached to two of the greatest legs I had ever seen on a cop. She had to be six feet tall if she was an inch, and my cop intuition told me she was worth the climb. Jeanne pressed the button for the penthouse and up we went.

"While you're with the task force, detectives, if you need anything, ask for me."

"Be still my heart. Anything?"

Jeanne smiled. "You've both been given full clearance. I was instructed by Deputy Chief Flaherty: whatever you want, you get."

"How about a date?" I asked.

"I don't date detectives," she replied.

"What happened to 'whatever you want, you get'?" The elevator came to a stop. The doors opened and we exited.

"Please wait here," she requested, ignoring my advances. "Let me get your task force IDs, and then I'll show you to the boardroom."

"Jeanne, would you mind also having this run for us?" Ron asked, handing her the license plate of the Mercedes we saw earlier that morning.

"Forget that," I said. "Why don't you date detectives?"

Jeanne let out a sigh. "You don't really want to know

why?"

I nodded.

"Fine, it's been my experience that when you date detectives, they screw like they shoot."

"What?"

"They pull their piece out too fast. They discharge their weapon too soon, and they never seem to hit the mark. Now if you have no further questions, I'll get those IDs."

I stood aside and watched her disappear down the hall. "She wants me, Ron. Have you ever heard a more desperate cry for help?"

"Hers or yours?"

The safe house took up the entire floor of the building's penthouse. In the living room and dining room were detectives and uniform officers, all seated at their desks. Tired of waiting for Jeanne, I asked one of the desk-sitters to point me toward the conference room. He motioned down the hall.

The conference room was a converted master bedroom. In the center of the room, a large, rectangular, exceedingly polished table was surrounded by chairs. Around the room's perimeter were four blackboards, each with diagrams drawn in different colored chalk. Goose was already seated. On the table in front of him was a pot of coffee.

Wilkins was standing with a group of detectives by one blackboard, colored chalk in hand. Each diagram displayed a trail of facts related to the case. Each group member made quick sequential marks on the board. It looked like a tic-tac-toe game gone bad. The pictures taped to the top of the diagrams were our victims. If we don't catch this guy soon, I thought, it's going to cost the city a fortune in colored chalk.

I found a seat next to Goose. "Didn't expect to see you here. Shouldn't you be doing the autopsy?"

"I'm waiting for you, dude," Goose blurted out. Then, lowering his voice, he said, "We gotta talk."

"We are talking, Goose. In fact, what we're doing now constitutes a conversation, remember? Or are you having another flashback?"

"I wish." He paused. "I gotta talk to you and Ron privately."

The way Goose said "privately" got my attention. He was nervous. He needed to talk, and I wanted to listen. But he was right—this was not the place.

"Meet us at the McDonald's after the meeting. I'll treat for breakfast and we'll talk."

"Let's go now."

"Can't. The briefing's about to start. Wait for us at McDonalds."

"Fine. Just don't forget, man. It's important."

Having made his point, Goose left the room. What could be bugging him so much that he felt it necessary to come here? Goose was usually easygoing. I leaned forward and poured myself some coffee just as Flaherty entered. People took their seats. Court was about to convene.

Other than Flaherty and Wilkins, no one looked familiar. Next to Wilkins there was a vacant seat. I assumed it belonged to his partner, Walt Greeley.

"Let's get started," Flaherty announced. "I don't want to waste time with introductions—most of you know each other. The two men seated to my right are Detectives Jerry and Ron Gold. They facilitated the apprehension of the Madam Murderer. They're here at my request. You are to keep them fully informed of all events. Understood?"

41

Heads around the table nodded.

"By now you should all be aware that last night another woman was murdered on the Upper West Side. We believe this murder is related to Susan Atwell's," Flaherty declaimed. "Detective Wilkins will get us up to speed."

"Right," Wilkins said. "The victim, Diane Westlake, age twenty-nine, female, Caucasian, was found bound, beaten, and with her throat slashed in her residence at 365 West Ninety-first Street at 1:35 this morning. There were no signs of forced entry."

Ron listened carefully and took copious notes. Ron was born with a photographic memory. Unfortunately, he was also born with a slight obsessive-compulsive tendency.

"We received an anonymous 911 call at approximately one a.m. today." Wilkins took a small digital recorder from his pocket and pressed "play." A female voice echoed through the quiet room.

"H-h-hello," it said frantically. The voice had a trace of an accent.

"This is 9-1-1 Operator 6-3-6-7—"

"—I'm calling from 365 West Ninety-first Street. Did you get that—365 West Ninety-first Street!

"Please try and remain calm. What is the emergency?"

"Diane and Corinne. Th-they were supposed to meet me for a New Year's Eve drink. They never arrived. She's dead. Diane's dead!"

"Are you at Diane's apartment?" the operator asked.

"Yes. It was dark. Except the second floor. She told me she wasn't working tonight. No one answered the door. I tried it, and it was open."

The woman began to cry. Her breathing became labored.

"Oh, Lord, it was open," she repeated again. "I went inside. Second floor. I-I found her. Please help!"

"Who? Who did you find?" the dispatcher asked.

"Oh Lord, please send some one!" The voice began to plead.

"A unit has already been dispatched. Are you at that address now?"

"Yes."

"Stay there. A car is on the way. What is your name, Ms.... Hello? Hello!"

The woman's voice was replaced by the buzz of a dial tone.

Wilkins stopped the recorder. "We're looking for the caller, but as of yet, no luck." He proceeded to the chalkboard. "The victim's next of kin, Alfred Westlake, her father, has been notified and is on his way down from Albany to make an identification," Wilkins said. Ron underlined the name in his notes.

"Chief, is it possible to get a copy of the Atwell murder report? I'd like to review the findings," Ron asked.

Flaherty pointed to the man sitting to his right. The man reached into his briefcase and slid two bound briefs towards us.

"If you'll turn your attention here, Gentlemen." Wilkins was pointing to the chalk-colored diagrams on the board. For the next half hour, he reviewed both murders thoroughly, comparing both their similarities and differences. I tried to pay attention, but the voice I had heard on the 911 call was bothering me. I kept replaying it in my mind.

Wilkins turned from the chalkboard, looked down at his notes, and continued. "According to a Mrs. Edders, who lives next door, Westlake was the perfect neighbor. Moved in about two years ago and immediately renovated the property. She was active in the neighborhood. There were never any disturbances and, according to Edders, she and Westlake shared interests in gardening and music. They were scheduled to go to Avery Fisher Hall tonight."

"Do we know if Westlake was employed?" Ron asked.

"Look at her house. Do you really have to ask?" Wilkins said. "She's a pro. A high-class pro at that. That townhouse must have cost a few million *before* renovations. Who else could afford something like that?"

"The daughter of Alfred 'Alley Boy' Westlake could," I replied. The name didn't register with Wilkins. "Alfred Westlake is a retired Wall Street arbitrageur. He's worth billions."

"You think they're related?"

"You'll know in a few hours," I said.

Wilkins tried to wipe the surprised look off his face. "So what if she is? Wouldn't be the first rich kid to become a madam."

"No, she certainly wouldn't," Ron said. "But before I'd tell the grieving father—"

"—the rich, powerful, grieving father—" I interjected,

"—his only daughter was a hooker, I'd want to be certain," Ron concluded.

"Damn certain," I added.

Wilkins nervously flipped through his notes. "Mrs. Edders believes Westlake was a computer consultant. She worked at home."

"Let's confirm that before we meet with her father. Check if she was working for a company or as an independent contractor," Ron said. "Let's also get a look at her bank accounts for the last six months."

"Will do," Wilkins said. "But I still think we're going to find she was a pro."

"Why?" Ron asked.

"Three years ago your perp snuffed hookers. If it's a copycat, the perp will duplicate the crime. It's how a copycat gets off—trying to imitate the sick person he idolizes. In this case, it's the Madam Murderer."

"Imitation is the sincerest form of flattery," I said dryly.

"Evanston's body was never recovered," Ron reminded us. "We might be looking for him."

"I'm not ruling it out," Wilkins stated. "But our caller said she saw lights on the second floor, and that Westlake wasn't working last night. You saw the second floor of that place. What do *you* think she meant by 'working'?"

"Let's not jump to conclusions because of what occurred previously," Ron replied.

I reached across the table for some coffee.

"Who's jumping to conclusions?" Wilkins yelled, slamming his hand down on the table. I spilled the pot of hot coffee all over the empty chair next to him, and watched sadly as the last of the precious liquid began to form a puddle on the seat.

I was about to give Wilkins hell when Jeanne MacDonald entered and angrily handed me a slip of paper. I ignored the spill and her attitude. After reading the note I turned to Flaherty. "It's been real, but Ron and I have a few things to check into." We got up from the table and headed for the door.

"Stay in touch," Flaherty barked.

As I left I asked Wilkins for the 911 tape. He handed me his recorder, assuring me there were other copies. I began for the door again. Without turning, I called back, "One more thing, Dave. You might want to check if prints from the phone at the Westlake apartment were taken."

He nodded. As we walked out, Wilkins called after us, "Aren't you going to wait for Lieutenant Greeley? Don't you want to hear his take on the case?"

"Not particularly."

Confused, Wilkins looked down at his partner's chair. As he watched the steam rise from the puddle of hot coffee on the seat, he called out, "It's his case. Don't you want to tell him anything?"

"Tell him I kept his chair warm."

7

"Where exactly are we off to?" Ron asked.

"We have a brunch date," I said, heading for the elevator.

"Since when do you do brunch?"

"Since now. We're meeting Goose at McDonald's." I handed Ron the slip of paper.

"The Mercedes parked in front of the Edders' house is registered to Corinne Moreland," Ron read aloud.

"Yup."

"Age twenty-eight. Resides at 70 East Twelfth Street. Wasn't a Corinne mentioned on the tape?"

"Yep. Some coincidence, huh?" I reached for the elevator button when I realized there wasn't one. In its place was a small gold plate with a slot. An aggravated Jeanne MacDonald appeared.

"You were supposed to wait for me," she said sternly.

"You missed me?" I replied tenderly. My charm was on autopilot.

"You were not to leave until you received these." She brusquely handed us two laminated ID cards.

"Jeanne MacDonald, I could listen to your accent all day long." I smiled.

"Then I'll tape her for you. We have to go," Ron said impatiently.

"Tape would work. But it-"

"-it what?"

"Hand me Wilkins's recorder."

"What for?"

"Humor me." Ron handed me the tape recorder.

"Listen to this, Jeanne." I played the tape. She listened carefully as the recorder relived the previous night's cries for help. When it was over I asked, "Where would you say the voice you just heard was from?"

"England. Manchester perhaps," she responded without hesitation. "It's definitely a British accent. What's left of it."

"You're certain?" Ron asked.

"Yes, but it sounds like she's been out of the country for some time."

"Because the accent is slight, like yours?" Ron surmised.

"Yes and because of the way she phrases things."

"Phrases things?"

"She no longer uses the term *flat*, for example. She uses the word *apartment*. She's Americanized, but not completely."

"Interesting observation. You're going to make a good detective one day," Ron said.

"I hope to."

"Not only is she gorgeous, she's brilliant too!" I added. "Jeanne, get a unit over to the Moreland address and keep us informed of what they find."

Ron gave her our cell phone numbers.

"If you'd only date detectives we could make beautiful music together." I turned to my brother. "But time's a-wasting. McBrunch awaits!"

8

I swaggered into McDonald's with the confidence only someone who had eaten thousands of Big Macs could muster. My health-nut brother followed, looking like a McFish out of water.

"You want something?" I asked as I gave my order to the girl behind the counter.

"Pass," Ron said, spotting Goose seated in the back, munching on french fries. I collected my order and followed Ron to the table.

"*Hola, amigo. ¿Que pasa?*" I said, taking the hamburgers from the bag. I passed one to Goose, sat down, and began to eat.

"How can you eat that?" Ron asked.

"They're out of McTofu."

"Do you know how unhealthy that is?"

"I don't care."

"Hey, dudes. I didn't meet you here to talk about food."

"What do you want to talk about?" I asked.

"Somebody's going through my desk, man."

"And you think it's us?"

"I don't know who it is," Goose said, placing his carton of fries on the table.

"What makes you think someone is going through your desk?" Ron asked.

Goose took a deep breath. "Look, I know I, like, sound paranoid, but I know where everything is in my desk. At first, when a few things were out of place, I, like, didn't give it a thought. I chalked it up to forgetfulness. I'd been putting in some late hours. But now—"

"—now *what*?" I pushed.

"My roach clip."

"Your what?" Ron and I said in unison.

"My roach clip. It's a clip at the end of a long leather strip with feathers. I use it—"

"—I know what a roach clip is for, Goose. Get to the point," I urged.

"I use it," he continued deliberately, "as a *reminder*. Whatever important notes or papers I have to work on next, I clip them together with the roach clip," Goose continued. "I always keep it in the top right drawer of my desk. A couple of nights ago, before I left work, I clipped a particular page from the Atwell report. When I came in the next morning, a different page was clipped."

"You're sure?" I asked.

"Of course I'm sure, man. I, like, know when my space has been violated." Goose was jumpy. Ron placed a hand on his arm.

"Let's all calm down. We're starting to act like we're at the center of a conspiracy," Ron said. He lowered his voice. "No one's going through your desk at night, Goose." Ron looked at me, then at Goose.

"What do we do, dudes?"

"Do *we* have any ideas, Ron?"

"Goose, what could you have discovered that would warrant all this attention?" Ron asked.

"I don't know, man. It's a murder investigation. Maybe everything is important, maybe nothing." He lowered his head and began to rub his neck.

"Think, Goose," Ron prodded. "Anything with the Westlake body strike you as odd?"

Goose stopped rubbing and looked up at Ron. "Westlake! Absolutely."

"Well, are you going to tell us or do we have to wait for the movie?" I asked.

"Westlake was sodomized."

"And that surprises you?" I asked. "The second victim three years ago was sodomized also."

"Yeah, similar to the second victim three years ago, except this time there was no sperm. But the perp did use a lubricant. And here's the kicker: not the same lubricant as in the original murders. The original perp used a petroleum jelly to perform the act and—"

"—and this time the perp used vegetable shortening," Ron interjected. "Probably Crisco."

"The shortening used for baking?" I asked.

"One and the same, man. How did you know, Ron?"

"I found traces of it at the scene but wasn't sure until now."

"Well I didn't think it was possible, but you've put me

off my food," I said, pushing my burger away. "Crisco. I may never eat cake again."

"Don't look so surprised, dude. Gay men have been using it for years. It's healthier than petroleum-based jellies. The *straight* S&M community just borrowed the knowledge."

Goose must have seen the confusion on our faces. "Am I, like, giving you first hand news? Surely you found these things in your original investigation?"

"We were looking for a prostitute murderer, not some S&M freak who went off the deep end," I said.

"But if this assailant is involved in S&M, he knows about little things—like what to do with Crisco," my brother said. "To catch him, we need to know what *he* knows."

"I'm with you, partner. But how did this guy know about the brand on her thigh?" I asked. "That news was never released to the press."

"The brands don't match," Goose said through a mouthful of fries.

"What do you mean?"

"I compared pictures of the victims from years ago to the marks found on Atwell and Westlake. They're close, but no cigar. Not a match. The marks on our victims are larger."

"Are you sure?" Ron asked.

Goose nodded.

"What made you measure the brands?"

"I was asked."

"By whom?"

"Mitch Palmieri."

"Head of the crime unit?"

Goose nodded.

"That's interesting," Ron muttered.

"Looks like we're leaning more toward a copycat every minute," I said.

"Maybe not. Times change. So could our perp. Maybe for the last few years he, like, satisfied his needs through S&M—and learned its ways," Goose opined.

"Maybe," I said, not really believing it.

"Anything you want me to do?"

"Does anyone know about the Crisco yet?" Ron asked.

"No. I just reported a lubricant."

"Good. Note in your report that the lubricant was Crisco, and leave the report in your drawer tonight. In the morning, submit it with one change: remove the mention of Crisco and replace it with 'specifics regarding lubricant to follow.'"

"Why, man?"

"Trust me. You don't want to know. Just do it."

Goose hesitated.

"Are you in or out?"

Goose looked at me, then Ron. "I guess I'm in. I guess we're all in."

"Deeper than we think."

9

I called Jeanne MacDonald from the car to check on her progress finding our missing car owner. A unit had been dispatched to the address, but no one was home. The super unlocked the door for the officers, who reported the bed didn't look slept in. They asked to be notified as soon as Corinne Moreland returned.

I thanked Jeanne and relayed the information to Ron. "I must have been the only one in the city who was at home last night," I said.

"You could have had dinner with Emily and me, but you said you and Cindy were spending a quiet night at home."

"We did. It just turned out to be in separate homes."

"You haven't been seeing her that long. Even you couldn't annoy someone that quickly."

"It's a talent," I replied.

"Flaherty thinks it's your greatest talent," Ron added. "You should never have left Nikki."

"Drive, Dear Abby."

"Where?"

"We have another appointment."

"With who?"

"You said we needed to learn more about the S&M scene, didn't you? We're going to talk to our old buddy Kirby."

"Kirby?"

"Lonsdale. Kirby Lonsdale. The third," I answered. "The one and only Pimp Ball Wizard of Prostitution."

"Why would he talk with us? He was our last collar. Is he even back out on the street?"

"Must be. We sent him away before we left and *we're* back on the streets."

"There's a sick logic to that."

"It's a gift. Come on, Ron. We're off to see the Wizard!"

Kirby Lonsdale III was a third-generation pimp. Like his father and grandfather before him, Kirby ran prostitution in Manhattan. When it came to sex in the city, no one got their piece until Kirby got his. And he always got his. At five foot nothing, the forty-five-year-old was actually more munchkin than wizard. But he guarded his turf like a junkyard dog. The only difference was that Kirby's bark was worse than his bite. He liked to play boss and was big on throwing fits and making threats, but he wasn't much on following through. And when threatening someone, follow-through is everything. Business had begun to stagnate until old man Lonsdale gave Kirby Red Donlan.

Red was six-three, with red hair and biceps the size of

my waist. On the streets, it was known that, unlike Kirby, Red's bite was worse than his bark. A fact easily proven since Red Donlan *had* no bark. He would attack without warning, striking as quickly as a cornered diamondback. Annoy Red Donlan and you never annoyed anyone again.

Our car turned the corner of Thirty-fourth Street onto Eighth Avenue. The streets were alive. People by were hurrying past the windows of discount stores. Workers were clearing out last night's trash from fast food joints. And on one corner, a few old winos were huddled around a fire burning in a wire garbage can. There's nothing like Manhattan for the holidays.

We were driving north on Eighth Avenue. To our right, I saw a large neon sign hanging over an amusement arcade. To our left was Port Authority, two blocks long. Newly renovated at an unthinkable cost, it was the end point for all travelers coming to the Big Apple or and the starting point for all those leaving. This multilevel monolith housed hundreds of buses, stores, and small shops, all to add to the traveler's convenience and bolster the city's revenues.

I watched as the well-dressed visitors poured out of Port Authority and into the waiting cabs that lined the curb. Many were on their way to work, or off for a day of sightseeing. Yet across the street from this costly Ellis Island of commuters were old, decaying two-story buildings embracing the last of the porn palaces and twenty-four-hour peep shows. Their suggestive signs and bright lights were the jewel in the crown of their sleazy allure. Below one sign, a homeless person was sleeping on the metal sidewalk grates, taking advantage of the steam coming from the subway below.

57

...Give me your tired, your poor,
Your huddled masses yearning to breathe free.
The wretched refuse of your teeming shore.
Send these, the homeless, tempest-toast to me.
I lift my lamp beside the golden door!

I wonder if Emma Lazarus knew when she wrote those immortal words over a hundred years ago, that the light coming from that lamp would, one day, be neon?

"Kirby's Virtual Reality Palace," the sign read. "What happened to the 'Penny Arcade' sign?" I asked as Ron pulled up to the curb. "Kirby changed the whole place. It used to be a cool little pinball arcade; now it looks like a casino."

"You never could handle change," Ron said.

"I'm all for change—as long as it doesn't include me."

Ron was about to ramble on about my inability to adapt when a tall, slender girl with dark shoulder-length hair and a long fur coat approached the car. She couldn't have been more than eighteen, but she looked at least twenty-five. She rapped on my window.

"Hey, honey, you looking for some action?" she asked as soon as I rolled down the window. She was bending forward slightly, exposing her ample cleavage. Before I could answer, she looked closely at us both.

"Are you two twins?" She got excited. "For fifty dollars we could have a real good time."

"I couldn't take your money," I said, smiling.

A fast smile came to her face. Unfortunately it came off even faster when she noticed the shield Ron was displaying in his right hand.

"Damn. You're a cop?"

"Cops. *Plural*," I said, showing her my badge.

"But...you're twins," she said, confused, as if the two

58

were somehow mutually exclusive.

"Life's full of surprises isn't it?" I answered.

"You gonna bust me?"

"Not today, darlin'. No time."

"This is a warning," Ron interrupted. "If I see you back here, you're a collar."

"I owe ya." She winked and then hurried down the street.

"When I think about the lives Lonsdale has ruined, I want to kill him!" Ron said.

"Depending on how things go in the next half hour, you might get your chance." I checked the clip in my gun. "Ready?"

"No."

"No?"

"Give me a second."

"Give you a second?"

"What are you an echo? I need a second."

"What for?"

"It's been a while since I questioned anyone."

"You're a lawyer!"

"I meant under these circumstances." Ron nodded toward my Colt.

"Is that all? Relax. It'll come right back to you. Like riding a bike."

"Do you think?"

"If not, we'll kill all the witnesses."

"Let's try not to kill anyone today, Jerry. If trouble breaks out, we'll contain it, not instigate it. Got it?"

"OK, but you're taking all the fun out of this."

Inside the arcade, lights flashed and kids screamed while playing video games. It wasn't my type of place anymore. Gone were the skee-ball machines and the constant dinging of pinball tables.

We headed toward the back, past all the games, to a hallway guarded by two goons. I could see the outline of their shoulder holsters.

The shorter, dark-haired one was built big and stood about six-foot-two. The other, who had bright orange hair, was about six-foot-five and built even bigger. Both were making time with two good-looking girls. *Why do beautiful women hang around assholes?* I thought. We attempted to pass between them.

"Where do you think you two are going?" said the redhead, grabbing my shoulder.

"We're here to see Kirby," I answered. "Don't trouble yourselves. We'll find our own way."

"Look, Butch. Twins!" Big Red said to his partner. Turning to me, he added, "Mr. Lonsdale don't see people."

"Unless he's gone blind, he'll see us," I said.

"Do I know you'se?" he asked through a heavy Brooklyn accent.

"I don't think we've had the pleasure," Ron said. "My name is Gold." He showed his ID. "Detective Ron Gold. This is my partner."

"You got to be kidding. You don't look like no cops," he laughed. Then his buddy began to laugh. Then the two women began to laugh.

"Laugh and the whole world laughs with you..." I said. Everyone stopped laughing.

"I don't know you'se," he said. "You know them, Butch?"

"No I don't, Sean."

"That's what I thought. Get lost."

"You know," I said as I straightened my coat where Godzilla had grabbed me. "Is it me, or is his hair the only bright thing on this guy?"

"What did you say?" Sean bellowed, moving his girl aside.

"A shame. So young. So stupid," I added.

"Mentally challenged is the politically correct term, Jerry."

"How insensitive of me."

Before I could offer an apology, Sean took a swing. I faded to my left and then landed a solid combination to his ribs followed by a fast right to his jaw. He went down faster than Monica Lewinski in the Oval Office. As I turned, Butch was coming for a piece of me. Ron intercepted him with a right to the head. He staggered backward, shook off the punch, and came at Ron again. Ron grabbed his attacker's arm, wrenched it behind his back, and hurled him face first into the wall.

"Now, which way is Kirby's office?" Ron demanded, placing pressure on the twisted arm. Stunned, Butch said, "Last door...end of the hall."

Ron turned to disperse the small crowd of kids that had formed when, without warning, Butch reached for his piece. As he aimed his gun at Ron's back, I aimed a roundhouse kick at the side of his head. I watched as gun and goon dropped to the floor. He was down for the count.

"I can't believe he went for his gun," Ron said. "He really isn't very bright."

"Mentally challenged is the politically correct term," I answered.

We continued down the hall to another door guarded by another Mr. Universe type.

"Kirby in?" I asked.

The guard smiled, "You need an appointment to see Kirby."

"So we've been told. But we're still going to talk to him." I flashed my badge. He wasn't impressed, either.

"I understand you're trying to do your job. We're just doing ours," Ron replied tactfully. "Step aside and let's all do this the easy way."

"No appointment, no talk." He spat on the floor.

"Another mental giant," I said.

"No appointment, no—"

Before he could finish, I landed a left in his midsection. He doubled over.

"Bodybuilders today don't spend enough time on their abs," Ron noted.

"So true." I kicked in Kirby's door, throwing Mr. Universe in first. Kirby was sitting behind a big desk in the far left corner of the room. Across the desk from Kirby was Red Donlan, nursing what seemed to be a cup of coffee. He recognized us immediately.

"What the fuck?" Kirby yelled, jumping from behind his desk. I sent the guard I was holding flying onto a sofa, which was unfortunate for the other two guys who happened to be sitting there. The three of them fumbled around.

"What are you two doing here?" Kirby screamed.

"Kirby, is that any way to treat a couple of old friends?" I asked.

Three years had sure taken its toll on Kirby. He was almost bald.

"Kirby, you look like hell. What happened to your hair?"

"It's called male pattern baldness," Ron informed me.

"He should look into another pattern. That one sucks."

"You comedians done?" Kirby shouted, facing his men on the couch. "Throw these bums out." The clowns on the couch got to their feet and started toward us.

"Kirby, you can't throw us out," I said, watching Red out of the corner of my eye. The three bozos didn't worry me, but it was unwise to lose sight of Red.

"Why? You ain't cops no more."

"Wrong, Kirby old boy." I pulled out my shield.

Kirby looked from my badge to the bodyguards. "I don't give a shit. Throw them out anyway."

Kirby's guys looked ready to start breaking heads when Red stood up calmly and waved them off.

"Let's not lose our cool here, fellas," Red said. "Kirby, what's a few minutes between old friends? Let's hear what's on their minds."

"Screw 'em." Kirby spat out. "'Cause of them assholes I done time."

"Cool down, Kirby." Turning to one of the thugs on the sofa, Red said, "Bobby, make Kirby a drink." Bobby did as he was told.

Kirby growled and sat back down behind his desk. He opened a humidor and lit a cigar.

"Cuban," Kirby said, pompously puffing smoke in the air. "You two know anything about Cuban cigars?"

"They're illegal," I replied.

"And that one puff cost more than your weekly pay," he retorted

"I hate when the little shit is right," I muttered to Ron.

"Let me handle this," Ron replied. Kirby and I eyed each other. "We need some information."

"What kind you looking for?" Red asked, heading back

63

toward his drink.

"What do you know about two women found dead, one a few weeks ago, and one last night?" Ron asked.

"I know a lot of women," Kirby said coldly.

"Two in particular. Both were into S&M."

"What should I know?"

"You're not cooperating, Kirby." I made myself comfortable, sitting on the corner of his desk.

"Maybe they're not in my stable."

"These women were into a higher-class clientele, but that wouldn't stop you from collecting your vig," Ron pressed.

"You thinking they was holdin' out on me so I snuffed 'em?"

"Bad for business to let the other ladies know your take can be negotiated," Ron added.

"Let me save you time, college boy," Kirby laughed. "The two you're askin' about ain't got nothing to do with me. I deal withsome kinky whores, but not them. Now get off my desk and out of my life." Kirby exhaled a large cloud of smoke from his cigar.

"Well, what do you know about them?" I slowly got up from his desk.

"I know they're dead." He smiled.

I leaned over and smacked the cigar out of Kirby's mouth. Red jumped from his stool and pulled out his gun, but mine was out first and already pointing at Kirby's temple. Ron's gun was covering the others.

"Red, you're slowing down in your old age. I remember you being faster," I said. Red smiled uncomfortably and slowly placed his gun on the bar. "Those two women had family and friends, Kirby. And they didn't die in their sleep,

64

so my brother and I want to know why."

Kirby tried to move away. I grabbed his collar with my free hand.

"Look, you sorry son of a bitch, if I don't get the answer I'm looking for by the time I count three, I'm going to do the city a favor and splatter your brains across the room. Assuming you have enough brains to reach that far."

"I don't know noth—"

"One..."

"Hey, you over there! Can't you control him? He's your brother."

"Kirby, when he gets like this, you're on your own."

"Two..." I cocked the hammer of my Colt.

"OK. OK. They weren't in my stable, and I didn't take a vig from them," Kirby cried out, sweat rolling down his face.

"That could be a reason to kill them."

"Nothin' like that. They were hands off. I was told to stay away."

"By who?"

"I-I..."

"Kirby, stuttering makes me nervous."

"You don't want to make Jerry nervous, Kirby. Not when he's holding a gun to your head."

"Vinny DiCenzio," Kirby cried out.

"*Senator* Vinny DiCenzio?" Ron repeated.

"Yeah. Him."

I pressed my gun deeper into Kirby's temple.

"I swear it's him. Now put down the fucking piece!"

I lowered my gun, patted Kirby's bald head, then started for the door. Not turning our backs on the group, I met Ron mid-room. Cautiously, we both backed up to the exit. Red nodded at us. He had lost this round, but he knew

65

there would be others. I looked at Kirby's three goons standing there, hoping Ron or I would make a mistake.

As Ron reached for the door behind him, Kirby called out, "You're gettin' old, too, Gold. You're in a bad line of work to be gettin' old."

"You an insurance agent, too, Kirby?" I replied.

"I see you again, Gold, you're a dead man!"

"You see me again, Kirby, and you'll wish I was."

"What happened to no guns?" Ron asked.

"Shit happens," I answered. I turned back to the crowd. "Gentlemen, we're out of here. Try and follow and I'll shoot the first one out the door. Got it?" They all nodded. "Good."

When we hit the street, Ron holstered his gun and got behind the wheel of the car. I joined him on the passenger's side, my gun still drawn.

"Hit the gas," I called out. Within seconds we were barreling up Eighth Avenue. I leaned back in my seat, relaxed, and looked over at Ron. He glared back at me, anything but relaxed.

"What I tell you? Just like riding a bike."

10

"Why are we heading uptown?" I asked Ron as he continued north on Eighth Avenue. "Turn this crate around and let's talk to DiCenzio!"

"There's something I want to check out at the crime scene first. Then we can go talk to the senator."

"Vinny has some explaining to do. I want to hear it now."

"Right after the Westlake house."

"No, DiCenzio's first," I insisted. "The house will be there tomorrow. I want to get to Vinny before that mental munchkin we just left can tip him off."

"Kirby's already warned him. Why do you think we weren't followed?"

"Because we're two of the meanest guys in town?"

"Or he was too busy dialing his good buddy, the

senator."

"Or that," I conceded. "I would love to know what DiCenzio has to do with S&M."

"I'm not going to question one of New York's top political figures until I'm sure what questions to ask."

"For starters let's ask him why a state senator is associating with Manhattan's biggest pimp. Or what his connection to Westlake is?"

"DiCenzio's a family man. How many married men do you know would admit to a relationship like that?"

"What 'alleged?' He told Kirby hands off."

"This is a delicate situation, Jerry."

"Come on, this isn't the stone age."

"Eighties, nineties, or now, infidelity is a delicate topic—especially for a politician."

"You're in a good relationship. If you were arrested for soliciting, you think Emily would be angry?"

"We're not married yet. And sure, she'd probably forgive me—by the time she had to give my eulogy."

"Stop exaggerating."

"You've never been married either," he countered. "We don't want to go after someone like Vinny DiCenzio and his political machine until we know exactly what we're doing."

As we drove I thought about what Ron had said. At fifty-two, Vinny DiCenzio was not only politically connected, he was adored by the Manhattan elite and loved by the working class. A moderate Republican, he preached fiscal responsibility but was laissez-faire on most social issues. Vinny believed in feeding the people as long as the state didn't foot the bill. He painstakingly juggled his politics so every constituent, rich or poor, felt they got their fair share: his platform had something for everybody.

Vinny was definitely on his way up. At one time there was even talk he would be the next Republican candidate for the U.S. Senate. From state senator to U.S. senator— maybe Ron was right. Perhaps patience would be prudent.

"OK. I'll tell you what, why don't we wait to see DiCenzio and go to the crime scene."

"Good thinking," Ron said as we pulled up in front of the Westlake townhouse. "I wish I'd thought of that."

The street was clogged with network news vans and reporters doing their stand-ups. I glanced at the WZAD van hoping to catch sight of Nikki. She wasn't there, which saved me the trouble of ignoring her.

Ron and I ducked under the blue police barricades. I checked the time: four p.m. I'd been up for over thirty hours, and I could feel my second wind slipping away. We displayed our shields to the patrolmen guarding the stoop and entered the foyer, where I found one of the cops who had been at the crime scene that morning.

"What are you still doing here, Brown?" I asked.

"Overtime. It helps pay for the Christmas gifts I couldn't afford last week. Or this week, for that matter."

"How's it going?"

"You tell me. You're the detectives."

"For the record, the investigation is making great progress," Ron replied.

"And off the record?" Brown pried.

"Who knows? We're only the detectives. But thanks for asking," I replied. I made my way upstairs. Ron stayed downstairs, talking to Brown.

The scene on the second floor was far more sedate than it had been that morning. The brass had left; only the members of the crime unit and a few uniforms remained. I started to nose around when I heard orders being barked behind me. I thought it was Walter Greeley trying to make an impressive entrance. Then I realized it couldn't be: the orders were concise and correct, two characteristics of command that had always seemed to elude the good lieutenant.

I turned to see Lieutenant Mitch Palmieri, head of the crime unit, causing a commotion. Mitch came from a family of cops. Like his father and brother, he was a no-bullshit kind of guy. Fifty-six and compact, the Brooklyn-born cop could nonetheless pack a punch like someone three times his size. Palmieri was big on bluster and short on tact. But that hadn't stopped him from handling the forensic investigations for some of the most famous murder cases in the city's history—including the Madam Murders.

As Palmieri approached, he stopped at a small circle of crime unit technicians and one uniformed officer shooting the breeze.

"Hey, you, officer—what's your name? Do you belong here?" Mitch yelled, knowing full well he didn't.

"Bannon. I'm with traffic control, lieutenant."

"Then, Officer Bannon, go play in traffic and get the hell away from my crime scene." The group disbanded immediately except for Bannon who looked as if he wanted to take on Mitch. Bad Idea, I thought to myself. One look into Mitch Palmieri's eyes and it was apparent this was a man who gave shit, not took it. On a closer look, Bannon must have seen that too and decided it wiser to go play in traffic. As Bannon headed for the door, Mitch moved on to his next unfortunate subordinate. This time it was a detective having a smoke.

"Crowley, what are you doing?"

70

"Nothing...."

"You think it's fair for the city of New York to pay you to do nothing?" He was leaning in toward Crowley's face.

"Ease up, lieutenant, I'm just finishing a smoke." Crowley stepped back to take another drag. As he raised the butt to his lips, Mitch grabbed it away.

"You got the balls to smoke at my crime scene?" Mitch exploded. "You got some kinda job security I don't know about, Crowley?" he said, accenting the last part of his name like a marine drill sergeant.

"You worried about second-hand smoke?" Crowley joked.

"I'm worried about your continued employment with the NYPD, you dumb son of a bitch. You don't know better than to contaminate my crime scene? Get back to work before I kick your ass up and down Broadway." As Crowley left, the ever-diplomatic crime unit chief turned his attention to me.

"Gold, right?" he asked as he offered his hand. "I don't know which brother you are, but I had a feeling it wouldn't be too long before one of you turned up. Been a while."

"We really should try and get together every two or three serial murders," I said, shaking his hand.

"You must be the wiseass brother.

"Jerry," I confirmed.

"That's it. Jerry.

"Right," I said, "Jerry The Wiseass Gold."

Palmieri grinned. "Where's your better half?"

"He's around somewhere."

"I hope so. Him I liked. You, Mr. Wiseass, I tolerated."

"Is that any way to talk to a crime-fighter extraordinaire?"

"That's the only reason I talk to you at all. What do you

71

want? I'm on a tight schedule."

"Information."

Mitch started down the hall. "If I got it, it's yours. Talk fast."

"You think this is Evanston's work?" I asked, following.

"That's some first question." Mitch continued walking, his eyes glued to the floor.

"I usually open with a joke, but you're in a rush."

Palmieri lifted his eyes and inspected the hallway. He seemed uncomfortable with its openness.

"Could it be Evanston?" he shrugged. "Yeah, it could be. And I could be the Pope, but I ain't. A lot of the details of these murders and the ones you investigated are similar. But what we got here is a copycat."

"What makes you think so?"

"Thirty-three years on the job. Thirty-three years of hard experience. That's what makes me think so."

I didn't reply. I kept my eyes locked with his. I wasn't one of his CSU underlings. He didn't fluster me. If he didn't know that already, he was about to learn it. I waited for him to say something worth hearing. I didn't have to wait long.

"Thirty-three long years I've been dissecting the acts of these murdering bastards," he said reflectively. No great revelation there, but I sensed there was a mother lode of information in there somewhere.

Mitch took a deep breath. "For one thing, the initials burned into this victim's thigh were not the same size as the ones in the previous murders."

"How do you know?"

"How do I know? What are we in, fuckin kindergarten? Don't play with me, Gold. You got a question, ask it."

"Fair enough. You had the M.E. compare the two?"

"So?"

"So who asked you to compare them?"

"Why do you think someone had to ask me?"

"Come on, Mitch, who's fuckin with who now? Stop screwing with me."

Palmieri grinned. We both knew serial murderers are very particular about how they do their killing. They always choose the same type of victim, perform the same rituals— and use the same tools over and over again.

"Look, I would have had them measured even if he hadn't told me to."

Pay dirt.

"He *told* you to? *He*?"

Mitch let out a laugh, but it wasn't because anything was funny. Not unlike a chess master who has been duped by his opponent, it was the sound of unconditional surrender. Chalk one up one for J. Gold, crime fighter extraordinaire.

"Yeah," Palmieri replied, knowing he couldn't skirt the issue any longer. "Sanchez asked for the comparison."

"Really? It's now standard operating procedure for a deputy commissioner to get involved in a murder investigation?"

"No, it ain't," Mitch said. "Look, I just did it sooner rather than later is all, just to get the guy off my back. He's a strange one, that Sanchez."

"In what way?"

"He thinks the whole case rests on that one piece of information. The guy has been a detective. But I'm the one who had to give him other possibilities."

"Like?" I asked.

"Like, what if Evanston *is* alive. Could be he lost the

original branding iron and got a new one. It's not like he could go to the local precinct's lost-and-found looking for it," Mitch added.

"Do you buy that story?"

"Fuck no, I wouldn't even rent it. Is Evanston dead? Yes. Can I prove it? No. My gut tells me this is the work of a copycat. My gut's never wrong."

I nodded.

"My gut also tells me it takes a real sick son of a bitch to do something like this. But it takes an even sicker son of a bitch to copy it. You'd better find this guy, pronto."

"One last thing?" I asked.

"I gotta get moving."

"You're always moving, Mitch," I heard a friendly voice say. It was Ron. He was coming toward us with a huge smile and an open hand that Mitch shook readily. "You'd better slow up and start to smell the roses. You're not getting any younger."

"Where have you been?" I asked.

"Around. How's the family, your father, your brother?" Ron asked.

Mitch growled. "I haven't spoken to my father or brother in five years, and I don't miss them."

"Kids OK?" Ron forged ahead, unsure if it was a safe subject.

"Oh my kids are wonderful, thanks for asking," Mitch said sweetly. "Those two kids are the best thing that ever happened in my life."

"Ron smiled with relief. "Your wife's good?"

"Actually, she's a royal pain in the ass," he howled. "Gold, you're married, right?"

"Almost," Ron smiled.

"How about you?" he said, turning toward me.

"Not even close."

"Good. Don't do it. Let me tell you my plan," Mitch continued. "In ten years, the girls will be out of the house, the dog will be dead, and I'm going to dump my wife. She can have whatever she wants, but she's got to go. Then I'm going to find a twenty-year-old babe with huge tits and screw my twilight years away. I'm just counting the days."

"Won't that be dangerous at your age?" Ron asked.

"Hell, I'm just reaching my sexual prime. It's my wife who's holding me back."

"I hate to interrupt, but I have another question I need answered," I said.

"I thought we were done."

"Answer this one and we are."

"Anything to get rid of you."

"Did you find a black book at either this site or the Atwell scene?"

"We found one at the Atwell scene. A leather-bound address book."

"Was it vouched and turned in to the property locker?"

"We dusted and bagged it. But it was never turned in. It was the only real lead we had. Greeley held on to it."

"Anything turn up from it?"

"You'd have to talk to the primary about that."

"The primary being Lieutenant. Greeley?" Ron asked. Mitch nodded.

"Does he still have the book?"

"I don't know, Ron. Once the evidence is out of my hands, I don't keep tabs on it. Greeley is responsible for the chain of custody."

"What about here?" I asked.

Mitch shrugged his shoulders. "Nothing yet."

"It's still early in the investigation," Ron interrupted as he grabbed my arm and started moving me toward the door. "Good seeing you again, Mitch. Let's go, Jerry."

"Let's go, Jerry? I didn't want to come in the first place. But since we're here, I'd like to find out who has that address book," I said, shaking Ron's hand from my arm.

"I think we found all we're going to find here," Ron said, brushing his coat pocket and looking me in the eye.

I relented. "Take care, Mitch. Thanks for the help."

Mitch grunted his acknowledgment and started down the hall.

We were about to leave when we heard a gruff voice roar, "What in God's good name do you two think you're doing here?"

I turned to see a white-haired, stoop-shouldered man moving our way. Lieutenant Walter Greeley, looking just as pathetic as he had three years earlier. Nothing about him had changed—not even his clothes. He looked like Alfred Hitchcock with a bad hairpiece.

"Palmieri, who gave you permission to talk with these two bozos?"

"That's Detective Bozos," I said proudly, displaying my shield. "We're ba-ack."

"Quiet!" Greeley sneered.

"Walt, is that any way to talk to an old friend?"

"We're not old friends."

"How can you say that? We go back a long time. Not as long as that suit you're wearing. But we have history."

Greeley's lip started to twitch, and his face turned crimson. "I thought I was through with the likes of you."

"Surprise," I said, flashing him my brightest smile.

"There's no place for a wiseass like you on my police force. Not then and not now."

"Your police force? You bought the NYPD?"

"I rent it from my son-in-law."

"And how is the Lieutenant Governor Denton, Walt?"

"Employed, which is more than the two of you will be after I get back to the precinct."

"If you get to the precinct as quickly as you get to a murder scene, I'll be able to retire first."

Greeley turned to Ron. "Gold, was your brother born a moron?"

"No. He was stricken with it later in life."

"Thanks for your support," I whispered."

"Don't mention it."

"Palmieri, answer my question. Who told you these guys could have access?"

"Don't put me in the middle of this bullshit. HQ told me that what these guys want, they get. You got a problem with that, take it downtown. I got work to do."

Mitch turned to leave when Greeley took him aside. Ron nodded toward the stairs.

"The way the good lieutenant likes to hear himself talk, we can be across town before he's finished with Mitch," Ron said.

Ron was right, but I wanted to see Mitch and Greeley go at it.

"Mitch," Greeley said. "We might have to have them here, but we don't have to work with them. They're not team players. Get what I'm telling you?"

"Yeah, I get what you're telling me. They're not team players," Mitch repeated indifferently.

"That's right. And they should not be privy to certain

delicate information because—"

"—we're not team players!" I interjected.

"Will you let the man do his own talking," Ron said as he elbowed me in the ribs.

"I thought this was like Jeopardy. You know, first one with the right answer buzzes in."

"They're not team players, Mitch," Greeley continued, ignoring us. "Right?"

"Wrong," Mitch replied. "I already told you, what they want, they get. I don't give a rat's ass what team they're on. The brass downtown wants it that way. Now, do you mind if I get back to work, or do you want to bench the entire investigation?"

"No, of course not," Greeley responded, suddenly cordial. "However, let me remind you, Mitch, that I am in a position to help you—and your career— should I ever have the opportunity. And I would gladly do that for a fellow team member."

"And if I'm not, what are you going to do, trade me?"

"'Trade me,'" I laughed. "Good one, Mitch."

Greeley was tugging at his collar, his eyes angrily moving between Mitch and me.

"Greeley, I got things to do."

Greeley watched as Palmieri made his way down the hall. He wasn't happy with Mitch's answers. But even Greeley, as dense as he was, knew enough not to mess with Mitch, even if he *had* made him look like a fool in front of us.

"Let's go, Ron. I've had enough fun for one day."

Greeley cleared his throat.

"Palmieri," he shouted authoritatively in an attempt to save what little face he had left. "Did those guys disturb anything here?"

"Just you, Walt," I said starting down the stairs. "Just you."

11

The thought of Mitch and Greeley going at it kept me smiling as we left the townhouse. It gave me such a warm feeling I didn't even notice the cold until I heard one of the uniforms push back a group of reporters heading toward us.

"Detectives," one called out, "any new developments inside?"

No, she's still dead I wanted to answer. "No comment," I said.

"C'mon, give us a break. We're trying to do our jobs," another called from the crowd.

"So are we," Ron replied. The reporters were beginning to move closer to the barricade. They clogged the entire right side of the street as they and their crews moved closer.

"You're not helping matters. This neighborhood is

trying to deal with its loss," Ron continued. "It doesn't need you obstructing the streets and feeding their fears."

"Yeah, why don't all of you get lost," I added.

"It's our duty to report the news!" a clean-cut kid replied as he tried to climb over the barricade. "It's our constitutional right to be here."

"Look, buddy," I said pushing him back. "You're not Jimmy Olson, this isn't Metropolis, and I'm not Superman. Try that again and you'll be sorry."

"Are you threatening me?"

"Do I need to?"

"Jerry, he does have his rights," Ron said.

"To be annoying?"

"You think you've got a monopoly on that particular Constitutional right? Let me handle this."

I stepped aside as Ron lectured the group on First Amendment rights and journalistic responsibility. I walked toward West End Avenue, where I noticed Officer Bannon, the traffic cop Palmieri had reamed out earlier, arguing with a motorist. He was motioning to a classic 1965 Jaguar E-type convertible in mint condition to turn around. The driver defiantly remained where she was. I was admiring the Jag's green racing paint and how it sparkled under the street lights as I listened to its twelve-cylinder engine purr. Bannon seemed less impressed. He continued yelling at the windshield of the unyielding auto.

It was a damn fine-looking machine. And stepping out of it came a damn fine-looking woman. She couldn't have been more than thirty-six—thirty-six, twenty-four, thirty-six—with long blonde hair, shocking blue eyes, and an air of sophistication that made her seem older than she was. She was wearing a black leather waist-length coat, tight jeans, and spike-heeled black boots.

Bannon was writing her a citation and threatening to have the car towed. Unconcerned, the woman abandoned the car, leaving Bannon fuming. She and her skin-tight jeans sauntered toward Dave Wilkins, who was leaning against one of the barricades. This woman knew how to work it. I watched in awe as her back pockets shifted gracefully as she walked. Then I remembered that Ron had something he wanted me to see. I tore myself away from the show and called out to Ron.

"Hey, Clarence Darrow, we have work to do."

"I'm almost done."

"Hey, guys," I shouted into the crowd, "the cop in charge is Lieutenant Walter Greeley. He's going to be out in a few minutes. Why don't you wait over there," I said, pointing to an area closer to the door. "He'll be glad to answer all your questions."

The group left Ron in mid-sentence and scrambled for a spot near the door.

"Done now?" I asked, walking back to Ron.

"Done."

"What did you want to show me?"

Ron reached into his coat pocket and removed a photograph of the late Diane Westlake in the arms of a smiling Senator Vinny DiCenzio.

"Vinny again," I said. "Where did you find this?"

"The third-floor bedroom. I took the opportunity to investigate while you were talking to Mitch. I was looking for Westlake's black book. Whether she was a pro or not, she needed to keep track of her appointments."

"You found her black book?"

"Not exactly." Ron reached back into his pocket and

removed a CD: Michael Jackson's *Thriller*.

"That's not a black book," I said.

"I was looking at her entertainment center when I noticed shelves of compact discs."

"So she liked Michael Jackson. Big deal," I said, examining the CD. "It's not a crime."

"I don't think she did. All the other discs in her collection were of classical music. Some of them were extremely impressive. I almost wish—"

"—Get to the point," I urged.

"Sorry. I digressed. It didn't seem right—only one pop disc among all that classical music—but I left the CD alone. Then I went into her bedroom. It had already been turned upside down by CSU. Mitch's people are very thorough."

"I'll tell him you're impressed next time we speak."

"I noticed a PC on her desk," he continued deliberately.

"How unusual for a computer consultant."

"Not unusual at all. A computer consultant would likely use a computer to keep her appointments—"

"—Damn good thought—"

"—but I couldn't check the entire system with CSU there."

I grabbed the CD. "Westlake backed up her computer files onto a compact disc."

"She was too smart to leave sensitive material on her computer."

I looked at the back cover of the Jackson disc closely. The sixth track on the CD—"Beat It"—was highlighted in yellow. I opened the cover. Resting in the jewel case was a homemade compact disc.

Ron put his hand in the air, and I was about to give him a high five, when the sound of a woman's voice stopped me cold. It was a familiar voice. It was the voice from the 911 tape. I turned to see where it was coming from, and there, arguing with Dave Wilkins, was the Jaguar Lady.

"Ron—that voice..."

"Voice?"

"Her," I said, pointing to the right of Wilkins. "She's the one who made the 911 call."

I starting to approach her when Greeley came storming down the steps, shouting my name. I didn't have time for this. Thinking fast, I called out, loud enough for the reporters to hear, "Lieutenant Greeley?"

The words were barely out of my mouth before the reporters rushed forward. Like water through a burst dam, they engulfed him—but not before he grabbed the collar of my jacket. As the reporters screamed their questions, Greeley tried to push them away.

"Get back!" he yelled. "Wilkins, Brown, move these reporters away!"

As the officer attempted to control the crowd, I attempted to get away. I needed to speak to that woman. But trying to get to her through the chaotic swirl of journalists was impossible. I felt like a salmon swimming against the current.

"Where is it, Gold?" Greeley hollered.

"Where's what?" I tried to keep moving forward, but I couldn't reach the woman. I was feeling more like a lox than a salmon. I'd just gotten screwed and I didn't even have to swim upstream. I watched as the woman tensed up. She turned and headed for her car, looking spooked.

"The picture!" he barked as he spun me around. "I know you took it, and I want it now."

"Later, Greeley."

"Now. I want it now."

Great, I thought. He picks *now* to start acting like a detective. I gripped him by the lapel and pushed him against my car.

"You don't know anything, old man. Now get out of the way." But he didn't let up, and the blonde-haired beauty slipped into her sports car.

"Hey, lieutenant, calm down. You're way out of line," Ron said.

I wanted to tell him to forget the old man and go after the woman, but I couldn't tip off Ron without Greeley and the rest of the world hearing. I heard the Jaguar's engine rev. There was nothing I could do. The Jaguar Lady put the car into reverse and backed down the street.

It took me a second before I addressed Ron and Greeley, both dancing with me against the car. "Wilkins," I screamed. "Forget the reporters and get this old man off me before you're minus one partner!"

Wilkins came running, getting between me and the lieutenant.

"Old man. Who are you calling an old man?" Greeley spit. "In my day, when I walked a beat—"

"—dinosaurs were roaming the planet," I yelled as I threw open my car door. Ron was already behind the wheel. The reporters tightened their circle around Greeley.

We were backing out when Greeley shouted, "I find out you stole that picture and you're through. Again. I'll have your jobs!"

"You wouldn't want my job," I shouted back. "I have to work with too many morons and one fossil!"

85

12

It was just past six. The winter streets of Manhattan had been dark for some time. This might have bothered many who walked the neighborhood where Diane Westlake was murdered. For them, the night came too soon. But not for others.

The Executioner welcomed the dark. The evenings afforded anonymity that the light of day did not. The Executioner was watching as the Gold brothers argued with the older detective, feeling invincible. The brothers would have to be dealt with. But they were not sinners, yet. They still walked the thin line between the righteous and the damned. A warning was needed. But more urgent matters first. *Only an avenging angel, doing God's work, would be able to walk the streets of Manhattan unnoticed,* the Executioner thought. *God has allowed me to dispatch another enemy.   Now it is time to prepare to take the next godless soul.* The Executioner reached into the pocket of the cloak and removed a photo of a woman with a black lily tattooed above her left breast. The hooded figure hailed a passing cab.

"Where you going?" the driver asked, looking into the rearview mirror.

"To work," the Executioner replied with a malevolent smile. "To work."

13

It was half past seven when we got to Ron's house in the suburbs of New Jersey. Metuchen is a quiet town southwest of the city that offers its residents a tranquility that Manhattan can't. And Ron insisted he needed tranquility to review Westlake's disc. I was still fuming about the Jaguar Lady, positive it was her voice on the tape. As I followed Ron into his colonial and down the center hall, I was having a hard time feeling tranquil.

"It's been a long day, Jerry. Relax for a while. I want to have a nice quiet dinner with Emily."

"She was right there and got away," I snapped.

Ron stopped in his tracks. Drilling his index finger into my chest, he said, "Calm down. Take a deep breath. Tomorrow is another day."

"Damn it, we had her."

"Why are you so sure she's the one? How could you hear her voice over all that street noise and still be sure?"

"I know what I heard. I'd recognize that British accent anywhere."

"Fine," Ron sighed. "I didn't hear anything, but I'll take your word for it. We'll track her down."

"Did you get a license number?" I asked, agitated.

"Don't need it."

"She's going to surrender herself?"

"Didn't you tell me Bannon was ready to tow her car? He had to have issued her a summons."

The expression on my face changed. Maybe this town did offer tranquility. "Let's call the station."

"Not tonight. All the information will be there tomorrow. Tonight, think quiet dinner, computers, and sleep," Ron said, calmly tapping the CD in his pocket.

"It's going to drive me nuts."

"That's not a far drive; it's more of a short stroll."

I followed Ron into his house, continued down the end of the hall, and entered the kitchen. To the right was a dinette and chairs; the table was set for four. Opposite the table was a sink and counter area. Across the room was a doorway to the family room. I heard Emily, but couldn't find her.

Ron and Emily had gotten together before Ron and I left the NYPD. I followed her voice and found her with a telephone tucked between her shoulder and ear. She was wearing a red Rutgers University football jersey, red sweatpants, and white running shoes. Her dark, shoulder-length hair fell to the side of the receiver. Her deep blue eyes acknowledged my presence. She flashed me what I called "*el grande*": a thousand–watt smile that could make a dying

89

man forget his problems. It wasn't a sexy smile but a warm, caring one that rose up from deep within her. It must have taken all of her petite, hundred–pound being to produce it. I pulled out a chair and sat down.

Just then Ron came up behind Emily and wrapped his arms around her waist and kissed her on the side of her neck, eliciting an inopportune giggle into the phone. She wiggled free of Ron's grasp and quickly recovered her composure.

"John, could we continue this discussion at the office?" she said, and then, "Thank you so much. We'll talk then. Good night." She crossed over to the far wall and replaced the receiver.

Emily was an anomaly. As legal counsel for MagnaFlex, a multinational conglomerate, she dealt with issues I couldn't even conceive of. But at home she wasn't a high-powered attorney—just a caring, giving woman who found time for everything and everyone in her life, including her sister's two daughters. Emily's sister Ann had divorced early and didn't always make time in her busy life for her daughters, Kate and Leslie. They were nine and five, respectively, and often spent time with Ron and Emily.

"I wish you wouldn't do that," she admonished.

"Ever?" Ron replied.

"Just when I'm on the phone," Emily laughed. "Now is OK." Emily turned toward him and they kissed. As the embrace ended, she looked at me and flashed me *el grande* again.

"I'm home, June," I said, "Where are Wally and the Beaver?"

"That's cute," she said, "Are you staying for dinner?"

"For the night."

"You mean you're mine for the night?" she joked, while making room at the table for one more. "How many women can say that?"

"How many would want to?" Ron added, as he headed out of the kitchen. "I'm going to say hello to the girls. You coming?"

"In a second. I'm saying hello to my brother's favorite woman."

"Your brother's only woman," he corrected.

"Ron, please get the girls ready for dinner," Emily requested. "They're staying the night too."

"Consider it done. Nothing like a nice quiet dinner with my family," he said, disappearing out the door.

Emily walked over to the kitchen door and watched as Ron crossed the adjoining dinning room to the family room until she heard the girls greeting him, with their giggling "Uncle Ronnies".

"What is going on, Jerry?" she asked. "Ron called me from the road. He sounded happy and said he had a surprise. But he didn't explain."

I reached inside my pocket and displayed my shield. "We're cops again," I said excitedly, as if I had just told her we had won the lottery. The expression on Emily's face said she didn't share my enthusiasm.

"We're cops," I said again, hoping that would invoke a smile. But my words just hung in the air, and a pensive silence overtook the room

"Why?" she asked softly.

"It's the Madam Murderer. They think he's back."

"No one else could handle this case?"

"Maybe," I said, "but not as efficiently. We're a team, and the city needs us."

Emily's cold gaze cut me off. "All right. I missed the excitement," I admitted, to her and to myself.

"Couldn't you get a hobby? I hear skydiving is exciting, and you don't need a partner."

"Too dangerous."

"And this isn't? You and Ron aren't kids anymore."

"It's not like we're breaking down doors."

"I worry," she said. I moved next to Emily and placed my arm around her shoulder.

"There's nothing to worry about. We'll conduct the investigation and then—"

"—then what? Give back your shields?"

"Are you jealous of the shield?" Hearing my words, I knew it was the wrong thing to say.

"The shield was your life," she said, moving away.

"Emily."

"Don't 'Emily' me. I know what I'm saying. That piece of metal may be a key to excitement for you. To Ron it was a badge of honor, and with honor comes the kind of responsibility that could get him killed."

"He's my twin brother."

"He's the love of my life; he's my best friend," she said with tears forming in her eyes. "And I won't let you take him so you can have your shield."

Uncertain of what to say or do, I watched as a tear slowly fell from Emily's eye. I gently wiped it away from her cheek, hoping that somehow I would remove her concern along with it. But no sooner had I wiped one tear away than another took its place. I realized how lucky my brother was. I reached for a napkin and was about to wipe away another tear, but Emily prevented me. I felt her need and hugged her in my arms as she wept softly.

"Emily," I said tenderly, "life is a day-to-day deal. I can't promise you what will or won't be tomorrow. When tomorrow comes, we'll deal with it. Ron loves you and that comes before the job. That I promise."

Emily slowly withdrew from my arms.

"I won't let anything happen to Ron. Before it comes to that, we'll walk away."

She took the napkin from my hand, dried her eyes, and attempted to display a smile. Not *el grande*, but a smile all the same. She kissed me on the cheek.

"In the meantime, think of all the perks of being a cop's babe."

"Like?"

"Like getting to sleep with an ace crime fighter."

Emily let out a reserved chuckle.

"Maybe he'll even handcuff you to the bedpost."

Her reserved chuckle broke into an outrageous laugh as Katie entered.

"Aunt Emmy, why are you getting handcuffed to a bed?" she asked innocently, causing Emily to laugh harder.

"Did you do something wrong?"

"Nobody's getting handcuffed, Katie," she said, trying to catch her breath. Katie accepted the answer and headed for her chair.

"Hey, don't I get a hello?"

"Hello, Uncle Jerry," she said from her seat, unfolding her napkin and placing it on her lap.

"And a hello right back at you," I responded.

"Good thing it was Katie," I whispered to Emily.

She nodded gratefully. Leslie was not as reserved and would have asked a thousand questions until she got all the facts. That one is a cop in the making.

93

"Where's your sister?" Emily asked.

"She's channel surfing," Katie answered.

"Channel surfing? She's only five," I said.

"I wonder who taught her that, Jerry?" Emily asked sarcastically.

"Who taught Mozart to compose? No one. She's a natural," I said, walking toward the family room to get her. There I saw a tiny five-year-old sitting on the sofa in front of a large-screen television flipping through every channel on the dial.

"Hey, cutie pie, it's dinnertime," I said from behind the sofa.

"Uncle Jerry!" A tiny voice greeted me as she climbed up on the couch to give me a hug.

"We don't climb on the furniture, Leslie," Ron reminded her.

I scooped her up, remote and all, and proceeded to return the hug.

"Uncle Jerry, this is the way you do it, right?" she asked, referring to the way she was quickly switching from program to program with the remote.

"Definitely a natural," I said with pride when Leslie stopped the channel selector on a news bulletin. There on the screen was Nikki Horn. Before I could figure out what she was saying, Leslie had changed the station.

"Slow down there, darling," I said. "You don't want to burn your little fingers out."

Ron took the remote from her surprisingly tight grasp and put the news channel back on.

"Isn't that you and Uncle Jerry?" Leslie asked Ron.

"Seems to be, honey," he answered.

"Turn up the sound, Ron."

Nikki was discussing aspects of the Westlake murder. It had to be expected, but media attention was not a good thing: it would only increase the pressure for an arrest. I looked at my brother and slowly shook my head from side to side.

"Don't start going nuts. It's not that bad," Ron said.

"No?"

The news cut to a video clip of Raymond T. Daley, the commissioner of police, with Nikki's microphone in his face.

"At least it's not the mayor."

"They're probably saving him for the eleven o'clock news."

Raymond T. Daley had been involved with the NYPD his entire life. At fifty-five, his lanky build and silver hair gave him a grandfatherly appearance. I was impressed by how comfortable he seemed in front of the cameras. He always maintained an informal posture. This evening his left hand was in his pocket, and his right hand rubbed his ear. It was like watching Jimmy Stewart. The picture played well with the press.

"Nikki," the commissioner was saying, "I have complete faith that everything possible is being done to apprehend the animal responsible for this abominable crime. We have our best detectives spearheading the case."

"That would be detectives Jerry and Ron Gold?" Nikki asked.

"It would. They have extensive experience in such cases."

"Your ex-girlfriend is becoming our personal press agent," Ron laughed.

"Just what we need. Now every nut in town will be trying to contact us." The news station began a segment about Ron and me, with clips of us as rookies and some taken of us this morning. Ron watched silently as Nikki delivered her stand-up. When it was over, Ron hit the remote and the screen went dark.

"Commissioner Daley's money is on us," Ron said softly as he handed me the remote and took Leslie in his arms, giving her a hug.

"So much for your quiet family dinner."

14

We were parked in front of the safe house, having arrived before sunrise thanks to my superior navigation of the New Jersey Turnpike. Ron was shuffling through the pages of a printout he had gotten from Westlake's CD. He hadn't shared the contents with me, saying he needed more time to review the data. I didn't press him, even though I could see the report was disturbing him.

Inside the safe house, we passed the kitchen and saw a lone figure with his back to the door standing by the coffee machine.

"Chief," I said, checking out the donut box on the table next to him.

Flaherty turned and gazed at Ron. He was dressed in a dark blue suit, blue and white striped shirt, and a blue and red tie. He looked frostily at my faded jeans, long-sleeve black sweatshirt, and Nikes.

"Well, if it isn't the George Clooney and Daniel Craig of the NYPD," he said, pouring himself some coffee.

"You saw last night's news," I replied.

"Me and the entire tri-state area. Weren't you two told not to talk to the press?"

"We didn't encourage them, chief," Ron said.

"You didn't discourage them, either. Or did I miss that part of the show?"

"Talk to my press agent."

Flaherty smiled. "Get into the conference room. You can brief me."

"Brief you?" I said.

"Brief me. Isn't there something you'd like to share with me?"

I opened the box and offered him the only substantial thing I could get my hands on. He reached in and took one. "Conference room. Now," he said, exiting.

Ron started to follow when he noticed I wasn't moving.

"You coming?"

"You can handle it. It doesn't take both of us to say we don't have squat."

"What about Kirby, the senator, and the—"

"Squat," I interrupted. "We don't know *anything*," I said "Get it?"

"Got it. What if he presses me?"

"Play stupid."

"Then you go. Stupid is more believable coming from you."

"I have other things to do."

"Like?"

"Like tracking down the good senator's itinerary for the

98

day."

"You're going to make an appointment?"

"No. But we don't want to have to track Vinny all over town before we find and grill him."

"You mean question him."

"Whatever."

"Jerry, we're not interrogating a street hustler. He's a New York State Senator."

"He's also a murder suspect."

"That's unsubstantiated."

"That's why we need to talk with him."

"I agree. But it has to be handled diplomatically."

"Fine. We'll talk to him at the U.N. Go take care of Flaherty."

Ron headed for the conference room. I headed for the coffeepot. I poured myself a cup of freshly brewed life with a little milk, then reached for the phone on the wall. Dialing the operator, I inquired after the whereabouts of Jeanne MacDonald. The woman on the other end offered to track her down. I thanked her and hung up.

I began to feel the caffeine surge through my body. I was silently thanking God for the coffee bean when Jeanne arrived.

"You wanted me, detective?"

A truer statement had never been spoken. She was a vision dressed in a dark-blue uniform, her slacks clinging to her body like chocolate syrup to an ice cream sundae.

"Be still my heart. If it isn't my sweet Scottish lass."

"It isn't," she replied curtly, "but since you brought the subject up I'd like to discuss something with you."

"I'm listening," I said, leaning against the counter.

"I found your behavior yesterday inappropriate."

"Really?" I said. "Well, perhaps a wee bit."

"Knock it off, detective. I take my job seriously, and *I* want to be taken seriously. It's difficult enough as a woman officer to prove myself without you making a fool of me."

I observed the serious expression on her face, the unspoken anger in her body language confirming my egregious error.

"You're right," I said quickly—too quickly.

"Don't patronize me!"

"I forget how tough the job can be for a rookie, let alone a female rookie. I'm sorry."

I offered her my hand. Jeanne eyed the offer skeptically, unsure of my motives. I put my hand down while she decided if they were honorable. A moment later she replied, "Apology noted."

"Good." I carried my coffee toward the corner table.

"I hope our conversation demonstrates that a policewoman can have a brain, detective."

"Absolutely. And sometimes its even packaged nicely."

"There you go again."

"It was a joke."

"I didn't find it funny."

"Are you a cop or a critic?"

"Did you hear a word I said?"

"I heard, 'policewomen can have brains.' But not a sense of humor? Forget I said it. I need you to—"

"—to what?" she interrupted. "Do your laundry, clean your house?"

"That was a joke. You do have a sense a humor," I said sardonically.

"You probably think a woman's place is in the kitchen."

I looked around our surroundings, noting how

comfortable she looked, but decided it wiser to keep the observation to myself.

"Let's get down to business," I said.

"Business?" she exploded. "I can just imagine what that entails. I knew talking to you would be a waste of time. I should have taken this up with Captain Flaherty."

She turned to leave.

"Listen officer, I don't give a rat's ass who you take it up with, but if you want to play in the big leagues you'd better start learning the rules, and if you want to play on my team, learn them fast. There's a difference between joking and business."

"The police bible according to Gold?" Jeanne's body tensed with anger. She started to leave and then decided there was more to be said. "Who are you to teach? You with your smart remarks and lack of respect for command," she shouted. "Without respect—"

"Screw that. You want to know what I respect, Officer MacDonald? I respect things that scare the hell out of me. And right now a murderer out on the streets killing innocent women fits the bill."

"Hardly innocent women. They're hookers."

"Get your head on straight, officer. They're human beings and deserve to be treated as such despite their vocational proclivities."

"I-I wasn't implying they shouldn't be," she said, drawing back. "I was just saying if you're going to break the law then you have to accept the risks. I'm not judging them. Don't put words in my mouth."

"Then let me put an idea in your head. This madman according to you is killing hookers, what happens when he includes others?"

"Why would he?"

"Because he can, and he knows he can. He knows we can't stop him until he screws up, and that may not happen until much later in his sick little game. This guy is just getting started. He's racked up two murders that we know about and we don't know much else, even about him. Anonymity is a real plus in his profession. We could search the city for years and never find him. He could be the boy next door, your best friend's fiancé, or maybe your brother. The possibilities scare the hell out of me, and you should be scared, too. Or haven't you seen the pictures hanging in the conference room?"

"I've seen them."

"Go see them again. Those women died horribly."

"That's not the issue here." Jeanne headed for the door.

"It sure as hell is," I said. "It's the only issue."

She turned toward me. "I may be a rookie, but even I can see you're taking this case way too personally."

"It's not the case—it's the act I take personally. This bastard didn't just kill them, he humiliated them. He degraded them. He took Diane Westlake against her will, stripped her naked, and tied her to a whipping horse. Then he beat her unmercifully until he was ready to kill her. You saw those pictures. You know the agony she endured. The horrific cruelty."

"I-I don't want to think about it." Jeanne turned her head.

"Not thinking about it isn't a luxury I have. And if you're going to work for me, it's not a luxury you have, either. Diane Westlake should be home listening to Beethoven and Chopin, not lying on an ME's slab. Am I getting through to you, Officer MacDonald?"

My eyes had been locked with Jeanne's, but now I looked away and attempted to regain my composure. "You haven't worked with me before," I said calmly, "so I'll tell you how it is. I kid around a lot. If that offends you, I'm sorry. I'm not great when it comes to etiquette."

"I hadn't noticed."

"Etiquette's my partner's job. But, then, that's not why the city hired me. They hired me to solve this case fast. And it just so happens that's what Ron and I do best."

The expression on Jeanne's face changed. I could see she was about to question if we were as good as I thought. I saved her the trouble.

"There are maybe two people in the country other than my brother and me who have half a chance of catching this psychopath. Those two don't know this city better than Ron and me. So you and the Big Apple are stuck with us until we nail this nut or until someone else does—which I find unlikely, since the city's alternative is Walter Greeley."

"Pretty scary thought," she replied.

"We're going to nail this guy, Jeanne. Ron and I did this once before, and we'll do it again, and anyone standing in our way is going to wish they hadn't. Your choice is simple: you're either on the team or off."

Jeanne had heard my offer, but her expression said she didn't take to ultimatums any more than I did.

"Officer MacDonald—Jeanne—I think you show dedication and a passion for the job. It would be a mistake to let our bad start dictate your decision. This case is bigger than your needs or mine."

"Are you asking me to stay?" she asked.

"I am. I need someone who knows how to cut through the red tape. You know this office like I know a donut shop."

"Thank you. I think."

"Don't thank me yet. There's one point you and I have to be clear about."

"That is?"

"When it comes to any aspect of this case, my word is law."

"Because of the needs of your arrogant male ego?"

"Because I'm the one who is going to climb inside this sucker's sick mind and because it's my ass on the line, not yours. I'll listen to what you have to say, but at the end of the day it's my call. *Comprende*?"

Jeanne stood staring into my eyes silently. I held her gaze. "Agreed?"

She hesitated. "Agreed," she finally repeated, extending her hand for me to shake. I did. "What do you need, detective?"

"I need you to locate Senator Vincent DiCenzio. I want his itinerary for today and a number where he can be reached. I also need you to reach out to an Officer Bannon. He was working traffic yesterday at the murder scene. I need to find him."

"Anything else?"

"Yes, pull the DD-5 from the Atwell murder. I need to locate an item of evidence."

"Any particular item?"

"Yes. But that's not your headache, it's mine."

"When do you need this information?" she said.

"The DD-5 by the end of the day."

"And the other?"

"Before I finish my coffee."

Jeanne grinned. "Let me see what I can do, detective," she replied, turning to leave again.

"Two more things."

"Yes, detective?" she said, waiting.

"One, call me Jerry, and two, welcome aboard, officer."

"Thank you...Jerry," she said, smiling, before turning and leaving.

I was refilling the coffeepot when Ron joined me in the kitchen.

"Meeting over?" I asked.

"Not much to meet about if you don't share anything."

"He bought it?"

"Would you?"

"No."

"Him either. I told him we're working—"

"—a lead from an informant. You name names?"

"No, but he's going to corner us for something by this afternoon."

"What's this afternoon?"

"Our next conference. Flaherty wants us to meet with the victim's father."

"Let him meet with Greeley."

"He did, which is why we we're meeting with him this afternoon. Do you have a problem with this?"

"Yeah, but I'll do it anyway."

"Fine then," Ron said sharply.

"Fine," I repeated. "Something bothering you?"

Ron hesitated then said, "I don't like lying to Flaherty."

"Get used to it. We're going to lie to a lot more people before this case is over." Ron's look turned somber. "That CD and picture is the first real break we've gotten. I'm not sharing it with anyone I don't trust."

"You don't trust Flaherty? He's on our team."

"After what Goose told us yesterday, I don't know who's

on our team. It's been a long time since we worked with Flaherty. Time changes people. For now, let's play it close to the vest."

Ron vacillated, then nodded. As he did, Jeanne slipped into the room, handed me an envelope, and turned and left without a word.

"She's quiet this morning," Ron noticed.

I opened the envelope. "Let's go."

"Where?" Ron asked following me out the door.

"To complain to our senator."

15

Our car raced toward the West Side Highway, and questions raced through my mind—questions I knew Vinny DiCenzio had the answers to. I also knew DiCenzio had no intention of sharing them willingly. Super-sleuth that I am, that didn't phase me. The senator had three choices for handling this interrogation. He could invite us in and graciously tell us everything he knew over donuts and coffee. He could invite us in and lie through his teeth to cover his own ass. Or he could refuse to speak with us at all. My gut reaction was that DiCenzio was a number-three man with a number-two backup. But I was going to speak with DiCenzio one way or another. I was driven, like a gambler ready to throw the dice at the craps table. I wasn't foolish enough to think I'd get all sevens or elevens. But for the first time in this investigation I was holding the dice, and no one was taking them from me until I had a turn.

"I can't wait to talk with our senator," I said, turning onto the West Side highway and heading north.

"Technically, Jerry, DiCenzio isn't our senator."

"Don't try to brighten my day." I stepped on the gas, weaving my way through the uptown traffic.

"What's your beef with DiCenzio?"

"I don't like the guy. He's an opportunist."

"So are most politicians. You think he's peddling his influence?"

"Far from it. I'm sure his dealings with Kirby Lonsdale are on the up-and-up."

"Anyone ever tell you you're a cynic?"

"Everyone."

"Well, cynic, if you're in a rush to see DiCenzio, why are you going uptown? The senator's office is downtown."

"He's not at his office. He spent the night at the Prince Town Club," I said.

"The Prince Town Club?"

I handed Ron the note Jeanne had given me earlier.

"That's the Princeton Club, and that's on Forty-third Street."

"Oh. Well, we're not going there yet anyway. I have to make a quick stop. I need to see a cop about a ticket."

I turned the car onto Diane Westlake's street and pulled as close to the front of her house as possible. As I did, Officer Bannon wrapped his glove-covered knuckles against my driver-side window.

"Can't park here, buddy," he said.

I answered, "It's you I need to talk to."

Bannon leaned over to take a better look at us. I flashed him my shield.

"I thought you looked familiar."

"From the news?" I asked.

"No, from Palmieri's yesterday. You're friends with that touchy son of a bitch?"

"Climb in the back and get warm."

Bannon opened the back door and got in. I cranked up the heat.

"What do you guys need?" Bannon removed his gloves and savored the heat.

"Officer," Ron said, "last night my brother observed you having a slight altercation with a motorist in an expensive sports car. Do you recall the name of the driver of that vehicle?"

"What?"

"He wants to know if you remember the dizzy bitch in the Jag who was giving you shit about parking," I translated.

"Hard to forget someone who almost runs you over, especially one that good-looking."

"Did you issue her a summons?" Ron asked.

"Damn right I did. Good looks take you only so far."

"Did you file it?"

"No. I'm doing it later today. You need to see it?"

"It would help," Ron replied.

Bannon retrieved his summons book from his back pocket. He began to thumb through the pages. When he came to the one we were interested in, he wrote down the necessary information and passed it to Ron.

"We owe you one," I said.

"Leave me the heat and we'll call it even." He reached for the door handle and got out. As I pulled away from the curb, I wanted to oblige Bannon and leave him the heat. I knew that after our discussion with DiCenzio, we'd be getting more heat than we'd know what to do with.

"You notice anything unusual?" I asked, speeding up to beat a changing traffic light.

"Like the Crown Vic that's following us?"

"Like that. Any idea who it might be?"

Ron looked into his visor mirror. "Hard to say. Lately we're so popular."

"I'm going to shake them."

"We don't have time. Let's get to the Princeton Club."

"What about them?" I asked pointing my thumb over my shoulder.

"'Keep your friends close, and your enemies even closer,'" he quoted. "Let them follow. We'll meet them soon enough."

Ron was right. Now wasn't the time. So I turned down Broadway and headed south to Forty-sixth Street, driving erratically to annoy our newfound friends. At Fifth Avenue I made a right, and then another right at the corner of Forty-third. There, in the middle of the block, among the prime Manhattan real estate, sat No. 15: the Princeton Club. I pulled over, leaving enough space for our tail to park, but it was nowhere in sight.

I was about to go to the revolving door and enter the plush lobby when Ron pulled me aside. "Remember why we're here, Jerry."

"I didn't develop amnesia in the last fifteen minutes. We're here to talk to the rat bastard senator." I resumed my path to the lobby.

"Wrong," Ron said, grabbing my arm again. "We're here to question a New York State Senator in a professional manner. I don't want a scene in here."

"What exactly *is* in here?"

"One of the most prestigious clubs in the country. It's for Princeton alumni, and some of the most famous people in America have been members. It has everything you can possibly imagine."

"I don't know about that, Ron. I have a pretty good imagination."

"It has rooms for overnight stays, a health club, barber shops—very posh."

"In that case I'll clean my sneakers before I go in."

"We are not going into a dive arcade to talk to a pimp. Let me take the lead on this one."

"Why? Because you're wearing a suit?"

"Because I'm more diplomatic than you."

He had me on that one. I stepped aside, motioning for Ron to lead on.

"One more thing," he said, "No guns."

"I'm not leaving it in the car."

"Just leave it in your holster. I don't care what happens in there, Jerry, you don't draw your gun."

"But what if—"

"—No buts. No guns. Just questions. Got it?"

"You're the leader," I said, shrugging my shoulders.

"Good. Keep that in mind for the next hour."

We finally entered the lobby. It looked just the way Ron had described it: expensive and elite. The floors were dark marble. The walls had dark oak paneling and held paintings of past university presidents.

Ron walked over to the concierge desk. I followed. Standing behind the desk was a tall, thin attractive woman with short blonde hair and deep blue eyes. She was wearing a white turtleneck under a blue blazer with a Princeton insignia pin on the lapel. Around her neck was the obligatory strand of pearls. The desk blocked my view of the rest of her, but I was certain her lower half was sporting something just as preppy. I'd even bet a two-week supply of donuts she went by the name "Buffy."

She carefully looked us over. Ron passed her inspection. Me she wasn't certain about. Although not openly hostile, she acted as if I might be an eccentric alumnus she didn't want to offend. I unzipped my jacket. She looked at my old jeans and instantly decided I was not now nor ever could have been Princeton material. She turned and addressed Ron.

"May I help you, sir?"

"We're looking for Senator DiCenzio," Ron said.

So far, so good, I thought. She looked down into her appointment book.

"I'm sorry. The senator can't be disturbed. May I take a message?"

Not so good.

"We must see the senator," Ron repeated.

"That's not possible. The senator is holding a press conference within the hour. He simply cannot be disturbed."

"He must be a little disturbed, otherwise he wouldn't have gone into politics," I commented. The preppy ignored me.

"I'm sorry to put you in this awkward situation," Ron said. "It is extremely important we speak with Senator DiCenzio now."

"I've told you..." she started to say when Ron displayed his shield. She looked toward me.

"Ditto, baby," I said, casually sliding my shield from my pocket.

"Excuse me for one moment, detectives."

She came around her desk and headed down the hall. She was wearing a dark pleated skirt and low heels. Just as I'd imagined.

"Now we're getting somewhere, leader. Let's have a seat." I walked across the room to the sitting area and took advantage of the comfortable burgundy Chesterfield sofa. Ron followed but didn't sit.

"You know, maybe I'll join this place," I said, leaning back and putting my feet up on the coffee table.

"I'm sure they'd love to have you. But you can't, unless you're a Princeton graduate."

"Do you think the police academy has a club like this?"

Before Ron could answer our concierge arrived with reinforcements. The woman at her side was a mid-forties version of Buffy.

"Detectives, I'm Linda Witherspoon, the senator's personal secretary. How may I help you?"

"By getting your boss down here," I said, standing.

"Excuse me?"

"I'm Detective Ron Gold. This is my partner, Jerry Gold. We're investigating a homicide, Ms. Witherspoon. We need to speak with the senator."

"I see, detectives, and the senator is always willing to help the police in any way he can. You know he's a staunch supporter of our men in blue. Unfortunately, now is not the best time. Perhaps I could contact you later, and we could set up a lunch?"

"Lady, we're not here to make a campaign contribution. My partner told you this is a murder investigation. Now where is the senator?" I asked.

"In his room getting ready," she said, slightly flustered.

"And the room number?" Ron asked.

"Gentlemen, there must be another way."

"There is," I said crossing to the concierge's desk. I thumbed through her book. "Room 414." I started for the elevators.

"Thank you, ladies," Ron said, joining me.

"Wait one moment," Witherspoon said indignantly. "I have fifteen of New York's top reporters waiting in the Woodrow Wilson Room for the senator."

"Let them wait," I said.

"That is not how it is done around here," she said, grabbing my shoulder.

I wished I hadn't promised Ron not to draw my gun.

"Now kindly leave. You've outstayed your welcome."

If that elevator didn't come soon all promises were off.

"You will not take that elevator," she insisted.

"She's right, Jerry." Ron nodded toward the stairs. I followed. Unfortunately, so did Witherspoon, nagging all the way. As we climbed the second flight of stairs, her voice began echoing through the stairwell. By the third flight it was echoing through my head.

"Ms. Witherspoon certainly is persistent," Ron noted, coming up beside me.

"*Annoying* is the word that came to my mind. Persistent was her major at Princeton," I replied, turning to climb the final set of stairs. Then I heard another voice ahead of us.

"Where do you think you're going," a heavy Brooklyn accent called out.

I looked up and there on the landing, blocking the access to the fourth floor, were two, muscle-bound gorillas. As if that weren't annoying enough, Witherspoon caught up to me.

"How did you get in here?" she screeched to the two gorillas, interrupting her own nagging.

"They're not alumni?" I replied.

"Hardly, detective."

"You two don't happen to drive a Ford, do you?" I asked.

"What if we do. What's it to ya?" the bigger one with no neck said, moving down the stairs toward us. His partner followed.

"Jerry, I think we found our tail."

"You think?"

"Mr. Lonsdale sends his regards."

"Wasn't that nice of Kirby?" I said.

"He also said to send you two a beatin'."

"Not so nice," Ron replied.

"What is going on here?" Witherspoon called out.

"If the broad don't want trouble, tell her to shut her mouth and take a hike," No-Neck said.

"Good luck. You try and get rid of her."

"Broad? Whom are you calling a broad?" Witherspoon said defiantly.

"Spunky little bitch, ain't she, Pat?" No-Neck asked his partner.

"Yeah, spunky."

"Spunky? Why I never.... That's it. I'm calling the police."

"Lady, we *are* the police," I reminded her.

"Then do something!"

"Talk to the leader." I nodded toward Ron.

"You sucker punched me last time we met."

"Come closer and I'll sucker punch you again," I offered.

115

With that said, No-Neck threw a right at my head. Unfortunately for my assailant, No-Neck also had no brain. He threw the punch from a few stairs above me and became completely unbalanced. I dodged the assault easily, grabbing his shirt and using his forward momentum to throw him down the remaining stairs. He landed hard at Witherspoon's feet, forcing her to retreat into a corner, screaming. No-Neck started to get to his feet, also screaming. I moved toward him, undecided whom to shut up first. Ron moved in behind me leading with a right jab. I turned to see No-Neck's buddy, Pat, frozen on the steps, blood pouring from his nose.

"You broke my fucking nose," he said, surprised. "I'm going to kill..."

Ron didn't wait for him to finish. He landed a flurry of combinations to Pat's mid section. As he doubled over, Ron kneed him in the head, and it was over—for Pat, anyway. I turned back toward No-Neck as he lunged at me, propelling both of us into the wall. He knocked the wind out of me. No-Neck stepped back to throw his next punch, but not before I landed a perfect side kick to his right knee. He went down hard, smacking his head on the iron handrail as he fell. I tried to catch my breath. Ron was sitting on the stairs above me, doing the same. I collapsed next to him.

"The senator!" Witherspoon cried out, looking at the human refuse lying at her feet. She sped past us up the stairwell and through the door.

"We should follow. Could be others up there," Ron puffed.

"Could be," I agreed, leaning back on the steps.

"Come on, Jerry, remember 'serve and protect'?" Ron headed up the stairs. I took another deep breath and followed.

Linda Witherspoon was standing in the hallway on the fourth floor with her back to what I assumed was the senator's room. Witherspoon was silent.

"Ms. Witherspoon," Ron called out. She didn't respond. "Something's wrong, Jerry."

I thought her silence was an improvement until I noticed that the senator's door was open. We ran for the room. As we got closer, I noticed that Witherspoon had turned pale. Her shoulders were trembling and her chest was heaving as if she were crying, but there were no tears.

"Ms. Witherspoon, are you all right?" Ron asked, approaching. She pointed toward the room.

"Stay with her, Ron." I slowly pushed the door open the rest of the way. The room was a fancy railroad flat. I could see everything from where I stood, including what had scared the hell out of Witherspoon.

A male figure was lying face down in a bloodstained bed. The covers were pulled halfway up his body. There in front of me, with a red ball gag between his teeth, lay Senator DiCenzio, his throat slit. I checked for a pulse.... None. I cautiously lifted the covers. The senator's hands were cuffed behind him.

I quickly canvassed the room. There were no signs of a struggle. I found his clothes hanging neatly in the closet. Inside his suit jacket was his wallet. It still contained credit cards and about a thousand dollars in cash. I was putting the wallet back when the picture fold came undone. Curious, I thumbed through them. There were family pictures followed by a photo of the family pet, a Siamese cat. In the final picture the senator was smiling widely, standing among five beautiful women, two of whom I

117

recognized as Diane Westlake and Susan Atwell. I slipped the picture into my pocket.

I left the room as carefully as I had entered to find Ron comforting Ms. Witherspoon at a seating area farther down the hall. Ron looked up and asked me with a stare if Vinny was alive. I shook my head no. Ron reached inside his coat pocket and removed his cell phone.

"Is...is...he dead?" Witherspoon managed to whisper.

"He's certainly exhibiting all the symptoms," I replied, kneeling alongside of Ms. Witherspoon, who was in shock. I was unsure how much of what had happened she actually comprehended. She looked down at her hands folded neatly in her lap. They began to shake violently. She was too strong a woman to allow herself to cry, so her body released her emotions.

"My God," she said, confused. "The press conference. The senator... He's going to be late."

"Ms. Witherspoon, the senator is about as late as he's ever going to be," I said. I put my arm around her. She leaned into me, burying her face into my chest. I could feel her pain seeping out.

"Jeanne, put me through to Flaherty," Ron said into his phone. While on hold he turned to me. "How do I start explaining to him what we were doing here?"

"Ask him if he's sitting down."

16

Ron and I watched as the EMS workers quietly removed the senator's body. The way they rushed him through the lobby made it seem like he might still be alive. Behind them, Wilkins and two of his team escorted Kirby's men, cuffed, to a waiting patrol car.

"What's shaking?" I said to Wilkins as he passed.

"CSU is finishing up at the crime scene, and we're going to book your two friends here for murder."

"You mean assault. They didn't kill us," I said.

"The murder rap is for the senator. For trying to take *you* out, Greeley wants to pin a medal on them."

"I don't believe they murdered the senator," Ron said. "They're not murderers, they're muscle."

"And pretty lousy muscle at that," I added. "Besides, if they wanted to kill us, they could have picked a better time, a better place. They've been following us most of the day."

"Well, they're all I got, so I'm taking them."

We followed Wilkins out to the street. I was leaning against the club building, checking my coat pockets for a cigar.

"See you back at the safe house," Wilkins said as his car pulled away.

"Yeah, sure," I replied, disappointed my hand had come out empty.

"He's wasting his time collaring those two for the murder, but I see his point," Ron said. "At least he's going back to the safe house with something."

"What are you talking about?" I asked, walking toward the car. "We got a dead senator. Doesn't that count for anything?"

"Ask Flaherty when you see him."

"You ask him. He likes you better."

I reached for the car door when two pops rang through the air, followed by the sound of shattering windows. My car windows. Ron took cover behind the passenger-side door. Instinctively, I rolled over the car hood and joined him as two more shots pelted the car. I waited for another shot but all I heard was tires squealing. I peeked around the fender and saw a Ford Crown Vic speeding around the corner.

"You OK?" I asked Ron as we stood. He nodded. "Did you see anything?"

"Besides my life flashing before my eyes. You?"

I nodded. "Ford Crown Vic."

"I'm starting to think it wasn't Kirby's men following us."

"Ya think?"

"No," Ron theorized as he scanned the street for

additional threats. But the danger seemed to have passed as quickly as it had appeared.

"Those shots were meant for us."

"What do you mean *us*, Jerry? They shot up your side of the car."

"Who would want me dead?" I asked, surveying the damage.

"Aside from Kirby, Red, and few dozen others, no one. Look at this car. Who's going to tell Flaherty his car's been shot up?"

"Mention it after you tell him about the senator."

17

It had been hours since the Executioner returned to the dungeon. The chamber was cold, dimly lit, and sparsely furnished, housing only items of necessity. Still, there was comfort among the old urn lamp, the mannequin in the corner that donned the black suit of death, and a leather chair from which the Executioner eyed the surroundings. Much had happened with the passing of the night. Another woman had been added to the wall of trophies.

The wall of trophies was divided into five areas. Each held numerous black-and-white photographs of five women dressed in provocative leather attire, posed in positions of domination. At the top of each picture set was an eight-by-ten photo of the woman featured below. All five could have been sisters—tall and slender, with long, flaxen hair. Susan Atwell and Diane Westlake's photographs were splattered with blood: their own blood. Blood from their severed arteries that had stolen life from their bodies and that, in turn, had been stolen by the Executioner.

"An eye for an eye," the Executioner bellowed with laughter, but the laughter was interrupted by the sound of metal upon metal. Entering the adjacent room, the Executioner observed the semi-conscious body of Corinne Morland lying on a steel-examining table. Still dressed in her New Year's Eve party attire, black leather slacks, black satin blouse and tall black stiletto heels, the table restraints were unfastened alongside of her. Only a black leather collar locked around her long, elegant neck and attached to a chain fastened her to the table.

Corinne Moreland seems peaceful, thought the Executioner. Appropriate that ketamine, an animal tranquilizer, would work so effectively.

"Too effectively. It makes my task effortless," the Executioner said to the sedated woman. "Imagine my good fortune to meet you at Diane's. How easy it was to convince you to meet me here."

Corinne's eyes slowly opened. Awkwardly, she tried to lift her head. The length of chain attached to her collar rattled against the steel table. The noise brought a sharp pain to her head. She lay still, trying to orient herself.

"I'm glad you decided to join us," the Executioner said.

Corinne tried to speak but couldn't. The pain in her throat was awful. She tried to swallow but her mouth was dry.

"Drink this," the Executioner ordered, handing her a glass containing a clear liquid. Corinne hesitated. "It's water. Drink."

She raised the glass to her lips and sipped slowly. The

cool water hurt going down but she continued to drink. The water cleared her head. She looked around the room—a doctor's private operating room. She let her fingers move up her body and feel the collar around her neck. She started to panic, but she was still too weak for words.

"No need for alarm," the Executioner said, moving a surgical tray next to the table. Removing a syringe from the tray, the Executioner prepared a hypodermic. Holding the filled syringe to the light, the Executioner tapped it as the plunger slowly moved inward, allowing a short stream of the liquid to escape. Unable to move from the table, Corinne Moreland's fear intensified.

"No, please," she managed to whisper as the injection entered her arm.

"Don't argue with the doctor," the Executioner said as the drug began to take effect. Corinne lay watching, unable to say or do anything. The Executioner lifted a scalpel from the tray and moved closer.

"I've injected you with a serum that induces temporary paralysis. You'll be happy to know it doesn't anesthetize the body. You may not be able to move, but you will most certainly be able to feel. I wouldn't want you to miss one exquisite moment of what is about to happen."

18

It was late afternoon by the time I placed the final period at the end of our report. Ron was absorbed with his Westlake papers. DiCenzio's murder was not good news for the investigation or for us, not to mention for DiCenzio. I stood to stretch my legs. The safe house conference room, as big as it was, was starting to close in on me. I headed for the door.

"Where are you going?"

"I need coffee. You want any?"

"No, but I'll take the walk."

We headed down the corridor. Turning the corner to the kitchen, I found a barren coffeepot sitting on a cold burner.

"The end of a perfect day."

Then Flaherty burst into the room, slamming the door behind him.

"No, *this* is going to be the end of the perfect day," Ron answered.

We watched as Flaherty's wrath began to build. He paced the length of the room. When he reached the far wall, he turned, his face red, his expression ugly.

"You heard about Senator DiCenzio?" Ron asked.

Flaherty did not answer. Walking toward us, he picked up the coffeepot and threw it against the far wall. It shattered upon contact.

"He's heard," I said, mourning the loss of the coffeepot.

The senseless act of violence did nothing to quell Flaherty's temper. He was still fuming as a clerk ran in asking about the noise. Flaherty threw the well-intentioned clerk out and slammed the door behind him. Then he turned to me.

"So you have nothing substantial to share with me," he said sarcastically. "Nothing at all?"

I shrugged.

"How about now? Anything?"

I shrugged again.

"You want to explain how you two happen to show up where a state senator turns up dead, and how that's not substantial?"

"Now that he's dead, it's substantial."

"You're damned right," Flaherty shouted.

"Have your gun ready, just in case," I mumbled to Ron.

"You may have a dead senator, but there's a live police commissioner, mayor, and lieutenant governor who want to know what the hell you were doing there, and why. In fact, I'd like to know. Perhaps you ace crime fighters might enlighten a simple deputy chief on that point."

"We don't know," Ron said.

"Yet," I added, before Flaherty went off again. "But we're working on it."

Flaherty, trying to regain his composure, went to the water cooler, ignoring the pieces of the shattered coffeepot on the floor, and filled a glass.

"What do you know?" he asked, tight-jawed.

"Nothing really substantial," I responded. Flaherty threw his glass at the wall.

"Don't use that phrase around me—not now, not ever. What do you *have*, goddamn it!"

"Speculatively," Ron interjected, "we believe DiCenzio had a connection with the Lonsdale organization. We were trying to follow the lead through, so—"

"—you two went to speak with the senator without my authorization."

"That about sums it up," I said.

"And the two guys found in the stairway. Do they belong to Lonsdale?"

Ron nodded.

"Are they good for the killing?"

"Doubt it," I said, at the risk of getting pelted by more pottery. "They wanted a piece of Ron and me."

"I know the feeling. Too bad they didn't get it. It might have knocked some sense into your heads."

"You still care," I answered.

"Where are those goons now, chief?" Ron asked, changing the subject.

"Being interrogated by Wilkins."

"What about us?" I wanted to know.

"What about you? You don't have enough on your plate? Let Wilkins handle them."

"He did get there fast, Jerry."

"Too fast. Hard to believe anyone that efficient could be Greeley's partner."

"He's efficient because he follows police procedure. Unlike you two clowns, he shares information."

"We should try that sometime, Ron."

"Not try it. Do it." Flaherty's face reddened again. "If anyone else you've interrogated without my knowledge turns up dead, you're through. So help me, I'll lock you up."

"How would that look on TV, chief?"

"I'll let your agent worry about that."

"How is the media handling the DiCenzio matter?" Ron asked.

"They're not. We've isolated the scene and we're keeping it quiet.

Before we could respond, Jeanne entered, carrying a file.

"Am I interrupting something?"

"I don't know. Do you want to read us our rights, chief?"

"More than you could possibly imagine," Flaherty grumbled. "What do you have, officer?"

Jeanne looked at Flaherty, then to me, uncertain if she should speak. I nodded for her to continue.

"Information Detective Gold requested." She handed me a file. I opened it to find a copy of the pink DD-5 form I had requested earlier, as well as the driving record of the beauty in the Jag.

"Thank you, Officer MacDonald," Flaherty said, escorting her out.

While Flaherty showed her to the door, I folded the driving record in half and placed it in my pocket.

"Since we're on an open communication policy now,

you won't mind sharing that with me," Flaherty said, grabbing the file from my hands.

"Our pleasure."

He opened the file and studied the pink DD-5.

"Why did you request this?"

"We're trying to track down Susan Atwell's black book."

"What's the connection?"

"We don't know. That's why Ron and I want to see it."

Flaherty was tapping the file against the side of his leg when we were interrupted by another knock at the door.

"Sorry to interrupt again, chief. Mr. Westlake is here to see the detectives," Jeanne said. "I made him comfortable in Conference Room B."

"Fine."

As Jeanne left, the chief handed me the file.

"Go to work," he said as he made his way toward the exit.

"Chief," I called out.

"What?" He didn't turn around.

"Since we're into open communication and sharing information..."

"Yeah?"

"Did Wilkins get anything from Lonsdale's men?"

Flaherty turned to face me, incredulous.

"Did he?" I repeated.

"Nothing substantial," he replied, then turned and left.

19

Ron and I entered Conference Room B. Waiting there was a well-dressed man standing behind the conference table, his arms folded across his chest. His thin, six-foot-four-inch frame intimated that he might have been a professional basketball player when he'd been younger. The dossier I had in my hands said otherwise.

Alfred "Alley Boy" Westlake had never played on a professional basketball team, but he could afford to buy one. As a Wall Street arbitrageur, Westlake amassed millions by purchasing undervalued companies, selling off or closing their unprofitable divisions, and retaining their core business, an operation that led to indecently large profits. He learned his craft, as he called it, out on the streets, despite his Ivy League schooling, thus earning the nickname "Alley Boy."

For over twenty years, Westlake bought and sold some of the world's largest companies. Wall Street loved him. Everyone involved in a Westlake deal profited, except the employees of the companies he closed down. Labor, therefore, held a different opinion of Alley Boy—or Gutter Boy, as they preferred to call him. Still, Westlake was one of the country's wealthiest men. He liked to keep a high profile, always being seen with movie stars, sports figures, and influential politicians. The man actually managed to make Donald Trump seem modest.

"Mr. Westlake," I said, extending my hand, "Detective Jerry Gold. This is my partner, Ron Gold."

"I know who you are," he said, shaking my hand. "And I know your brother." He reached for Ron's hand.

"We're very sorry for your loss, sir," Ron said.

Westlake nodded. His grip was weak, his frame fragile, his blonde hair displaying more than its fair share of grey. But it was his eyes that kept my attention. They were blue, piercing blue. They were the same eyes as his daughter's. Up close, Alfred Westlake looked much older than his fifty-nine years would suggest. Losing your only daughter can do that.

"Would you like a drink, Mr. Westlake?" Ron offered, feeling the man's grief.

"Thank you, no." He sat.

We sat too and waited for him to begin. This was his meeting, after all. We didn't have a long wait.

"Why is my daughter dead?" he asked unemotionally.

"We don't know why, only how," I replied.

"I know how, damn it." Westlake's voice began to rise, taking on a strength he didn't seem to have. "Lieutenant Greeley explained that."

"What else did the lieutenant explain?" I queried.

"The lieutenant is under the impression this might have something to do with me."

I didn't like the way this was going. I knew that once Greeley had confirmed who the victim's father was, he would see a motive spelled out with dollar signs.

"Is that the way you see it too?"

"No sir. We're not concentrating on that theory," Ron answered.

"Mr. Westlake, when was the last time you saw your daughter alive?" I asked.

"Two weeks ago. I was in the city on business. We met for dinner."

"Did she seem distraught?" Ron asked.

"Dee? No. She was always bubbly, always involved in a new cause, a new charity. That's why she went into psychology. Even as a child she was giving, always wanting to help."

"Psychology? We were under the impression she was doing freelance computer consulting."

"Computers were her hobby. Her passion was psychology." Westlake saw my confusion and smiled. "You're wondering how a bastard like me wound up with an angel like Dee for a daughter?

I was wondering, but I kept my mouth shut.

"Dee was raised by her mother, my first wife, Alison. I married her before I was a player, while I was still learning my trade. She divorced me before I became successful. The woman couldn't handle what it entailed. She died in an auto accident while Dee was in graduate school."

"What college did Diane attend?" Ron asked, looking up from his notes.

"Barnard. She insisted on being in the city. I insisted on Columbia University."

"Was she seeing anybody? Did she have any boyfriends, romantic interests?"

"Not that I knew."

"Was she working?"

"My daughter didn't need to work."

Ron switched directions. "How did she occupy her time?"

"Charities, mostly. She was always fund-raising for a homeless shelter or organizing a skills workshop for the long-term unemployed."

"Did Dee have many friends?" Ron called the victim by her father's nickname for her. Westlake seemed appreciative. His tone became softer, more reflective, and less antagonistic.

"She was always popular. But I don't know many of her friends personally."

"Can you write down the ones you do?"

I passed Westlake a pen and paper. As he wrote, he spoke. "I've answered your questions. Now answer mine. Why did my daughter die?"

Ron looked at me. I motioned to tell him.

"We believe your daughter was the victim of a serial killing. She was the second to die in the same manner."

"Is this the sex bullshit Greeley's assistant was telling me? That my little girl was involved in kinky prostitution. Bullshit! I would know if that were the case."

"I'm sure you would. Detective Wilkins has to check all the possibilities, even the unpleasant ones, as do we."

"Cut the bull. My people tell me you caught a murderer like this once. You can do it again. Whatever it costs, I'll pay

133

it. Whatever you need, I'll take care of it."

"Mr. Westlake, that's not the issue," Ron said delicately. "Investigations take time."

"Time. Let me tell you about time. Within the week I'm going to bury my only child," he said angrily. "I want this animal caught before then."

Westlake stood, put down the pen and slid the pad in front of me. He walked across the room, stopping at the door.

"Detectives, I am a very powerful man. But you know that, don't you?" He gazed at the dossier on the table. "At my age, I can afford to be very generous with my friends—and very, very vindictive toward my enemies. Which will you be, detectives? You have until I bury my daughter to decide."

He turned to leave, his left hand clinched into a fist pounding against his leg. That was when I noticed the ring. "Mr. Westlake," I said.

"Detective?"

"Do you know Vincent DiCenzio?"

"Why do you ask?"

"Do you, sir?"

"I know the senator."

"How are you acquainted?" Ron asked.

"Vinny DiCenzio was my college roommate."

"The college you both attended wouldn't happen to be Princeton University?" I pressed.

"Yes. What could that have to do with this?"

"Nothing," Ron said. "Thank you for your time."

Westlake nodded. "Until I bury my little girl, detectives." He turned and left.

"What made you ask that, Jerry?"

"His college ring. The stone looked identical to the stone in the pin the preppy at the desk of the Princeton Club was wearing."

"Good catch."

"Did you also catch that he's unaware of the present state of his old roomie?"

"I did. Let's get out of here before he finds out and wants more answers we don't have."

Ron agreed. He grabbed the dossier. I grabbed the pad with the names. One name jumped off the page. Dropping the pad on the desk, I removed the driving record Jeanne had handed me earlier.

"What's the problem?"

I placed the record next to the pad.

"Check this out."

Ron looked over my shoulder. There, in black-and-white, on both sheets of paper, was the name Elizabeth Drake—the Jag Lady.

20

Night overcame the city. The harsh sunlight that hours earlier had poured down onto an unprotected Fifth Avenue had been replaced by the soft glow of street lamps and the piercing streaks of passing headlights. Ron and I stood in front of the safe house watching as Manhattan changed from an austere center of business to playground central.

"You want to get something to eat?" I asked.

"No, thanks. I need to get home."

I nodded and tossed a set of keys to him. "Take what's left of Flaherty's car."

Ron removed a new set of keys from his coat. "It's being repaired. Flaherty lent me another. Do you need to be dropped off anywhere?" He pointed to a parked black-and-white.

"I'll take the train."

Ron unlocked the car door. "Jerry, maybe we need to rethink our plan of attack. Maybe we should split up and broaden our efforts."

"Maybe."

"How do you see it?"

I didn't answer immediately. I liked the fact that we'd cover more ground apart. What I didn't like was not having my brother to cover my back.

"Tomorrow I'll interview the Jag Lady," I said. "You keep working on Westlake's computer printout."

"Who's going to follow up on DiCenzio?"

"Our dead senator isn't going anywhere. We'll wait for Wilkins's report. Let's decide about the split after tomorrow."

"I'll keep in touch by phone."

"Right."

I watched Ron pull away into the sea of traffic and join the blur of headlights. Without my brother, I felt isolated and alone in a crowd of eight million New Yorkers. Ron never seemed plagued by such emotions. He was smart—he had Emily. He had a life. I stepped off the curb to hail a cab.

Before I'd ever heard of the Madam Murders, before Nikki Everhorn had become television anchorwoman Nicole Horn, I'd had a life, too, and it started and ended with Nikki. She had everything I'd wanted in a woman. Intelligent, attractive, and sensitive, she knew how to play like an innocent child or tease like a wild seductress. Nikki grabbed my heart as easily as Michael Jordan grabbed a rebound. I should've known then that I was in trouble. But when I was around her, I wasn't sure what I knew except that I didn't want to leave.

A night out with Nikki was as unpredictable as the fifth

race at Aqueduct. Once, when she was working late, I surprised her with a bag of Chinese food and French pastries. She suggested we eat in her editor's office, which had a great view of Central Park that only an office on the thirty-third floor of a Manhattan skyscraper could offer. I felt awkward, but since the only person around was Ramona, the elderly cleaning woman, I figured, what the hell.

As I removed our dinner from the bags, Nikki shut the office door and closed the blinds to the window to the newsroom. Then she found an empty corner on our mock table and sat with her legs crossed. She was wearing an Anne Klein dark-blue blazer with matching skirt that rested suggestively high above her knee. Her blouse was plain white and her shoes had high dark-blue heels. I watched as she removed her blazer and began to unfasten her blouse.

"You came bearing gifts. I thought I might bare something, too," she purred.

With that and her bra off her chest, Nikki grabbed my shirt and pulled me toward her hungry lips. Dinner was served. Pressing her tight body against mine, our tongues explored each other. Her fingers rifled through my hair as my hands methodically read the contours of her body like a blind man reading Braille. The energy mounted as I helped peel away the rest of her clothes, feeling the softness of her skin.

As I lay Nikki across the desk, she reached for the pastry box and removed a long, slender chocolate éclair. She allowed the pastry to graze her lips. Then she bit it in two, coating her lips with the thick custard. She streaked the cream down her soft neck to her supple breasts, her erect nipples poking through the custard like cherries on top of a vanilla sundae.

"Would you like to start with dessert?" she teased.

I lunged at her lips like a starving man, devouring every inch of this breathtaking appetizer. Good thing I wasn't diabetic. I could hear her shallow breathing as my hungry mouth made its way down the creamy path. I engulfed her and was still licking her breasts when I heard the cleaning woman outside the door. I backed away. Nikki pulled me closer, whispering, urging, "Take me now."

I heard my lover's urgency. I also heard Ramona's mop coming closer. Explaining to a sixty-something cleaning woman why I was violating a beautiful young reporter on her editor's desk was not something I relished. Nikki didn't seem to care. She began to rip at my clothes. I had to make a quick decision: Ramona or Nikki? I drew Nikki toward the end of the desk. She spread her legs, beckoning me to feel their warm embrace. I placed my hands on her hips as she raised them, begging me to enter her. Moving as quietly as I could, I obliged her need, nervous that at any moment we'd be confronted by the cleaning woman.

"Nikki—Ramona..." I whispered a warning.

But Nikki's body become more animated. The danger of being discovered turned her on. She started to push harder against me, crying out after each thrust. I'd never heard her scream. For a moment I thought her backside was caught in the top desk drawer. Nikki's aria of pleasure became louder and louder until it peaked with a final high note: "Oh, God. Yes!"

As Nikki climaxed, she grabbed at the first item in reach: a Napoleon. In a frenzy, she hurled it at my chest. Its cream exploded over my torso at the same moment I came.

As our bodies became limp, I looked toward the door,

certain Ramona had witnessed our intramural office activity. But there was no Ramona—just Nikki and me. And that was all I needed, back when I had a life.

Distracted by screeching car brakes, my thoughts of paradise faded quickly and parked themselves back on the lonely pavement of Fifth Avenue. There, the sight of a beat up old cab welcomed me. The driver was a short, balding man in his early sixties. He had a large stomach and seemed to have trouble seeing over the steering wheel. He invited me in as only an old-time New York cabbie could.

"You getting in or posing for a picture, buddy?"

"What if I am?" I replied, trying to capture one final image of that night with Nikki. "I'm not asking you to hold the camera."

The cabbie laughed as I got in. "Where you going?"

But the site of Dave Wilkins walking down the street distracted me. He stopped beside a black Ford Crown Vic and unlocked the door.

"Not for nothin', but I got the meter runnin'."

"Home. New Rochelle."

"Up in Westchester?"

"Yeah."

"Your dime, buddy." The cabby threw the car into drive. "I got all night."

"Me too," I said as Wilkins faded behind us.

We made good time through Manhattan. In the Bronx, I saw Yankee Stadium—the new Yankee Stadium—to my right. The House That Ruth Built had been torn down by real estate developers. Either way, it was still a hell of a sight.

"I can't believe those bums didn't make the series last year. You think the Yanks got a shot this year?"

"I hope not," said the cabbie. "I'm a Mets fan."

"Do you mind turning up the heat back here?" I rubbed my hands together.

"Sure. Your comfort means everything to me. I suppose you're going to want me to carry you to your doorstep, too."

"If I'm frozen by the time we get there you won't have to."

I slid my hands into my coat pockets. Something sharp jabbed me. It was the corner of the folded paper with the Jag Lady's address. I stared at it. Tired as I was, something was telling me to check it out. Now. I told the cabbie to turn around.

"What?"

"You heard me. We're going back to the city."

"You sure?"

"No, but do it anyway."

"It's still your dime."

Back into Manhattan I told the driver to head west. A short time later we pulled up in front of 375 West Seventy-second Street. Climbing out of the cab, I paid the fare and flipped the driver a Jackson.

"Twenty dollars? Sport, you ever need a cab to tour the city again drop a quarter. Here's my number." He slapped the outside door of the cab. It read "All Right Cabs. Murray Hill 2-2232."

"You ask for me: Ben Carlucci. Benny for those that tip like you."

"I'll do that, Benny." The cab started to roll away. "Hey Benny, you ever consider updating your sign. Nobody writes phone numbers that way."

"It's an old cab," he yelled back.

I smiled as Benny and the yellow dinosaur turned the

corner into the Manhattan night. I was alone on the street, taking in the architecture. There was a silent grandeur about the building. The late nineteenth-century structure exemplified a time when opulence, rather than economy, ruled. Looking into the second-floor windows, I could see the high ceilings and spacious rooms that working-class New Yorkers could no longer afford. Apparently, the Jag Lady did all right.

I eyed the picture on Elizabeth Drake's driving record as I stood in the cold. Maybe she wasn't home. Maybe she was sleeping. Maybe I should come back when my head was clear. It was eight o' clock. I was beyond tired but not sleepy. I needed to be sharp for this interview.

I folded the paper with the address back into my pocket and was turning to leave when I saw an attractive blondee in the vestibule rummaging through her tan Coach shoulder bag. I compared the picture with the woman leaving the lobby. They looked similar, but the woman I remembered from yesterday was taller. Then again, it was dark and this lady wasn't wearing come-fuck-me spike-heel boots. Tonight she was dressed like the girl next door: loose-fitting blue jeans, white Nike sneakers, and a yellow down parka. She was still a knockout. If the girl next door looked like that when I was growing up, I'd still be living at home.

"Here's looking at you, lady," I said, doing my best Bogey impersonation. I came up beside her. "Ms. Drake?"

She looked at me nervously, then hastened away.

"Ms. Drake," I repeated after catching up to her again.

"Yes?" She continued walking toward West End Avenue.

She may not have looked the same, but she sounded the same. I heard the English accent and was certain she was the one who had made the 911 call. Well, almost certain. If she were a little taller and sluttier, I'd be certain.

"Ms. Elizabeth Drake of 375 West Seventy-second Street?"

"Actually it's Dr. Drake. Do I know you?"

"We need to talk. I'm hoping you can help me with a problem."

"I'm a child psychologist. I don't work with adults."

"That's not what I've heard, doctor."

"Who are you?" she asked, breaking her stride just long enough to run her eyes over me. When my mission wasn't forthcoming, she nervously clutched her bag and tried to leave. I placed a hand on her right forearm. When she turned to confront me, she encountered my badge.

"Detective Gold, NYPD."

"Detective, what could we possibly have to discuss?" she asked apprehensively.

"Diane Westlake."

"Diane?" she whispered, becoming visibly upset.

"Diane. Where can we talk?"

21

I accompanied Dr. Drake to a local tavern.
Appropriately christened the Speakeasy, it lived up to its
name. The interior was designed like a 1920s saloon.
Knock-off Tiffany lamps lit the dim room. A highly polished
bar took up most of the left wall; booths ran the length of
the right Tables were scattered in the middle. The place
wasn't crowded. A guy dressed like Edward G. Robinson in
Little Caesar greeted us. After requesting a table in the rear,
we followed Eddie G. to a booth in the far back corner of the
room. It wasn't a table but then he wasn't Edward G.
Robinson, either.

I watched as the doctor shed her coat and slid across
the mahogany bench until she was hugging the wall. She
had better curves than the Indianapolis Motor Speedway
and was probably just as fast and dangerous. Still, I

couldn't help thinking what a great ride it would be. I slid into the bench across from her and fastened my seat belt.

"Can I get you something from the bar?" a waitress dressed like a 1920s flapper asked. I looked across at the doctor.

"I don't drink," she said curtly.

"What do you do when you're thirsty?"

She didn't laugh. The waitress seemed to find it amusing. But she was working me for a big tip. It was working. I waited for the laughter to subside.

"Bring us two coffees—leaded, no decaf," I said, flashing the waitress a friendly smile. She followed my lead, smiling back, and then headed for the bar.

"You drink coffee? Or do you have enough stimulation in your life?" I asked.

"Do you think you can afford coffee on a cop's salary?"

"No. Thank God for kickbacks."

She reached into her bag, removing a pack of cigarettes. I watched as the slender white stick greeted her mouth, her red lipstick indelibly marking the filter like a seal pressing into hot wax. Striking the flint of her gold lighter, she held the flame just beyond the tobacco.

"Mind if I smoke?" she asked with a hint of sensuality.

"I don't care if you burn," I said, stealing an old line from the immortal Jackie Gleason. "Unfortunately, the City of New York does."

Indignantly, she closed the lid of her lighter, leaving the unlit cigarette hanging from her lips.

"That's a classic joke. Lighten up."

"You come up to me on the street insisting that I talk with you. Now you bore me with your ancient jokes and ask me to lighten up. Are all detectives this forward?"

145

"I tend to be an overachiever."

"Your wife must find you amusing?"

"I'm not married."

"I'm not surprised."

"There you go. *That's* a joke, right?"

"Ask your questions, detective. I don't have all night."

"Fine. I can do this the easy way or I can do it the hard way. It's your choice."

"I like it hard, detective. *Rock* hard." Her tongue moved slowly across her lips. "How hard can you make it for me?"

I reached into my pocket and tossed Diane Westlake's morgue photo onto the table. The doctor looked at the horrific picture. What she saw registered instantly. She averted her eyes and turned toward the wall. When she looked back there were tears.

I guess I had made it hard enough. She couldn't seem to compose herself. Her tears were now flowing freely. Unsure what to do, I waited. The self-assured doctor, curt just minutes before, now seemed lost. I slid her my napkin. Taking it, our fingers touched. She felt soft, warm, and vulnerable. I pulled back. She desperately held on. It was as if she were struggling to purge the pain from her soul and using my hand as the conduit. Maybe it was working. I felt like hell.

"Diane would never hurt anyone," she cried. "How can she be dead?"

That was the second time tonight I couldn't answer that question. Before I had to admit it the waitress arrived with our coffee. Looking into the pained eyes across the table, I pushed my cup aside.

"Bring me a Jack Daniels," I said to the waitress. As she turned to leave I grabbed her arm. "Better make it a double."

146

22

While I waited for my drink, I watched the doctor try to collect herself.

"Why, detective?" she asked, wiping her eyes.

I decided to give her the official version of what I knew, which wasn't much. When I finished, the tears that had formed earlier made way for anger.

"You're never going to find the person who did this to Dee, are you? To you she's just another corpse."

The waitress came with my drink. I didn't wait for her to serve me. I lifted it off the tray and took a shot. It was warm going down I had to resist the temptation to keep drinking—a decision I would probably regret.

"I've seen a lot of corpses," I said, "each with a different story they couldn't tell. My job is to tell it for them. By the time I'm done with this investigation, I'm going to know

Diane Westlake inside and out. And I'll know who murdered her."

The doctor continued to stare at the photo.

"But I doubt I'll understand why. Life is cheap out on the streets."

"Dee wasn't out on the streets. She wasn't a prostitute!"

"I didn't say she was. But she was into *something*, and I think you can help me understand what it was."

"I can't," she replied, looking away and trying unsuccessfully to hold back more tears.

"You called the police the night of the murder. You helped then."

"I-I don't know what you're talking about," she stammered.

"No games, doc. You're too smart, and I'm too tired."

"You must be mis—"

"—I recognize your voice," I said firmly. She glanced down at the table. "If you're afraid of me, don't be. It's not you I'm after."

"Detective..."

"Jerry. My name is Jerry."

"You can't possibly understand what you're about to get into, Jerry."

"Help me to, doctor"

She reached for her coffee. Her hands were shaking so badly she couldn't get the cup to her lips. I placed my hands over hers to steady them.

"Liz " she said, barely audible. "My name is Liz."

She placed her cup down and gently removed her hands from under mine.

"Help me, Liz. Help me help Diane."

"I don't feel comfortable talking here. Could we discuss

this privately?

"Where?"

"My flat?"

I finished my drink and motioned for her to lead on. As I watched her head for the door, I got an uneasy feeling in my gut. I was hoping it was the Jack Daniels. But I wouldn't bet on it.

We left the Speakeasy and headed west on Seventy-ninth Street. The night sky was clear. Liz and I walked side by side to West End Avenue. I had the urge to place my arm around her shoulder, to console her, to feel her leaning against me and to smell the freshness of her long, flowing hair. I opted to put my hands in my coat pockets instead.

"Dee wasn't a hooker," she said again, suddenly.

"I never said she was."

"She didn't need money. Do you know who her father is?"

"Yes."

We walked a little farther in silence. I sensed she wanted to tell me something but didn't know how to start. I didn't push. We turned down West End Avenue. She was looking straight ahead, tears forming in the corners of her eyes. We stopped for a traffic light.

"I know she wasn't a prostitute," Liz said.

"Then when you called 911, why did you say she wasn't 'working tonight'?"

"We often called our sessions work or playtime. It was something we did. It meant nothing."

"How can you be certain Dee wasn't a prostitute?"

"Because I'm the prostitute."

The light changed, but neither of us walked. She was glaring at me through wet, reddened eyes. She trembled and enfolded herself in her own arms, unable to move. I heard myself sigh as I wrapped my arm around her. Embarrassed by her admission, she attempted to turn away. When she saw I wouldn't retreat, she relented, collapsing against me as we walked.

"You heard what I said?"

"Yes."

"Well?"

"I don't work vice, and I'm not a career counselor. I'm trying to find a murderer."

"And you would trust a whore to help?"

"I would trust anyone who cares as much as you do about her friend. Liz, I'm no one to judge. Most of us get by the best we can a day at a time."

She nodded and wiped her eyes.

"You want to tell me how you got involved?"

"Dee."

"Diane?" She nodded yes.

"I met Dee while I was completing my doctoral thesis at Columbia University. She had spent a few summers touring Europe, and I found we frequented a few of the same pubs back home in London. She made me feel less homesick. As we became friendlier, she invited me into her circle. She seemed to know all the American aristocracy."

"America doesn't have an aristocracy," I said.

"Perhaps I'm using the wrong word. What do you call the wealthy elite here?"

"Assholes."

"Yes, well," she laughed, "perhaps we can agree on 'upper class'?" Her laugh was strangely warm and childlike.

"Perhaps we can agree Diane Westlake got you in with her rich friends."

"Yes."

"And how soon after did you start screwing them?"

"I beg your pardon?"

"Am I using the wrong nomenclature? How long have you been living in the city?"

"Five years."

"Then you should understand the term 'screw' or do you prefer the term bang, how about fuck?" Liz removed my arm and pulled away.

"Maybe I should translate into British? When did you begin to shag them?"

"You may use whatever vulgar synonyms you wish. I never had sex with any of them."

"You tell me you're the prostitute, not Diane, but you didn't screw anybody?"

"Does that concept challenge your shallow mind?"

"Actually it does. What did you offer them?"

"I was their domina." Liz saw my confusion. "Their dominatrix. I am a professional dominatrix. Dee's friends would pay handsomely for a session with me. And in the beginning, I quite enjoyed the D&S scene."

"D&S?"

"Dominance and submission. Some refer to it as B&D— bondage and discipline. Or S&M."

"I'm familiar with that term. How does D&S differ?"

"It doesn't really," she explained. "D&S includes all the facets of the others."

"Did Diane teach you this trade?"

"No. I learned that back in London."

"So basically Westlake's friends paid you to beat them."

"Not all of them. Some merely got off by being humiliated."

151

"And what got you off?"

"The power." Her voice had a hard edge to it. "I enjoyed the power I had over those powerful people. Most women will never experience that type of dominance in their chosen professions."

"Unless they choose to be a dominatrix," I added.

"Most times not even then."

"Did Diane get off on the power?"

"Yes. She was a lifestyle domina. Dee met with the same people. She called it her "adult playgroup." I did it for the money, with different people."

"Was she paid?"

"Lifestyles are offered tributes—a gift for their services."

"Was Corinne Moreland part of the play group?"

"Yes. I was supposed to meet up with her at Diane's that night, but she never came. I tried to call her, but there was no answer."

"It appears Diane was killed during a D&S session. We found her bound to a whipping horse. Her backside was flogged raw and her throat was cut. Do you think Corinne or someone in her playgroup got out of control?"

"Those involved rarely lose control, and Corinne and Dee were as close as sisters," she said.

"Sisters fight. Maybe they had too much to drink during an impromptu session?"

"You don't understand the nature of this beast. The entire scene is all about control. Nothing but control."

"You're telling me the players never drink?"

"The players don't use alcohol or drugs. They don't want to risk the possibility of losing control. Jerry, to them, total control—or being totally controlled—is the high."

"So no sex?"

"Correct. It's never about sex."

"So maybe this time things got out of hand," I pressed.

"There are safeguards to prevent that."

"For example?"

"A safe word."

We were approaching her building. Liz rummaged through her bag and removed a key. "As a psychologist, I must tell you this D&S phenomenon is fascinating. It has been around for centuries. The participants characteristically are extremely wealthy over-achievers with extraordinarily high I.Q.'s."

"How do they meet?"

"Through clubs. Or the Internet is an excellent means. But participants follow a specific protocol before a domina takes on a submissive."

"I'm listening."

"To begin with, the submissive completes a questionnaire, which can be awfully extensive. If the two seem compatible, the submissive is interviewed. And if that goes well, a contract is drawn up."

"You're kidding?"

"I'm very serious. The scene is very structured."

"Go on."

"Once the submissive's fantasy has been established, a safe word is chosen. When spoken, it tells the dominant partner that the submissive has reached his or her limit and to stop the scene. The word is always confirmed each time any play begins."

"And you don't think Diane's dominant partner could have missed hearing her safe word?"

"Never," she said softly, her voice cracking with emotion.

We entered her lobby and headed for the elevator bays.

"How can you be sure?" I followed her into the waiting elevator. She pressed the button for the fifteenth floor.

"Because Dee would never bottom."

"Bottom?"

"She was never submissive. She would only work as a top—the dominant partner." The elevator door closed. I leaned against the wall absorbing everything Liz said.

"I don't believe this was a session gone wrong. Nor did Corinne have anything to do with harming Dee. Talk with her and you'll see."

"I wish I could."

I followed Liz down the hall into her apartment. I stood in the foyer and looked around as she hung our coats in a closet large enough to be a studio apartment. The place was big. Directly ahead, two steps down, was a huge sunken living room, complete with a fireplace surrounded by built-in bookcases. To the right was an elegant dining room about three-quarters the size of the living room. To the left was an eat-in kitchen, and off that was a hall I assumed led to the bedrooms.

"This is not a cheap place."

"I know. I paid for it."

"In cash?"

"Some."

"What does a dominatrix make?"

"Considerably more than a cop." She sat down on the living room sofa.

"Are you attacking my masculinity?"

"Not at the moment," she said, smiling. "Would you like to join me?" She patted the sofa seat next to her.

I sat in the oversized armchair to her right. It looked

safer. "You didn't answer my question."

"I never enjoy talking finances."

"Who does?"

"Very well. Last year I earned nine hundred and fifty thousand dollars."

"What?"

"Do you need me to translate that into British pounds?"

"That's a heavy sum in any currency," I said.

"It was a slow year."

"Sorry to hear that." I paused.

"Why are you asking me these questions?

"They're the only ones that come to mind right now. Hopefully they'll lead to other questions that might lead me to a killer."

The word *killer* caught her attention. The mood in the room turned somber.

"Liz, you don't strike me as a woman driven by greed. Why become a dominatrix?"

"I'm not concerned with money. I still work at the same children's clinic I was employed at during my days at Columbia."

"Why D&S?"

"At first it was fun. I met interesting people and, as a psychologist, I knew how to play the control game. I was good at it. It also afforded me constant company. I don't like being alone."

"Why turn pro?"

"My clinic got hit hard by city budget cuts. We were on the verge of closing down. When I learned how much I could earn by charging—"

"—you figured you'd be able to support the clinic."

"Yes. I also encouraged many of my friends to donate,

which they did gladly."

"On the street before, you called yourself a whore."

"What else would you call someone who spends years learning to heal mental illness and uses the gift to entertain D&Sers?"

She stared at me, waiting for an answer. Not having one, I walked over to her bookcases and glanced around. They were mostly classics. She went to the bar.

"Would you like a glass of wine?"

"Sure." I picked up a copy of Dickens's *A Tale of Two Cities*.

"A cop who reads Dickens?" She handed me my wine.

"It is a far, far better thing that I do, than I have ever done..." I recited.

"Impressive. Very impressive." She placed her wine glass down. "Would you excuse me while I change?"

"It's your place."

While she was gone, I replaced the book and called Jeanne from my cell phone. There was still no sign of Corinne Moreland. I told her there was a good chance Moreland had been abducted and to send a team to her apartment to go over the place with a fine-tooth comb.

I hung up and sat on the sofa. A picture on the coffee table—of a young girl playing in a park—caught my eye. I studied it.

"Is this picture of you as a girl?" I shouted.

"My daughter," Liz said, entering the room.

The resemblance was amazing.

"That was taken five years ago, when she was nine. She lives with her father back in London. I see her when she's on holiday."

"She's adorable."

I turned my head. There was Liz, dressed in black spike-heeled boots and a tight one-piece latex number. She looked as though she had been poured into it. There were shiny metal chains wrapped around her.

"Do you wish permission to touch me?" She approached.

Taken by surprise, I began to laugh.

That wasn't the reaction she was going for. She became incensed. "How dare you laugh at me," she growled.

"It's easy in that outfit."

"Do you know how many I've paddled for less?"

"If your income is any clue, I'd say a lot. I'm surprised you don't suffer from tennis elbow."

She went to slap me. I caught her open hand in midair. Our eyes locked. I didn't see contempt—I saw embarrassment. I pulled her toward me and kissed her. There was no resistance. I felt the wetness of her lips and the intense warmth of her desire. I stepped back and headed for the door.

"Don't go—please."

"I shouldn't be here. I think it's a good idea to—"

"—be alone? Please," she pleaded, "stay."

I knew I should leave, but her argument was as compelling as her lips were inviting. Against my better judgment, I took her in my arms. As she rested her head on my shoulder, I felt her warm breath on my neck. I kissed her again.

"I'll stay, but I don't want to spend the night with a woman who has more chains around her than a snow tire. I want to be with Liz," I said as I unzipped her suit. I ran my fingers lightly down her neck, stopping above her left breast to admire her tattoo—a black lily.

157

She took my fingers from her breast, brought my palm to her lips, and gently kissed it. I wasn't sure who was using whom for what, but for now I didn't care. There would be time to figure all that out in the morning.

23

It was four a.m. I was lying next to Liz in her giant brass bed trying hard not to disturb her sleep or the remnants of my euphoric state. I looked around her bedroom, my attention divided between the fire dancing on the logs in the fireplace and the satin covers moving gently up and down with Liz's breathing. Even asleep, she was picturesque. I felt a soft hand touch my chest.

"Hello," she said, smiling. She replaced her hand with her soft cheek.

I leaned forward and kissed her.

"Don't you find these moments awkward? After last night I feel as though we should be more than what we are," she said.

"What are we?"

"Strangers."

"I think we're a little past strangers." I got out of bed.

"You *do* find this awkward, don't you?" she chided as she lay face down on top of the covers.

"A little," I admitted, watching the soft light from the fire envelop her body.

"There's no reason to be. We're consenting adults, and I had a wonderful time, Jerry. But I don't want to make more of this than it was. I was lonely. You were lonely. We filled a need for each other for a night."

I stood at the foot of the bed wondering if I should care that she was kissing me off. It had only been one night. But this woman was special.

"Are you asking me to leave?"

"I'm telling you to do whatever makes you comfortable."

"Do you often have this conversation the morning after?"

"I don't invite a great many men into my bed, if that's what you're asking." She sounded hurt. I sat beside her and stroked her hair.

"I wasn't suggesting that."

She pressed her cheek into my hand. As we leaned closer our lips met, and our tongues began to collide again.

"Do you want to come back to bed?" she teased.

"We are in bed."

"In that case, would you like to defile me again, detective?" She threw her arms up in mock surrender. "My virtue is yours."

"I have to work this morning." I pulled the covers over us.

"It's not morning yet." Smiling devilishly, she slid under the blanket, her moist tongue gliding down my body.

I was about to object when her hungry lips found what

160

they were searching for.

"On the other hand," I sighed, "What's a little defiling between friends?"

* * *

I woke up alone. It was ten a.m. I called for Liz. No answer. I got out of bed and went into the living room and called for her again. Silence. I found my clothes neatly folded and placed on top of a decorative teakwood sawhorse. Unlike a conventional sawhorse, this one had an upturned triangular top bar with a horse's head carved at the end. It sat in the corner of the living room under two hanging plants. A note was attached. It read:

J.,

> Couldn't sleep and thoroughly knackered. Thank you for last night. I have an early appointment at the clinic and didn't want to wake you. Help yourself to anything in my flat. My morning appointment should end by one this afternoon. Would you like to meet for lunch? Come by my office—113 W. 57th St., Suite 659. The number there is 212-555-7643.

Love,

L.

P.S. Since I was up early, I took the liberty and did your laundry.

I put the note aside, gathered up my clothes, and headed for the shower. What luck. I had found a domestic dominatrix.

161

24

I was heading south on the FDR Drive for my lunch date with Liz in Midtown. After leaving her apartment I went home to New Rochelle to check my messages and saddle up Baby. Baby is my 1966 Mustang GT convertible with a high-output 289-cubic-inch V-8 engine. She has 271 horsepower with four-on-the-floor and a posi rear. My next-door neighbor, Mickey G., helped me rebuild her from an old heap. Thanks to his tools, his gas station, and his mechanical genius, Baby was breathing leaded fuel again and going from zero to sixty in six seconds. The only thing she was missing was a new paint job to cloak the reddish-brown primer presently covering her once-sleek exterior.

I called Liz's clinic from my cell phone and was informed she was waiting for me at the King Cole Bar at the St. Regison Fifty-fifth Street and Fifth Avenue. Fancy. I stepped on the gas. Exiting the FDR Drive at the United Nations, I was heading crosstown when my cell phone beckoned. It was Ron.

"What's up?" I said into the phone.

"A few things. We need to go over the data I got from the disc."

"Whenever you're ready, bro," I replied. "What else?"

"Flaherty's office called. He wants to see us."

"Somebody else turn up dead?"

"Always a possibility these days."

"I have to do something first. I'll meet you there in about two hours."

"See you then. By the way, the prints came back on the knife we found at the Westlake house. They are definitely Evanston's."

"Interesting."

"Isn't it though?"

"Even dead the man can't keep his hands to himself. Anything else?"

"That's not enough?"

"Keep me posted."

"*No problemo.*"

I was about to hang up when Ron asked, "Did you make contact with the Jag Lady?"

I contemplated my answer as I turned up Sixth Avenue. "You could say that," I replied.

"Did you get anything off her?"

"I think it's safe to say I did."

"Well?"

"We'll talk later at Flaherty's."

I dropped the line and pulled up in front of the hotel. The valet, a young kid in his late teens, opened my door.

"Nice wheels, man."

I thanked him with a ten dollar bill and told him to take good care of Baby.

I saw the bar entrance halfway into the hotel lobby. As I made my way toward the crowded room, a beautiful blonde caught my eye. Her short red silk dress was clinging to her body. I walked over to her. She leaned over and kissed me.

"Thank you for coming, Jerry," Liz said.

"Thanks for doing my laundry."

"Shall we get a table?" she laughed.

I nodded and followed her through the lobby toward Ducasse. The maître d' looked disapprovingly at my jeans and sneakers, but then saw I was with Liz. He greeted her by name.

"Come here often?" I asked.

Liz smiled. "Hello, Claude," she said to the maître d'. She turned back to me. "As a matter of fact I conduct business here from time to time. Today I'm planning a fund-raiser for the clinic. We decided to have the event here. Claude has been kind enough to offer his assistance with the menu. What did you think I was doing here?"

"I thought you might have been 'working.'"

"Jealous?"

"Uncomfortable. It's hard for me to cope with the fact that the woman I slept with last night is a dominatrix."

"Well, the woman you slept with last night *is*. That's part of who I am. I'm also other things." She reached out and touched my hand.

"Liz, you're a kind, giving woman. I can't believe you do those things. I don't know what to make of this business."

Before she could answer, the waiter interrupted us.

"Dr. Drake, may I get you a drink?"

164

"That would be lovely, Victor."

"The usual, doctor?"

"Please," Liz said.

Victor turned to me. "The same," I said.

Hesitating, Victor looked at Liz as if waiting for her approval before taking my order.

"What gives? Is he one of your..."

"Not at all," she laughed. "You don't know what my usual is, Jerry."

"Not a clue. But unless it's decaf coffee, I'll give it a shot."

"Two Scorpion Mezcal Gran Reservas, Victor," Liz said.

"Very good, Dr. Drake."

"Do you enjoy mezcal?"

"I might if I knew what it was."

"Mezcal is a distilled agave spirit. The premium mezcal you are about to have is aged for seven years with a scorpion in the bottle. It is considered a great honor to eat the scorpion. Some believe it acts as an aphrodisiac."

"Good to know."

Victor left to get our drinks. I waited a moment and then asked, "Now about this domina..."

"Perhaps we should lower our voices," Liz suggested. "If we're going to discuss this in public, we should do so quietly."

"Why?"

"Although many people accept the scene for what it is, others are not as...forward-thinking."

"Meaning me?"

"No."

"Who, then?"

"People in your line of work, for starters." Liz's eyes

broke contact with mine and drifted around the room. When they returned to me, I saw anguish in them.

"In many places, you can be arrested and prosecuted for involvement in D&S—even if it's between consenting adults."

"In many places sex in anything other than the missionary position is illegal, not to mention confusing for the narrow minded," I replied.

"But *those* laws are not enforced," she remarked sharply. "One of the women in my...circle...was in the midst of a nasty divorce and custody battle. Her husband hired a private detective who obtained pictures of her during a D&S session. The magistrate gave her husband sole custody of their child."

"The magistrate was doing what he thought best."

"The magistrate was an ass. She was a good mother with a good job—that is, until it was all made public."

"She lost her job?"

"Her job, her family—everything that mattered."

She paused and turned away. When she looked back, I could see disgust building inside those beautiful blue eyes.

"Do you know what really galled me? Her husband, that self-righteous, hypocritical, lying bastard, was involved in the scene as well."

"Nice guy. What ever happened to your 'friend'?"

"Always the detective, aren't you?"

"Occupational hazard," I said as the waiter placed our drinks on the table. He asked for our order. I told him we needed a few more minutes. "Your 'friend,' I prodded after the waiter disappeared.

Liz lifted the mezcal to her full, soft red lips and slowly took a sip. Returning the drink to the table, she stared at the glass.

"My friend decided to spare her daughter further embarrassment and came to America to conclude her studies—and left behind the most precious thing in her life. Doesn't seem quite fair, does it?"

"Every so often society needs someone to persecute."

"That makes it right?"

"Makes it what it is."

"And what about Dee? Now people will believe we're all homicidal maniacs." Liz's jaw tightened.

"It's a violent game you've chosen. It lends itself to those conclusions."

"You make it sound as if we are all bloodthirsty control addicts."

"You told me yourself you enjoy control—that you want that control."

"Most doms are giving, caring people; otherwise they couldn't give of themselves to fulfill their submissive's needs."

"Come again?"

"Did you know most doms come from altruistic professions? They're nurses, teachers—"

"—psychologists," I interjected.

"Yes, even psychologists."

"Liz, if you give of yourself to fulfill the sub's fantasy, how are you in control?"

"Therein lies the dichotomy of the game," she smiled. It wasn't a warm smile. "Control is an illusion."

I continued listening.

"In the D&S scene, the submissive designs the fantasy and can end it anytime. We are really doing what *they* want."

"And what does the dominatrix get out of this?"

Liz didn't answer. Looking down at her drink, she brushed her forefinger up the thin crystal stem of the elegant glass. She studied the remaining gold liquid and how it swayed at her touch. As she observed her drink, I observed her. She was expressionless, but her eyes filled with resignation.

"What does she get, detective?" Liz repeated, bringing the glass closer to her lips. "Why, she gets the illusion of control," she said, consuming the remaining mezcal with one long tip of her glass. "And the heartbreak of losing her child."

I wanted to console Liz though I knew it wasn't possible. I went to sip my mezcal and noticed the remains of a scorpion in my glass. As the waiter came for our order, my cell phone rang. Ron was wondering where I was. Unable to speak, I assured him I'd be at the safe house soon and ended the call.

"Liz," I said putting my phone away, "I have to go. Will you be all right?"

"Of course."

I got up to leave.

"Will I see you tonight?" she asked. I didn't respond immediately. "I see," she said, mistaking my silence for a no.

"Liz..."

"Please, Jerry. I'm an adult. I understand."

"No, you don't. What I was about to say is I might be working late. If I'm not, I'd like to see you."

She smiled. "Maybe for drinks?"

"You bet," I said, looking at the scorpion resting on the bottom of my glass. "After all, who doesn't love a great piece of tail?"

I was heading south on Fifth Avenue, feeling confused about Liz. I enjoyed her honesty and warmth, but her involvement in the D&S scene troubled me. Downshifting to second, I tried to keep my mind on the investigation, but it kept wandering back to Liz. I was beginning to believe they might be one and the same.

25

The conference room was abuzz. Greeley was off in the corner arguing with Flaherty. I couldn't hear him, but from the way he was waving his arms, it was clear there was a problem. Ron was sitting at the conference table talking into his cell phone, and one seat down Goose was talking to himself. I made myself comfortable between Ron and Goose.

Ron hung up his phone. "Got the word back from the lab. The bullets they pulled from Flaherty's car were .22's."

"Small caliber for a—"

"—hit?" Ron said. "But the right size for a warning. Any further information on the lady in the Jaguar?"

"I'll get you caught up later," I said uncomfortably, nodding toward Greeley. "Why are we here?"

"I don't know. I didn't call this meeting."

"Hey, Goose," I said. "Sorry to interrupt your

170

conversation. You have any idea what's going on here?"

"Hey, Jerry, like, how's it hanging, man?"

I looked at Goose and smiled. "How long has he been here?" I asked Ron.

"Since the seventies."

"Like, guys, I had another visit last night."

"Did you follow our plan?" Ron asked.

"To the T, man. But it still creeps me out—not to mention that it, like, blows my mind."

"I think it's a little late for that, Goose."

I was about to suggest to Ron that we get the hell out of there when Flaherty took his seat at the head of the table. Greeley sat to his left.

"Now that the prodigal son has returned, maybe we can get this show on the road. Unless of course you have an objection, Detective Gold?" Greeley was speaking directly to me.

"I have a lot of objections, Walt, but I wouldn't want to overburden your brain."

"Isn't that, like, real considerate," Goose said.

"Shut up, hippie," Greeley barked. "All I want from you is those reports, which are late. I don't want no mouth!"

"I have two words for you Greeley..."

"Jerry," Ron interrupted.

"...mandatory retirement."

"I thought you were going to use two other words," Ron said, relieved.

"Fuck you," Greeley yelled.

"Those two?" Goose asked.

"Where do you come off keeping us waiting? And why did you speak to Westlake after I interviewed him?"

"Relax, Walt, no need to have a hemorrhage."

"What did he talk to you about?"

"Flaherty didn't tell you? Westlake wants to buy the NYPD. He was asking me how we could downsize the staff."

"Downsize?" Greeley was puzzled.

"You know. What jobs could be eliminated. But don't worry, Walt, you'll always have a job here because for the life of me we can't figure out what the hell it is you do."

"You're a real wiseass," Greeley hollered, jumping from his chair. "I'll teach you to crack wise!"

"I don't need you to teach me, I already know how."

"Enough, you two," Flaherty said.

"You going to let him talk to his superior like that, Tom?"

"Enough," Flaherty repeated, standing to meet Greeley's glare. "You have anything else we need to discuss?"

Greeley didn't answer. He just stood there, grinding his teeth.

"Good. Then you have a murder to solve."

Seething, Greeley headed for the door. Flaherty sat back in his chair.

"What's the word, chief?" I asked after Greeley had departed.

"The word is since you two came aboard we're not any closer to a suspect and more people are dead. They're dropping like flies. I'm getting pressure from downtown. They want answers."

"Can't blame them. One dead senator demands more attention than two dead women and a possible kidnapping," Ron said.

"Don't put words in my mouth." Flaherty leaned forward in his chair. "I expect that from your brother, but not from you."

"And I expected you to shield us from the heat longer," I said.

"A senator is dead and you two happen to be in the vicinity. If it were anybody else, you'd be emptying parking meters on Staten Island. I'm doing plenty of shielding, but there's plenty of heat. In fact, Commissioner Daley's office called. He wants to meet with you two. Five sharp at his home."

"We'll be there," I said.

"You're damn right you will. You are going to change first." Flaherty said, pointing to my attire.

"Why?"

"Why do I bother?" Flaherty muttered. Then he turned his attention to Goose.

"Doctor, any information on the senator's death?"

"Preliminary—the labs aren't back."

"I'm listening," Flaherty responded.

"Death was due to the injury sustained..."

"Hey, Goose," I interrupted, "It's only us."

"Sorry. Somebody slit his throat."

"With what?"

"With the same kind of instrument used on our other victims, dudes." After Goose finished, I brought the room up to speed on my meeting with Liz—excluding the personal details. When I was done, Flaherty looked pleased.

"Now I remember why I hired you in the first place," he conceded. "Is there a connection between the two dead women, their live friend, and the senator?"

"We're working on that now," I replied. "We have a few things to follow up on before our afternoon meeting."

"Go."

Ron, Goose, and I got up.

173

"Goose, you need a ride?" I asked, heading for the elevator.

"No, I'm cool. I'm going back to the lab, even though it freaks me out. I'm thinking maybe I should bring these break-ins to somebody's attention."

"You did: Ron and me."

"I mean like Flaherty."

"Why? You're not in any danger," I said.

"I don't want to end up like the senator."

"We wouldn't let that happen."

"That's real reassuring. Did you tell that to DiCenzio?"

"I didn't have time."

26

We had an hour to make the thirty-minute drive to Forest Hills Estates, so I stopped to pick up a couple of Cokes. As we headed east through the Midtown Tunnel, Ron stared at his side view mirror. I opened the bag holding the sodas and offered him one. He declined.

"Did you notice we're being followed?"

"Black Ford Crown Vic?" I said, sipping my soda.

"You noticed."

"No, it seems to be the car of choice for tailing us this year. When did he pick us up?"

"A few blocks from the safe house."

I looked into the rearview mirror and confirmed it was a Crown Vic.

"Kirby's men again? He tends to be persistent."

"More like annoying. Shoot out one of his tires," I

suggested.

"For being annoying? I don't think so."

"Getting soft on crime?"

"I'm not filing three hours of paperwork because Kirby Lonsdale annoys you."

"Whatever," I grinned.

"What is with you and that stupid grin? Did you get laid last night or something?"

"Just because I happen to see the humorous side of life, why do you assume I have partaken in sexual intercourse?"

"'Sexual intercourse'... 'Partaken,'" Ron laughed. "You did get laid."

"All night long and most of the morning."

I turned onto Continental Avenue slowly enough for our friends in the Crown Vic to follow.

"Anyone I might know?" Ron asked.

"You might say that."

"Nikki. You got back with Nikki."

I shook my head.

"Not Nikki? Who then?"

"Her name is Elizabeth Drake," I heard myself say cautiously.

"Why does that name sound familiar?" Ron took a hit of my soda. "Elizabeth Drake...the Jag Lady!" Ron spit out her name along with his soda.

I nodded.

"You screwed a potential suspect in an active murder investigation. Are you crazy?"

"No. Just morally weak."

"You're certifiable."

"Since you put it that way."

"What other way is there to put it?"

"It wasn't planned."

"You just happened to find yourself in bed with her last night?"

"Yes."

"Remind me to tell that to Internal Affairs when they bring us up on misconduct charges. 'Hey, guys, it just happened.' You really crossed the line this time."

I didn't like Ron's attitude. Probably because I knew he was right.

"She didn't kill those people, Ron. She couldn't have. She's a psychologist."

"Since when are serial killers vocationally selective?"

"They're not. But they are gender selective. It's rare to find a female serial killer."

"It's rarer to find a detective who sleeps with his suspects."

"I don't think she's capable of murder."

"I didn't think I was either until now!"

"She's being very cooperative."

"I'll bet."

"My gut's telling me she's not the one."

"Are you sure that's not another organ talking? What you did may very well have compromised our entire investigation *and* that woman's safety. Didn't it occur to you that if we could find her, so can others? Like the killer—assuming she's not."

"She's not. I'd bet my career on it."

"You already did. And mine, too."

I turned Baby left onto Greenway North. We were looking for the commissioner's house in the affluent neighborhood on the outskirts of the city. The houses were large stone Tudors, and they all had perfectly manicured lawns. I pulled up in front of a house third from the end of the block. A small plaque announced "449 Greenway North."

"Made it with ten minutes to spare," I said, shutting down Baby's engine. "You see our tail?"

"No, but I'm sure it's around."

"We have a few minutes. You want to catch me up on Westlake's disc?"

Ron reached into the backseat and grabbed a file from his briefcase. It held printouts, each of which had four columns. The first column had one word. The second and third columns consisted of six numbers with slashes after every two. The fourth column consisted entirely of numbers in different groupings, composing paragraphs of gibberish.

"What am I looking at?"

"I don't know for sure," Ron answered. "But my guess would be Diane Westlake's black book."

"That's great."

"Some of the data looks corrupted."

"Not so great."

"See this," Ron said, pointing to the first column on the page. "These could be nicknames."

"Reasonable assumption. You certainly wouldn't put someone's real name in a book like this. It might fall into the wrong hands." I grinned.

"Right. I figure she has to have a key or dictionary for what the nicknames mean." He continued, "Columns two and three are most likely dates."

"I'm with you so far. What's the last column?"

"That's where I think the file got corrupted. Those numbers should be words."

"What do you want to do?"

"I can try to convert the file again using a different code-breaking algorithm and see what comes out. I must have done something wrong—unless that data is encrypted."

"Keep working it."

"Maybe we should revisit Westlake's house to see if she kept the key in a different place?"

"Let's go to our meeting," I said, looking at my watch. "We'll come back to this after you have another go at it."

We made our way up the winding slate sidewalk to the front door. I leaned over the iron handrail and took a quick look into the window. I couldn't see much other than a grand piano.

Ron reached for the bell. I stopped him. "Don't you find it unusual that Greeley screamed at Goose for not getting his reports?"

"He's entitled to the information."

"That's not my point. Wilkins is actually running the investigation. Why hasn't *he* requested the reports?"

"Chain of command. He asks Greeley, Greeley asks Goose...or—"

"—or?—

"—or maybe Wilkins never asked Greeley—

"—because he was already aware of what the reports contain."

"Wilkins could be Goose's midnight caller," Ron agreed. "Uh huh."

"But why?" Ron went to ring the bell again. Again I prevented him.

"Let's assume Wilkins is visiting Goose's desk nightly."

"Fine, since we're never going to get inside," Ron said,

resting on the handrail.

"Then why did Greeley yell at Goose about not receiving information fast enough?"

"Could be a clever move on Greeley's part to throw us off the track."

"Greeley clever? Ron, we're talking about a man who thinks a menstrual period is a musical hour."

"True, *clever* and *Greeley* are two words that will never be synonymous. But you don't have to be that clever to act upset." Ron rang the bell.

As we waited, I contemplated his theory. Could Greeley be that smart? Could he only be acting dumb? Greeley couldn't be that good. Sir Laurence Olivier wasn't that good. If Dave Wilkins was filching information, where was it going?

My questions would have to wait. The front door opened and a woman in a simple black dress covered by a frilly white apron greeted us.

"I'm Detective Gold," Ron said, displaying his shield. "This is my partner. We have an appointment with Commissioner Daley."

The woman stepped aside, allowing us entrance to the foyer.

"You're expected. If you'll follow me to the parlor."

"Thank you," Ron said, as she showed us in.

"If you'll be good enough to wait here."

The room was large and stately, with dark hardwood floors. Bookshelves with art—originals, not reproductions—and rare first editions lined the walls. To the side was a curio cabinet containing trophies for marksmanship. Among the awards was a picture of the commissioner's wife handing her husband a blue ribbon. To the far right was

180

the grand piano I had seen from the window: a Steinway. Its top was open; it looked as if it was played often.

"Good evening, gentlemen," a pleasant alto voice called out. "I'm Rose Daley. Welcome to our home."

A slender woman about five feet eight inches tall with light hair and dark eyes approached. She was dressed in an elegant, dark-colored pantsuit. She looked youthful and athletic, as if she spent a great deal of time on the tennis courts. Though I knew she was the commissioner's age, she didn't look a day over forty. She extended her hand graciously.

"You must be Detectives Ron and Jerry Gold. I've been expecting you."

"*You've* been expecting us?" I asked. We both shook her hand.

"The commissioner is running a bit behind. He asked me to entertain you until his arrival."

I nodded.

"That's not necessary," Ron said.

"Oh, but it is. It's not often I have detectives of your reputation in my living room."

"Our reputation?"

"Please don't be modest, Ron. Did I get that right? You *are* Ron?"

Ron nodded.

"You both ended the horrible reign of the Madam Murderer. It's not my intention to embarrass you, but you are celebrities."

"Celebrities?" Ron smiled awkwardly.

"Although I am a professor of music, I have always had a keen interest in criminology."

"Is that how you met your husband," Ron asked.

"No, but it is one of the things that fascinated me about him. As the wife of the commissioner of police, I meet a great many detectives. Until this moment I've never been impressed. May I just say, bravo, gentlemen."

Bravo? I didn't know if I should thank her or take a bow.

"Would you like an autograph?" I asked.

Ron elbowed me in the ribs. Mrs. Daley flashed me a smile. When you're a star, everything you say is magic.

"I truly believe you both are gifted with perhaps the most intuitive minds in the criminal justice system today. Oh, my..." she interrupted herself. "I am forgetting my manners." She noticed we were still standing. "Please make yourselves comfortable."

I couldn't help noting Mrs. Daley's style and grace. She seemed to glide toward the sofa. It must be something the rich learn during prep school. Perhaps a class in Wealth 101.

"May I offer you a drink?"

"We're fine, thank you." Ron said, refusing for us both.

Listening to Mrs. Daley talk, I began to understand why the commissioner had married her. Every politician needs a wife who complements him. George Washington had Martha, Abraham Lincoln had Mary, and Raymond T. Daley had Rose.

Rose van der Meer Daley was a descendant of one of New York City's oldest families. Like her father and grandfather, she was an unabashed supporter of conservative causes, and, given the commissioner's marksmanship awards, the Second Amendment.

"May I call you by your first names?"

"Certainly."

182

"Thank you, Ron." She paused. "How is the investigation going?"

"It's going, ma'am."

"How *would* one go about catching a serial killer? What's your secret? And, does it apply to this case?"

When Ron remained silent, Mrs. Daley said, "Forgive me. Of course you can't discuss the facts of an active investigation. I'm fascinated by this case, but there are certain issues I don't understand."

"Issues?" Ron asked.

"Yes. I don't understand the fascination with...how shall I put it...the 'scene' the victims were apparently involved in."

"Scene?" Ron asked.

"I believe the papers during the Madam Murders call it the S&M scene?"

Ron nodded.

"I know I'm old-fashioned—that what two consenting adults do in private is their own business—but I can't condone such behavior, especially if it leads to murder. Can you explain the scene to me?"

"I believe Jerry would be more able to answer your questions." Ron turned to me. "Didn't you have an intense meeting with an expert on that subject last night?"

I felt explaining S&M to the commissioner's wife would be like taking a debutante to a porn film. I'm sure it's done; I just didn't want to be the one to do it.

"I hope this isn't embarrassing you?" she laughed. "I believe if one wishes to understand the psychological workings of a serial killer, one must understand his fascinations. Of course, you can't give me any insights into this particular case, but it would be interesting to understand the mind of such a person."

I began to explain as obliquely as I could. She asked questions, all of which I answered. When I was done, she sat there, not appalled but fascinated.

"Ron, your brother truly did his research."

"Yes, he really went under the covers on this -."

"-perversion. I don't wish to appear judgmental, but what else could you call it?" she asked me.

"I don't deal in semantics."

"Do you believe violence is wrong?"

"Do you believe it's violence if you're giving someone what they want?"

"No," she said thoughtfully. "I don't believe it is. For a person who doesn't deal in semantics, you're very clever. Perhaps if we exchange the word *violence* with *behavior* we could agree?"

I shrugged.

"I find it hard to accept a culture that thrives on this abhorrent behavior."

"Fortunately for everyone, Mrs. Daley, they don't seek approval."

"Fortunate, indeed," she acquiesced as headlights from a car flashed through the window. "That must be my husband. I'll let him know you're here. It was a pleasure meeting you. I do hope we will meet again."

Within a few minutes a harried Commissioner Daley entered. We stood to greet him.

"Detectives, please remain seated," he said, shaking our hands. "Excuse the delay."

"Your wife kept us entertained, sir," Ron said.

"Good. Can I get you anything to drink? Soft drink? Perhaps something stronger?"

"No, thank you. Mrs. Daley already offered."

"Then shall we get down to business, detectives?"

About time, I thought.

"I was skeptical when it was suggested your services be enlisted. But I'm the first to admit when I'm wrong. Actually, the press is usually the first," he laughed. "What I'd like to speak about doesn't directly relate to your case."

"What would you like to discuss, commissioner?" Ron asked.

"I understand you found Senator DiCenzio's body."

I nodded.

"The senator was a well-respected man in our political party. It would be unfortunate..." He hesitated, stood, and shut the mahogany doors to the study. He chose his next words carefully. "...If unfounded speculation made its way into the media."

"And what if the *facts* found their way there?" I asked.

"You aren't a rookie, detective. Allow me to be blunt. This is an election year. If a scandal ensued from the DiCenzio incident, it would hurt our party. I'd hate to see that happen to our mayoral candidate."

"Would *you* happen to be the party's candidate?" Ron asked.

"My name has been suggested for the position, yes."

"Are you aware the senator's murder could be related to the murders we're presently investigating?" Ron queried.

"I see no ties presently. I think we can agree that to assume any connection would be premature."

"With all due respect, sir, I don't agree," Ron answered.

"What *can* we agree upon, then?" Daley said heatedly.

"We can all agree the senator's dead," I said.

"Can we also agree this situation should not be

unraveled in the press?"

Ron nodded.

"Good. So may I be comfortable in the knowledge you will keep this investigation under wraps?"

"You mean *secret*?"

"Shall we compromise on *discreet*?"

"Commissioner, although Ron and I can be the souls of discretion, we didn't catch the senator's case."

"I see." The commissioner glanced at his watch. "I am pressed for time. Nevertheless, gentlemen, I think you understand me." He showed us to the door. "Your discretion will be remembered and appreciated."

Inside my car, I scrambled to start Baby, hoping to get her heater going. We headed back to the expressway. Ron checked his side view mirror. "Looks like our tail is gone."

"Probably fell asleep waiting for the commissioner to get to the point," I said.

"And what exactly was the point?"

"The point is that the commissioner thinks *we* caught the DiCenzio case and not Greeley, and that he appreciates our discretion. In short, there is no point," I recapped.

"That's what I thought. Take me to Penn Station. It's late, I'm tired, and I want to go home."

We drove the next hour in silence until Baby pulled up in front of the train station.

"I'll call you tomorrow morning."

"Where are you off to tonight?" he asked.

"Home."

"Alone, right?" Ron asked firmly.

I nodded.

"Good. See you in the morning."

As Ron disappeared into the station, I disappeared

toward the West Side Highway and my warm evening with
Liz. Like the commissioner, I also appreciate discretion.

27

It was a little past two in the morning; Liz and I were resting contentedly in each other's arms. I began to stroke her hair as she lightly brushed her fingertips across my chest.

"You don't like what I do?" she said.

"I liked what you did tonight."

"I was referring to the whole D&S scene. You're quite opposed to it."

"What makes you ask?"

"When we were playing earlier and I asked you to take me over your knee, you seemed surprised. Is it because you've never spanked a woman before?"

"I've never spanked anyone before. I guess I'm against physical forms of punishment."

"Acquiescing to my request wouldn't have been punishment. It would have been giving me what I was requesting. I would have maintained control."

"Then let's say it's violence I'm against."

"You've chosen an odd profession to deplore violence."

"I deal with it. I don't *play* with it. Besides, you're a top. I thought dominants didn't like to be spanked?"

"Yes, but sometimes I switch. Dee and her friends..."

"The friends who got you into the scene in New York?"

"Yes. He introduced me to the world of bottoming. Occasionally, he enjoyed taking my knickers down and giving me six of the best."

"Really?" I yawned.

"Am I boring you?"

"No," I laughed, "I just hate talking shop in bed."

"You are incorrigible."

"Do continue," I responded in a proper English accent, mimicking hers. "Did he take your knickers down often?"

"Not often. But the few times he did, I began to understand the appeal. Someone else is in control, and for a short time I didn't have to deal with any decisions. It was as if I were a little girl and I didn't have to worry about anything."

"Did Dee's friend feel the same way when he was bottoming?"

"I'm sure Vincent did." She yawned, snuggling closer to me. "I'll ask him tomorrow. I have an appointment with him first thing in the morning."

"Vincent?"

Liz didn't answer. She tensed up. I asked her again.

"Jerry, that was indiscreet of me. I can't very well give you his surname."

"Even if I promise to give you six of the best?"

"Well," she giggled playfully. "You do make it hard to resist. But I mustn't. It's against my personal and professional ethics. You do understand?"

"I do, and I hope Vinny DiCenzio appreciates it as well."

"I'm sure he does appreci—"

She stopped short. But it was too late for her to take back what I heard. The late senator Vinny DiCenzio was Liz's introduction to the scene. Seeing that a breech of professional etiquette visibly upset Liz, I tried to console her.

"Liz, what you tell me in bed will stay between us. Trust me when I tell you Vinny will never know."

"Are you acquainted with him?" she asked, calming down.

"I ran into him at the Princeton Club."

"You won't tell him I said anything?"

"Even if I did, knowing the state Vinny's in right now, he wouldn't listen."

"He's been campaigning ardently. He must be exhausted."

"Dead tired. Try and get some sleep."

"I can't believe I let that out," she said, rolling on her side.

"Perhaps you should be spanked?"

She turned towards me, her eyes wide with excitement.

"Perhaps I should!"

28

Morning found me in an awkward position. I was on my way to the kitchen to tell Liz that her morning appointment would be late. Permanently. When I turned the corner I was struck by the *New York Times*—literally.

"Hey, why did you throw the paper at me?"

"You knew, didn't you?" With moist eyes she looked at the paper down at my feet. The headline read, "Senator DiCenzio Found Dead" in big bold letters. "You knew and you didn't tell me," she cried.

"I couldn't."

"Don't lie to me."

She retrieved the paper and began to read aloud:

State Senator Vincent DiCenzio, fifty-two, was found dead yesterday morning in a room at the Princeton Club. The case is being investigated as a homicide, according to New

York City Police Commissioner Raymond T. Daley. Sources close to the investigation confirmed that twin brothers Ron Gold and Jerry Gold, the detectives well-known for handling the "Madam Murders" in 2008, have been assigned to the case.

"Do you want me to continue?"

I took the paper from Liz's hands. Sure enough, according to the paper, we had caught the case.

"I don't care what the paper says, Liz, Ron and I are not working the case."

"You must have known. Why would the paper say otherwise?"

"Good question."

"First Susan, then Dee, and now Vincent." Liz began to shake. "Jerry, what is going on?"

"I'm trying like hell to find out. Could this be the work of one of your clients?"

"No."

"Why not?"

"What would be their reason? They have money and power."

"How about an acquaintance? How many women did DiCenzio recruit for his circle? How many played with him on a regular basis?"

"Five that I'm aware of—Susan, Dee, Corinne, Judy, and me."

"Judy?"

"Judy Russo is another university friend of ours. But she couldn't possibly be involved. She's been in Italy for the last six weeks working on an architectural project for her thesis."

"All smart women. Do you have any stupid friends?"

"Just the one I'm sleeping with."

I ignored her last comment. "When is Judy due back?"

"In a few weeks."

"Give me her address. I want to talk to her. You haven't heard from Corinne since that night?"

Liz shook her head no. There was a long pause and then she asked, "Jerry, am I in danger?"

"I don't know. The one thing in common among the murders seems to be the Senator."

"A coincidence."

"I don't believe in coincidence. Can you disappear for a while?"

"I was planning to see my daughter in London this weekend. She's on holiday."

"Pack your bags. You're leaving today."

Liz was confused. Too many things were happening too fast. I attempted to comfort her. She moved away. "Don't, Jerry."

"You can trust me."

"I'm not sure whom to trust," she cried.

"Trust that I won't let anyone hurt you."

Liz threw herself into my open arms crying. I held her tightly.

Another great catch.

29

It was eleven-thirty in the morning, and Newark Liberty International Airport was already a half hour behind me. Continental Flight 107 from Newark to London, England, had departed on time, with Liz on board. Before she left, she gave me a kiss.

I told her to have a good time with her daughter and to call before returning—that I would meet her at the airport and give her a ride home. My offer was not entirely unselfish. I didn't want her back in the city until I was sure it was safe.

I was sitting in traffic at the approach to the Lincoln Tunnel when I received a call from Ron. He confirmed that the DiCenzio case was definitely ours. He also reminded me I was to meet him at the safe house by noon. I was minutes away, but to save time I asked him to meet me on the street with a cup of coffee and a donut. I had skipped breakfast, and crime fighting builds up an appetite. Once through the tunnel I put my siren on the dashboard and let it blare. As the blood-red light spattered my windshield, the city traffic began to part. I flew across Forty-second Street, and within minutes I was turning right on Fifth Avenue and pulling toward the curb, where Ron was standing empty handed.

"Where's my breakfast?" I asked as he got into the car.

"Where did you leave it?"

"Thanks a lot, partner."

"That's right. I'm your partner, not your butler."

"We're a little touchy this morning."

"No, *we're* a lot touchy. I went to sleep last night working on one homicide we can't solve, only to be told by the *New York Times* this morning that we're in charge of two we can't solve."

"Vinny would have wanted it that way," I replied, attempting to console him.

"Vinny might have, but Emily doesn't. She's complaining she never gets to see me as it is."

"Tell her I see you all the time, and it's no great bargain."

"You think that's funny?"

"Best I can do when I'm hungry. Let's get some breakfast."

"Later. First we are going to Forty-fifth and Third. We have a meeting at the Fleet Street Cafe."

"Kirby Lonsdale's place?" I pulled away from the curb and merged in with the traffic.

"Yes. And coincidentally, our meeting is with Kirby."

"The same Kirby who said the next time he saw us he'd kill us?"

"The very same."

"What changed his mind?"

"Maybe he found God."

"Kirby couldn't find his ass without a search party. I doubt he found God."

"Get us there and we'll see."

"Right after I get my coffee."

I guided Baby toward a Dunkin' Donuts coming up on our left.

"You can eat later," Ron said grabbing the wheel and preventing me from pulling over.

"What if I'm not hungry later?"

"Risk it."

I grudgingly headed south on Fifth Avenue and made the left on Thirty-fourth Street. Heading east, I counted all the donut shops we passed. I turned uptown on Third Avenue. Less than five minutes later I parked on Forty-fifth Street between Second and Third Avenues, right under a large sign which was kind enough to inform me parking was not permitted.

"You're illegally parked, Jerry."

"So?"

"Do you want to get towed?"

I engaged the flashing lights on the dash. "Happy now?"

I got out of the car.

"You're going to kill the battery."

"Risk it."

We entered the cafe and stood by the coat check. The place was nice enough. The dining area was two steps down and ran the entire length of the room. It was designed for the white-tablecloth business crowd. It was also empty. At the bar sat Red Donlan, his back to the wall, with a cup of coffee in front of him. Two of Kirby's men were sitting alongside him. When they saw us, they approached. Like Kirby's other crews, these two also looked as if they lived at a gym.

"Red, what's the story? Kirby own a steroid factory?" I said as the taller one began to pat me down. Red continued sipping his coffee and looking straight ahead.

"They're carrying, Red," the taller of the two said, feeling my gun in my shoulder holster.

"What kind of a cops would we be if we weren't?"

He went for my gun. I grabbed his wrist and held it twisted in an extremely uncomfortable position. Uncomfortable for him that is.

"Get your own gun," I said. "Red, Kirby should supply the help with guns instead of steroids."

The other guy tried to move in but Ron stepped in front.

"Hold on, Joey," Red called calmly. "There's not going to be trouble, is there, Golds?"

"You tell me, Red—it's your party." I applied added pressure to the wristlock. The goon dropped to one knee in pain.

Red shook his head. Joey immediately backed away. I released the goon. He stood, shaking his wrist as he begrudgingly backed off. Ron and I headed for the bar and pulled up a stool alongside Red.

"You guys want a drink?" Red asked, leaning behind the bar. I noticed him pouring coffee from a pot with an orange handle.

"Decaf?" I asked him.

He nodded. "Everybody tells me it's healthier."

"I'll have the same." I said, sighing. Got anything to go with it?"

197

"Scotch."

"As healthy as that sounds, I'll take mine black."

While he poured Ron looked around.

"Lunchtime in Manhattan, and this place is empty, Jerry."

"Maybe Kirby cooks as good as he pimps."

"Where is Kirby?" Ron asked.

"Hiding. In back." Red slid a coffee in front of me. "Kirby's convinced he's the next one to bite the bullet."

"What makes Kirby think so?" Ron asked.

"DiCenzio going down rattled him."

"How rattled?" I asked.

Before Red could answer, bald little Kirby barged through the swinging kitchen doors yelling at someone by his side.

"I want this place sealed off, damn it! Get more guys."

"That rattled." Red motioned toward Kirby.

As he impatiently made his way toward us I tried my coffee. It was awful. I should have added the Scotch.

"Where have you two been? It's been hours since I called."

"We're here now. What do you want?"

"Don't you read the papers, Gold?"

"As a rule, he doesn't," Ron answered. "But that's *his* problem. What's yours?"

"DiCenzio!" he shouted. "Vinny's dead."

"Bad luck. Do you think it will affect his campaign?" I asked.

"Crack wise if you want, Gold. But Kirby Lonsdale III ain't gonna be next."

"I feel better knowing that, Kirby."

"Why would you think you're next?" Ron asked. I

courageously took another sip of coffee.

"Before I talk, I want protection."

"Excuse me?" Ron said.

"You heard me. I need protection."

"From what, the coffee?" I pushed my cup away.

"From the person who snuffed Vinny."

"You know him?" Ron asked.

"I might, but I say nothing until I get protection."

"And that's your last word?" I said.

"Damn straight."

"In that case, thanks for the coffee. Let's go Ron." We started for the door.

"Hey, where're you going?"

"Kirby, if you're not going to talk, there's no sense in Jerry and me hanging around."

"Yeah, we're important people. We have people to see, places to go, and so forth." I continued heading for the door.

"What about me?" Kirby hollered. "How are you going to catch this nut?"

"We just developed a new plan. We're going to stake out your place."

"And?" Kirby asked.

"And when he snuffs you, we grab him."

"*Then* you grab him?"

"Then we grab him," I repeated. "We'll probably get promotions."

"What kind of fucked-up plan is that?"

"Granted, it's not one of Jerry's best, but it's viable."

"Viable? You get a promotion, and I get dead. Ain't you got no other plans?"

"I was planning to get breakfast after we leave here. You want to tag along?"

199

We were at the door when Kirby cracked like an egg.

"OK. OK. They killed DiCenzio as a warning to me."

"Who are they?" Ron asked.

"Vinny's friends."

"Kirby, you want to narrow that down for us?" I said.

"I can't."

Ron and I looked at each other and then turned for the door again.

"I can't because I don't know, damn it," he screeched.

"Let me get this straight. I'm missing breakfast because you think one of Vinny's friends wants you dead. But you don't know which one?"

"Right. So go find him. How hard can it be?"

"Not everybody is friendless like you."

"Another dig, Gold? You think this is funny? I can wind up dead."

"Don't try to cheer me up."

"See, Red, I told you they're all out to get me. No one cares if I die."

"Kirby, I'm sure somebody somewhere cares if you die," Ron said compassionately, "though at this moment I'd be hard pressed to say who."

"I'm telling you two, they killed him as a warning to me."

"Why kill a senator to scare a pimp?" I said. "It doesn't make sense."

"I knew Vinny was into the kinky sex stuff. I arranged for him to use one of my old buildings as a party pad."

"Party pad? Kirby, nobody calls it that anymore."

"Fine. He used it as his dungeon. You like that word better?"

"Much," I said. "If you're going to be a professional, talk

like one."

"Screw you, Gold!"

"Much better. Now he's getting the hang of it," I said to Ron.

"Kirby, did the senator ever invite you to one of his parties?" Ron questioned.

"No. I ain't into that shit."

"You never saw him with anyone—no friends that might be into it?"

"I told you I ain't into that shit. Kirby Lonsdale don't need to beat women for a good time."

"Although beating them for business is no problem," I added.

"Hey, business is business. Sometimes you got to show 'em who's boss."

"Great, Ron, we got the only pimp with a conscience in Manhattan."

"And I'm going to stay conscious."

"I said conscience, not conscious, you mental pigmy."

"Who you calling a pigmy?" Kirby lunged at me. Red grabbed him before he made contact.

"Hey, Red. You work for me. What do you think you're doing?"

"Saving what's left of your life." I said.

"Could we calm down here, gentlemen?" Ron shouted.

"And he's using that term loosely, Kirby."

"Fuck you, Mr. Dictionary."

"Kirby, concentrate for a second," Ron said. "Did you ever see Vinny with anyone out of the ordinary lately?"

Kirby shook his head as he sat back on a barstool.

"What about when you gave him your place?"

"I didn't give it to him. I rented it to him. I'm no charity organization. I got overhead."

"He's breaking my heart, Ron. Let's go."

"Wait a second. *I* didn't take him to the place. My mouthpiece did."

"Your lawyer?"

"Yeah, my lawyer."

"Did *he* ever see anyone with Vinny?" Ron asked.

Kirby clammed up.

"Talk to them, Kirby," Red said. "Save us all a shit-storm of grief."

"He was with two attractive ladies."

Now I was shouting. "But you never met them, you lying—"

"Never! My mouthpiece told me."

I went to smack him. Ron held me back.

"OK. I sent one of my people to check these two chicks out. I figure this kinky shit is big money. I take them into my stable and get a piece of the action. When Vinny found out, he told me 'hands off.'"

"Give me your lawyer's name, number, and address. I want to talk to him," I said.

"I get my protection now, right?" Kirby began scribbling on a cocktail napkin.

"You have Red. That's all the protection you need. I never thought I would say this, but keep him healthy, Red. The city may need him."

Red nodded.

"You going there now?" Kirby's voice trembled.

"Right after breakfast."

Ron dragged me toward the door.

Then again maybe before.

30

Kirby's mouthpiece had an office on the fifty-third floor of a prestigious Park Avenue address. On its glass doors were stenciled the names *Kalian, Moss, Reigert, and Frazier* in gold lettering. I compared this lettering to the name I had on the wrinkled napkin Kirby had given me. R. Taylor Frazier was a match.

The offices were lavish and screamed Park Avenue shyster. The floor was covered with a plush taupe-colored carpet. Expensive furniture and art filled the waiting area. Across the room was a glass wall separating us from the firm's library. To our right was the reception area. The receptionist was young—right out of college. With a telephone headset glued to her ear, she courteously answered each call with a pleasant but hasty, "Kalian, Moss, Reigert, and Frazier, how may I direct your call?"

While Ron waited for her to direct the calls, I directed myself to the corner of her desk next to a decorative bowl filled with the remains of the firm's holiday candy. Under the scrutiny of my partner, I unwrapped a miniature Nestlé Crunch bar, and with all the skill and precision of a true junk food addict, devoured it.

"What do you think you're doing?"

"Just my little part to end world hunger."

I reached for another. Ron reached for the bowl. My weakened condition brought on from a lack of breakfast gave him the edge. He moved the bowl to the other side of the desk as the receptionist finished her call.

"May I help you, gentlemen?"

"We're here to see R. Taylor Frazier. I'm Detective Ron Gold and my partner—"

"—is hungry, so move it."

"Do you have an appointment?"

She was about to press a button on her console to answer another call. I prevented her by gently taking her hand in mine.

"Honey, we're the police. We don't need an appointment."

"I'm sorry, but everyone needs an appointment."

Borrowing the young lady's headset, I engaged the office intercom and began shouting into it. "R. Taylor Frazier, report to the lobby. This is the NYPD."

The receptionist snatched her headset back as my voice reverberated throughout the office. "I never saw the police do that on TV," she laughed.

I was smiling modestly as an attractive black woman in her early thirties entered the reception area. She was about five-foot-four with short, dark hair. She wore an expensive charcoal grey skirt and blazer.

"What is going on out here?"

"You're R. Taylor Frazier?" I asked.

"I'm Robin Taylor Frazier, yes. And you are—"

"—here to speak to you."

"You'll have to excuse my socially inept partner. He was expecting to speak to a man," Ron said, displaying his shield and credentials.

She read it carefully and then looked to me. Grudgingly, I reached into my pocket and gave her a glance.

"Do you usually get the attention of someone you're meeting with these juvenile antics, detective?"

"Usually I just arrest them."

"Attempting to intimidate me?"

"Just answering your question honestly. Now how about answering a few of mine, Miss Frazier?"

"It's Ms. Frazier, and I can't imagine how I can possibly be of help to you, so if you'll excuse me, I'm expecting two important clients at any moment."

She pointed toward the door to dismiss us when two well-dressed men, one tall and thin, the other short and heavy, entered the office. Judging from the expression on her face, her important clients had arrived.

"Mr. Sanders, Mr. Jones." She extended her hand to them. Before she could say another word, I took out my cuffs and slapped one onto her outstretched wrist.

"R. Taylor Frazier, you're under arrest. You have the right to remain silent—"

"What's the meaning of this?" the short visitor said.

"Gentlemen, these are two old friends of mine. Please give me a minute," she said smiling until she turned her attention towards me. "Follow me?"

"To the ends of the earth."

"To the library."

"Don't you love it when she takes charge?" I asked her clients.

"I don't actually know what to say," Mr. Jones replied.

"Nothing to say. When our little Robin gets in these moods she's a wildcat. In fact, in college that was her nickname: 'Wildcat.'"

"The library. Now!" Frazier repeated.

"Always good to meet some of Robin's clients," I said, shaking their hands.

Both men smiled uncomfortably.

"You ever need a ticket fixed while your in town, I'm your man."

More uncomfortable looks and smiles.

"After all a friend of Robin's is a friend of mine," I said, turning to follow Frazier.

The men nodded.

"Enjoy your stay," I said as Ron dragged me away by the collar of my jacket.

We trailed Frazier to the conference room. "I think you got her attention," Ron said.

"I have a way with women."

"Kirby has an attractive mouthpiece."

"That's some nice piece, period," I said under my breath as I watched her glide to the conference room.

As the door closed behind us, Ms. Frazier didn't waste any time.

"How dare you embarrass me like that," she began, my handcuffs dangling from her wrist.

I reminded her we were being watched. I pointed through the glass at her clients.

"Take this off immediately, do you hear? Immediately!"

"Ms. Frazier—"

"I have never been so ill-treated before. I am an officer of the court," she spat out.

"Then act like one," Ron replied.

"She's hot when she's mad," I said.

"Quiet," Ron said.

"She does mad better," I replied.

"Don't make me take out my gun and shoot you in front of the nice lady."

I put my hands up and backed away. Ron ignored me.

"Ms. Frazier, we came here for information that might help us catch a serial killer. We don't have the time or the inclination to deal with your feigned outrage."

"Yeah, so you can either answer our questions here or at the station. Your choice."

"Do you have any idea how many high-powered clients I have in this city?"

"How many will you have after they've heard you've been arrested for protecting a serial killer?"

R. Taylor Frazier looked at us, then out to her waiting clients. She made a hand gesture assuring them she'd be out momentarily. Her facial expression did not exude the same confidence.

"What exactly is it you need to know?"

"For starters, what is it you do for Kirby? You don't look like a criminal attorney."

"Because I'm not a man?"

"Maybe."

"That's a sexist remark."

"Answer it anyway."

"My specialty is real estate. My firm handles Mr.

Lonsdale's property holdings."

"Do you remember renting a particular unit on the Upper East Side a few weeks back?"

"I don't handle his rentals."

"I think you'll remember this rental," Ron said.

"It was to Senator Vincent DiCenzio," I added.

Our arrogant attorney became visibly uncomfortable.

"I may have."

"May have?" Ron replied.

"I deal with a great many people."

"Are many of them state senators?" I quipped.

"Some." She was no pushover.

"You're not being cooperative, lady," I said, dangling my handcuffs in front of her.

"I'm doing the best I can, detective."

"I don't think so, and since I'm the one you have to impress, I would forget about Laurel and Hardy out there and talk to me."

"My brother tends to have a short attention span, Ms. Frazier," Ron said. "Unless you'd like to continue our discussion downtown, I'd suggest you speak up."

I never rented a property of Mr. Lonsdale's to the senator."

"That's it. Let's go."

"You can't—"

"—he can—"

"—and he will," I said.

As I moved in to cuff her again, she stepped behind a chair.

"I'm telling you I never rented a property to the senator!" Her voice became more urgent as I got closer. "I rented it to a friend of the senator's."

208

"Not to the senator?"

"No. He met me at the apartment building with three ladies. The apartment was for one of them."

"What ladies?" I asked.

"Does that matter? Detective, this is a very delicate issue for the senator."

"Dead men don't have any delicate issues," my brother remarked.

"What ladies?" I insisted.

"I met the senator at the building on the Upper East Side. He arrived with three women."

"You're certain it was three?"

"I can count to three." Now she was annoyed. "In fact, I remember thinking they might be sisters."

"Why is that?" Ron asked.

"They looked very much alike. Except the third." She looked from me to Ron and back again and smiled.

"What was different about the third?"

"She had long, dark hair. She was the one who rented the apartment."

"Do you remember anything else about them?"

"They were all well dressed and stunning."

"It didn't strike you as odd, meeting Senator DiCenzio and three beautiful women to rent an apartment?"

"I've been a lawyer in this city too long to find anything odd."

"So nothing struck you as unusual?"

"Not unusual for the male of the species."

"Why not?"

"Detective, don't act naive, and don't think I'm naive. I was under the impression the senator was renting a residence for his mistress."

"Are any of these women the ones you're talking about?" Ron showed Frazier the pictures of our two female victims. She looked closely at the photos and then nodded yes.

"She was the one I thought he was having the affair with." Frazier pointed to the shot of Diane Westlake.

"Why?" I asked.

"He had his arm around her."

"And the other two?"

"This woman was quiet," she said, pointing to the picture.

"Did you get her name?" I asked.

"I didn't. This one was another story," Ms. Frazier said pointing at the picture of Susan Atwell.

"How so?" Ron pushed.

"She was very demanding and extremely combative. She seemed jealous of the attention the senator was giving the woman whose photograph you showed me first. From the minute we entered the apartment, all she talked about was redoing it. She kept barking orders. I began to wonder which one was going to occupy the apartment."

"Is she the one on the lease?"

"Yes."

"We'll need a copy of the lease and a key to the apartment," I said.

"I can't release a copy of the lease without Mr. Lonsdale's permission."

"Call him," I said. "He won't have a problem with it."

"And the key?" Ron asked.

"I don't have a key."

She raised the phone on the table and forwarded our request to her assistant.

"Have you been back to that apartment since?" Ron asked.

Frazier didn't answer immediately. She began to tap her fingers against the conference table. The silence had grown uncomfortable when a clerk entered with the lease. She took the file and dismissed the subordinate with an obligatory thank-you.

"I was there one other time."

"For?" I asked impatiently.

"It was for a party."

"A D&S party?"

"Yes. The senator called it Hellfire Night." She averted her eyes.

"Where?" Ron asked.

"The duplex. The basement was converted into some type of...well...dungeon. Everyone wore masks and..."

"And?"

"And I...I didn't stay long." Her voice betrayed her embarrassment as she held the door open.

"Did you recognize anyone there?" Ron questioned.

"Detectives, this is a very delicate matter."

"We can be very discreet," Ron assured her.

"No, you can't."

"Try us," I said.

Knowing there was no way to elude the question, she allowed the glass door to close.

"Detectives, everyone at the party wore hoods and masks. I couldn't identify anybody except the senator, and only because he wasn't wearing his hood when he greeted me."

"You must have seen something?"

"I didn't see anything."

"Or didn't want to?" I added.

"Fine, I didn't want to see. Now that I said it, please go."

"We can protect you," Ron said.

"I don't need protection because I don't know anything. I was not comfortable with those people. That's all there was to it."

"That's all?"

"Detectives in my line of work I meet many people—high-profile, powerful people—and they don't scare me. These people scared me."

"I understand why you didn't stay, but why did you go in the first place?" Ron asked.

"When someone as influential as Senator DiCenzio requests your company, you don't disappoint him."

"I suppose not."

"Are we done, detectives?"

"For now," I replied.

"Thank you for your time," Ron added.

Frazier didn't respond as she showed us out.

"You know you blew it, lady," I said.

"I beg your pardon?"

"Ambitious as you are, you should have stayed at the party."

"What would my clients have thought?"

"You could've asked them. They were probably all there."

31

On our way to the apartment I made Ron stop at a McDonald's so I could finally pick up some food. As he drove Baby north up Third Avenue, I unwrapped my Big Mac, knocked off the top bun, and replaced it with my Filet-O-Fish sandwich. I took my first bite.

"What are you doing?" Ron asked.

"I call it the McJerry Surf-and-Turf. You want some?"

"Pass."

"Your loss," I said and continued eating as Ron turned east on Seventy-eighth Street. At a red light, he reached for the file on the dashboard.

"You want to tell me about this person whose place we're about to burglarize?"

"Why do you assume I know anything?"

"Usually I don't assume you know anything. However,

213

back at Frazier's office you asked for a key. You wouldn't have done that unless you knew someone wasn't going to be home."

"The person could be at work."

"Then you would have been more aggressive about finding out how to contact them. I'd say you know this person is incommunicado."

"*Incommunicado*? Did you learn that in law school?" I gulped down the last of my sandwich.

"You're evading the issue. *That* I learned in law school."

"The apartment we're about to visit at 382 East Seventy-eighth Street belongs to a lady named Judy Russo. She was the fourth to be enlisted by DiCenzio through Diane Westlake. She's thirty-three years old, five-foot-seven, with blonde hair and dark eyes. According to my source, she's been in Italy for the last six weeks and isn't expected back anytime soon."

"Your source is well informed."

I shrugged and looked out the window.

"Too well informed. You saw the Jag Lady again, didn't you?"

I continued looking out the window.

"Liz heard about DiCenzio. It rattled her. I went to comfort her."

"I bet you did."

"Think what you want. We're friends, that's all."

"No, that's not all. She's a friend involved in a murder investigation."

"She's not involved."

"Then let's go see if she has a key."

"We can't."

"Why?"

"Why what?" I said evasively.

"Why can't we see if she has a key?"

"I sent her home to England."

Ron slammed his hand against the steering wheel.

"She thought she'd be next."

"So does Kirby, and you didn't ship him to England."

"She thought—"

"—I don't care what she thought. She's involved in a murder investigation."

"What would you have done if it were Emily?" I asked.

The car became quiet. Ron was staring hard at the road while I stared hard at him. He parked Baby in front of an eight-story prewar apartment building.

"I would have done the same thing," he finally said, getting out of the car.

I followed him up a short flight of stairs into the building's foyer. To our right was a row of mailboxes, and above each of them was an intercom button.

"Any ideas on how to get in?"

"Give me room." Moving Ron to the side I began to press each of the intercoms until we heard the click of the door being unlocked.

"Never fails," I said. "There's always one person who's expecting visitors and doesn't bother to ask who it is."

As we walked down the hall to Apartment 1A, Ron and I put on latex gloves. When we got to the door we found it, as I had expected, locked.

"Well, work your magic," Ron said.

Reaching into my back pocket, I took out a small leather pouch containing my tools. I selected two small picks and removed them with all the precision of a master pool player removing his cue from the rack.

"You're wasting time. This lock is too sophisticated to pick."

Smiling, I slid my thin instruments into the lock and began to manipulate the tumblers. "Some locks are too sophisticated." I felt the tumblers fall in place. "This lock, however, is not one of them."

"You missed your calling. You should have been a thief."

"One lawyer in the family is enough."

Ron followed me into the apartment, and for the next hour we searched the first floor of Judy Russo's home. The three-bedroom apartment had thick brown wall-to-wall carpeting throughout, and very little else. The furniture was old and weathered. The place looked as if it were decorated in Modern Depression. No wonder she had a cheap lock.

Her furniture and exposed belongings were all covered by a thick layer of dust. Nothing else seemed out of the ordinary. Nothing, that is, until we descended the curved stairs to the basement. There, as R. Taylor Frazier had described, was a complete do-it-yourself home dungeon.

"Enormous," Ron said, turning on the lights. "It must span the entire width and length of the building."

I nodded as my eyes raced across the room. The walls were all mirrored, like in an upscale city gym, except instead of muscle-building equipment was equipment for another type of training.

"Welcome to Disney World de Sade," I said. "Please watch your step as you enter. We wouldn't want anyone getting hurt unintentionally."

"Anything look unusual, Jerry?"

"Everything looks unusual."

One side of the room was lined with wooden stocks of

various sizes. All had similar indentations for immobilizing the head and hands; however, each had a differently shaped bench extending from its base to expose the part of the victim's body to be punished. Beyond the stocks were two wooden whipping posts. Three feet around and twelve feet high, manacles hung from either side. In another area was a large wooden cross with leather restraints at all ends.

"Ron, when a person leaves this place and says they're whipped, they're not kidding."

"The time and money wasted on machines designed to cause pain. Who thinks these things up?"

"I don't know, but judging from this room they are kept busy."

"Jerry, look at this."

Ron was standing next to a circular stone fire pit filled with dark coals. Alongside was a steel bucket filled with numerous iron rods.

"Cold," I said, placing my hand over the coals. Touching one, I realized they were ceramic. "This isn't a real fireplace."

"It's probably gas."

"For what?"

"For this," Ron responded. He pulled one of the rods out of the bucket.

"To heat the pokers?"

"Look closer at the tip, Jerry."

The tip was shaped as a letter *S*. I immediately began to examine the remaining rods.

"Branding? These people actually brand themselves?" I asked."

"Or others. Do you see any with the letter *R*?"

I was about to tell Ron no when I heard something

move. I looked beyond all the chains and devices and saw a spiral staircase to the right and a door to the left. I wasn't sure where the sound had come from. No one was on the stairs. We looked toward the door. Ron signaled for me to go first. I nodded and we both drew our guns. Ron positioned himself behind me and to the left. Cautiously, he pushed open the door and covered me high as I knelt low.

I entered quickly, my gun moving in sync with my senses. The room, like the main area, was mirrored, and I almost opened fire at my own reflection. I took a deep breath and then continued probing the strange surroundings. To the right, a large leather examination table, complete with restraints. To the side, a tray filled with a multitude of medical instruments—some I could identify, and others I didn't want to. Along the back wall was a cabinet and tabletop. The place resembled a doctor's office. The doctor wasn't in.

"Jerry, the tray."

Among the instruments was a row of extremely sharp scalpels.

"Ron, I'm getting an uneasy feeling in the pit of my stomach."

"That's your lunch."

I was about to respond when we heard footsteps overhead. Ron tore out of the room with me in close pursuit.

He pointed to stairs in the back corner.

"Where do they go?"

"How should I know? I'm a cop, not an architect."

I scanned the walls. "They probably lead back to Russo's apartment."

"Don't think so," Ron said, inching toward the stairs.

"*Now* you're an architect?"

"Russo's place can't be the size of the entire ground floor."

"So?"

"So those stairs are too far behind where Russo's apartment should end."

"So?"

"So go ahead I'll keep you covered," Ron said pointing forward.

"You go ahead. I'll keep *you* covered."

Neither of us moved. Standing against the wall on either side of the stairs, we strained our eyes, looking up for any signs of life. Ron still didn't seem too eager to make a move. Neither was I. We both knew once we committed to going up the stairs there was no cover. If something were to go bad it would go really bad.

"How many do you think are up there?" Ron wiped the sweat from his brow.

"One, maybe two."

"We should have secured the exits and entrances."

"Too late."

"Or called for backup."

"Too late."

"The apartment—the carpet didn't have footprints, and the dust was undisturbed. This dungeon is clean. We should've known whoever uses this place enters from somewhere else. The members must have keys. They come and go as they please."

"Ron, if we're still alive later," I whispered, "I'll be glad to continue this conversation. Right now can we deal with getting up these stairs?"

We both raised our guns.

"On three," Ron whispered.

I held up one finger, then two, then three.

"Going up," I breathed as I let my gun lead me up the circular staircase to a confined landing. Ron was close behind. In front of us was a closed curtain. Ron and I positioned ourselves on either side of the drape and listened. Cautiously, I moved the curtain. It was too dark behind it to see anything.

"I'm going in," I said. "Shoot anything that moves."

"Got it."

"Except me."

"Got it."

I turned to go but Ron grabbed my arm.

"Don't do anything stupid.."

"Don't worry," I whispered, pushing the drapes away.

I navigated the darkness cautiously, my back to the wall. As I felt my way around the room's perimeter, I sensed I wasn't alone. Ten steps into my journey, my left shoulder brushed against a light switch. Deciding I had had enough of this cat-and-mouse game, I reached for the lights.

As the room lit up I dropped to one knee. In the glare was a figure dressed in black.

"Freeze," I yelled, summoning up all my concentration not to blow him away.

The figure didn't move. It couldn't move. It was a mannequin dressed in executioner's garb. Relieved, I waved Ron in. Then I saw a door on the far side of the room; it was slightly open. Cautiously, I moved closer. Taking a deep breath, I kicked it open and lunged forward. I found myself alone, looking up a stairwell leading to the street.

"Damn it!" I shouted. Ron stood behind me, gun drawn. "Whoever it was is gone."

"At least you caught *him*." Ron motioned to our

inanimate friend with his gun.

"It's a dummy," I said going back inside.

"Takes one to catch one."

"What's it doing here?"

I took a swing at the mannequin's shoulder. The black statue rocked from the impact. Then I heard something hit the carpet. Lying next to the statue was a poker with the letter *R*.

"Let's take it to the lab and see if matches the brand on our victims."

"Jerry, you can't do that. We don't have a search warrant."

"Who's searching? I found what I want."

I took a pair of latex gloves from my pocket and put them on. Carefully I picked up the poker.

"Illegal search and seizure," Ron said.

"What are you crying about?"

"This is illegal search and seizure. We have no search warrant. What happens if we catch this guy? The court will discover we were led to him by evidence we obtained illegally, and any conviction won't hold up."

"We won't tell anybody how we found it."

"I can't do that. I am an officer of the court."

"And a royal pain in the ass."

I felt like putting my fist through the mannequin's face. I wanted to hit something. Instead something hit me. An idea. I took out my cigar lighter and struck the flint.

"You're going to smoke?"

"What?"

"I hate when you smoke."

Ignoring my brother, I put the tip of the poker into the flame.

221

"Give me your belt."

"What for?"

"Give it to me."

Ron slid his belt from around his waist. I placed it on the floor and proceeded to brand it with the hot poker.

"That belt is handcrafted leather!"

"And now it has your initial."

"Clever. You're going to give the lab the brand on the belt."

"And they'll match it from there."

"You ruined my belt."

"Considered it the price you paid for being an officer of the court. Let's get out of here."

"Aren't you going to get CSU down here?" Ron asked.

"No," I answered, heading for the door.

"Bad protocol," Ron replied.

"Chances are this guy didn't leave prints, and I don't want this place turned upside down yet. Leave it as it is and let's see what develops."

Out on the street I looked back at the dungeon. At what point had all the fun and games turned to murder?

32

It was a fast shot down the Jersey Turnpike to the tollbooth at Exit 12. It was nearly midnight. Sandwiched between two tractor-trailers, we impatiently waited to pay the toll.

"If the brand on my belt matches the brand on our victims, our killer is either a member of that club or had access to it," Ron thought aloud. "Jerry, we need a membership list."

"Easier said than done. These people like anonymity and are powerful enough to get it. They're not going to turn over a list to us."

"We'll subpoena them and force them to comply."

"You'll get the subpoena, but you won't get a list. It's a secret society. They give you a list—no more secrets."

"Nobody is above the law."

"Some of these dudes make the law. You want a list? We need to take another route. Our key is Russo."

"What about Moreland? Let's concentrate on finding her."

"There's already an APB out on her. Either she's been taken, or she's in hiding."

"I don't blame her. What about Liz? Wouldn't she have a list?"

"Liz wasn't a member. She used the facilities when she played with Vinny. Russo is the way to go."

"You said Russo was out of town during the murders."

"The entire time?" I asked.

"You think she returned to the country?"

"Why not? You never heard of jet-setters? Let's get Jeanne to check with customs and see if Russo was around during the murders."

"First thing in the morning, Jerry."

I inched up to pay the toll.

"If you're right, Jerry, it means—"

"—that we have a female serial killer."

"It's a long shot. Female serial killers are rare."

"So are classic Mustangs, and we have one of those." I patted Baby's dashboard proudly. "It's no coincidence that all our corpses were members of this club, and all were invited to join by DiCenzio."

"What could Russo's motive be?"

"Supremacy. Maybe she went off the deep end and decided there was only room for one ruling mistress."

"Maybe." Ron was unconvinced. "If you're correct, it may have been a mistake to send your friend out of the country."

"Why?"

"If Russo is aware of Liz's location, she could be in danger. We can't protect her in England."

My mind began to race. "Could we protect her here?"

"She's not here."

"If she were, could we keep her under surveillance until the murderer went to strike? Liz could bring the murderer right to us."

"You'd use your friend as bait?"

"You want to catch a predator, you need bait. You said yourself we can't protect her in England."

"And what if we can't protect her here?

"We can." I paused. "I know what I'm suggesting."

"Then suggest something else. We could get her killed."

"That's not an option."

"Not for us, but others might not share our goals."

"We'll keep her safe."

"'Keep her safe,'" Ron echoed, disgusted. "Jerry, are you listening to yourself?"

"I know what I'm saying, damn it."

"I don't like it."

"You don't have too. We'll keep her safe."

"Jerry, *hiding* her will keep her safe—not flaunting her."

"What kind of life is she going to have in constant hiding?"

"That's not for us to decide. Why are you being so persistent?"

"I don't hear you telling me it won't work."

Ron didn't answer. I pulled into his driveway and shut off the engine. Ron got out and came around to my window. "You coming in?"

Ignoring his offer, I said, "I know what I'm suggesting is risky, but I don't see an alternative. And you're right, we can't leave Liz in Europe."

"We don't have to exploit her, either. Let's keep working the CD from the crime scene."

"You've had no luck deciphering it. We need an alternative plan, Ron."

"And you just happen to have one?"

"Planning is what I do best. Get back to work on that disc. Tomorrow have Jeanne run the check on Russo and get the belt to the lab," I said, firing Baby back up.

"And while I'm doing all this what are you doing?"

"I'm going to London."

33

I pulled up in front of the airport, 'Airport Diner' that is, on the corner of Eighth Avenue and Forty-sixth Street. I needed to meet with somebody before I left for London. Despite the inconvenience of a last-minute invitation, the woman I called agreed to see me. This was going to be tough, so I decided to take control from the beginning.

The diner was jammed with late-night customers—an after-theater crowd, mostly. I spotted my mark in a booth in the back; I dodged my way through the crowd to the seat across from her.

"Thanks for coming," I said firmly.

"I knew you would need me sooner or later."

A waiter came and placed two cups of fresh coffee in front of us.

"I thought you could use a fix. I assumed you're still

drinking regular?" Nikki Horn gloated over her coffee.

I nodded I did.

"Sorry. They don't have éclairs," she added.

I let it pass. "I wasn't sure you were going to show."

"Wouldn't miss this for the world. You have any new leads?" Nikki asked.

I gave her the once-over. She was wearing a tight black pantsuit with a white blouse and low-heeled black shoes. Barely visible through her blouse was a white camisole. Simple but elegant. Typical Nikki.

"I need a favor."

"I'm listening."

I took a folded paper from my pocket and pushed it across the table.

"I need you to report this in tomorrow's newscast."

Nikki read the note carefully, more carefully than I liked.

"This woman you're going to London to retrieve—is she involved in the Madam Murders investigation?"

"Possibly," I said.

"How possibly?"

"Like it says in the note, we're bringing her back for questioning. We believe she's a material suspect. Satisfied?"

"No. You just decide to call me out of the blue to give me this tip for no particular reason?"

I nodded.

"Sure you did," she said. She wasn't convinced. She reached for her coffee and took a sip. "If I decide to run this tip, Jerry, we'll be working together. There are things we have to discuss first."

"You and I are not working together. Ron and I work together. You're doing what you do best: reporting a leaked story."

My words stunned her almost as much as they did me. Despite the noise of the surrounding diners, a cold, black aura surrounded us. I saw the other diners' mouths move, but I was aware of no sounds—just the silence between us. I finally broke the unnerving stillness.

"You want to talk? How about starting with *why*?" I asked, sounding more hurt than I wanted to. Nikki didn't insult my intelligence by asking what I meant.

"Because I love you, Jerry."

"That wasn't an easy question for me to ask. Don't dismiss it with an easy answer, Nikki."

She looked into her coffee as if the answer were floating on the surface.

"I was in love and—"

"—and what?"

"And ambitious," she shouted.

"Really. And did that make you happy?"

Nikki slid her cup into the center of the table, her eyes fixed on the remaining black liquid inside. I waited for her to continue, but she just stared at the cup. I didn't know what to say, so I said nothing. Finally I reached over and touched her hand.

"Ambitious," she whispered softly to herself. "Ambitious. I can't tell you how much that realization cost me in time, money, and therapy. Lying to yourself isn't cheap."

"I trusted you, Nikki."

"I know, and I betrayed that trust. I saw what you and Ron were going through. I knew what the department was doing to you was wrong. What they did with Evanston was wrong. The department should have let you bring the suspect in alive. They should have promoted you. Instead I watched them condemn you. I thought by making the story public I'd be helping you."

"Everyone thought Ron and I leaked the story. What I told you I said to my lover, not to a reporter."

"I used the story to get even. The department had to be held accountable. I labored over the decision."

She didn't have to go any further. I saw it in her eyes: the deciding factor had been her ambition. It was the story that made her career.

"I'm sorry I hurt you and Ron," she said.

I didn't answer. I didn't have an answer.

"Are you ever going to forgive me?"

I said nothing.

"What do I have to do, submit to a public flogging before I'm absolved?"

I remained silent.

"I see," she said, regaining her composure. "I'm not giving up on you, Gold."

"It's more complicated than that, Nikki; I'm involved with—"

"—another woman?"

I nodded.

"That's OK. I've been the other woman. Competition doesn't scare me, Jerry."

"What does?"

Nikki ignored the question. She gathered her purse, stood, and said, "Consider this done. I'll go with your story." She took the paper from the table. In return, I get first crack at anything that breaks."

"Agreed."

"And don't think I buy for one second that she's a

230

material suspect."

She turned to leave, and I should have let her. I followed her to the door. Then I heard myself ask, "Why then?"

"You asked me to trust you. And I do." She looked past the confusion in my eyes and gave me a gentle kiss on the cheek. When I tried to speak, she placed a silencing finger to my lips. "And I guess I always will." She turned and left.

So much for taking control.

34

I lucked out and made the 11:59 p.m. flight. Six hours later I was standing in Heathrow Airport waiting to clear customs. The airport looked just like JFK, but everybody at Heathrow spoke with an accent. While queuing, as the Brits call it, I called the number Liz had left for me.

She was at her "flat" in the heart of London. I hailed a cab and looked out the window as we left Heathrow behind. The British winter wasn't as bitter as the weather I'd left behind, but it wasn't the Caribbean, either. I hadn't slept on the flight, but I wasn't tired. The thought of Liz in my arms again warmed me up. I could hear her gentle laugh and the intoxicating smell of her perfume. I couldn't wait to hold her, to make love to her. My desire was clouding my senses; I had to force myself to remember why I was in England. Lives depended on it. Liz's life depended on it.

The cab came to a stop in front of a tall glass building at 22 Liverpool Street. I paid the cabbie as a doorman wearing a top hat, black overcoat, and white gloves opened the cab door. He looked two years younger than God. He was short and jovial—someone right out of a Dickens novel. He escorted me into the building.

"I'm looking for Dr. Elizabeth Drake's apart— her flat," I said, correcting myself.

"You're from the States, aren't you, sir?" the doorman replied.

"Nothing gets past you Brits."

"Not much," he replied cheerfully.

"What gave it away? The accent?"

"The rudeness."

"You got me."

"I spent some time in the States in my youth. When I was there—"

"—there were only forty-eight states?"

"A laugh a minute, you Yanks are," the doorman laughed.

"Laugh and the world laughs with you," I said. "Dr. Drake's apartment?"

"Thirty-fourth floor."

"Which...?"

"The *entire* thirty-fourth floor. Shall I announce you?"

"No," I said taking a ten-pound note from my pocket and handing it to him. "I want to surprise her."

"Thank you, guv'nor," he said, tipping his hat.

"Do all Brits call Americans 'gov'nor'?" I asked as I made my way to the elevator.

"No. We do that because you yanks expect it."

"What do you usually call us?"

233

"If I told you that, you wouldn't have given me the tenner," he said as the "lift" door closed.

Honesty, what a concept.

The thirty-fourth floor had a large entranceway with Italian marble floor tile and equally costly furniture. As I walked down the hall, I could hear someone shouting. I turned the corner and saw a man grabbing Liz. The assailant was about six feet tall, two hundred twenty pounds and dressed in a business suit. He looked like a Fleet Street type who had played rugby "at university"or whatever the hell they play here.

"Get out!" Liz cried.

"Or what?" he replied.

He raised his opened hand and prepared to slap Liz across the face. I grabbed his wrist and twisted it. He released Liz as he stumbled backward into me. I pushed him out of the way.

"Jerry," Liz cried, folding into my arms.

"You bastard. I think you broke my wrist," the man shouted.

"I don't think so—and I've broken enough to know. Can you wave your hand like you're waving good-bye?" I asked calmly.

He started toward me, leading with his right. I moved Liz to the side just in time to block his jab, turn, and kick his leg just behind the knee. He went down, clutching his leg.

"You broke my knee!"

"I don't think so, guv'nor. And I've broken enough knees to know that, too," I said, picking him up by his collar.

"Do you know who I am?" the man shouted as I

dragged him toward the elevator.

"The Queen of England? Because I have to tell you, you fight like a girl." I pressed the button for the elevator.

"This is my home, damn you, and that is my wife!"

"This is *my* home, and I am not your wife anymore," Liz corrected.

I looked him in the eye. "Rough break, old man. Because this is a good-looking place, and she's a great-looking woman," I said as I threw him into the waiting elevator.

"This isn't over!" he yelled.

"Yeah, it pretty much is," I replied as the elevator doors closed.

I turned toward Liz. She pointed and shouted my name. An arm grabbed me around the neck. I instinctively used her ex-husband's weight to flip him over my hip. He went sailing into the wall and slid to the ground. I lifted him by his collar, twisted his right arm behind him, and escorted him to the elevator once again.

"You bastard! I'll be back, and not alone."

"Are you mentally impaired," I said, ramming his nose into the doorframe. "I hurt people for a living."

"You broke my nose," Liz's ex cried as blood flowed from his nostrils.

"*Now* I think you're starting to get it. You may be right. And if you come back you'd better bring an army with you. Because next time, I will break your wrist, your knee, and then your neck."

I grabbed his hair and stared deep into his eyes.

"Take a good look, because what I'm telling you is what you stockbrokers call a 'sure thing.'" I could see the fear in his bloodstained face. "I hear this pretty little lady is unhappy because of you. Next time, I'll kill you. Now get lost."

I threw him into the elevator and watched as the doors closed.

"My hero," Liz said, folding her arms around me and kissing me.

"There are other ways you could thank me."

"And I intend to. My bedroom is over here."

"Bedrooms are nice. Actually, I was thinking of taking a trip together."

"A trip?" Liz asked as she unbuttoned my shirt and nibbled on my neck. "Where can we go that would be more like heaven than my bedroom?"

I felt Liz's hands moving down my body and unbuckling my belt.

"We need to go," I said, sounding a little less certain than I wanted as Liz's hand made its way down my jeans. "I need to get you to New York."

"I need to get you into the bedroom," she giggled. Her warm hand was driving me crazy.

"I'm going to make this the best trip of your life," she added, smiling. Her hand found what it was searching for in my jeans.

"We need to get to Heathrow."

"Really, Jerry? Not all of you seems to want to go." She squeezed me gently.

"Alright. First the bedroom. Then New York."

Liz dropped to her knees. "First right here," she teased. "Then the bedroom...."

"Then New York," I managed to get out.

"Then New York," she agreed.

Honesty, what a concept.

35

Her hand in mine as we touched down at JFK. By the time we retrieved the bags and found where I had parked Baby, it was two in the morning. The trip and the day's events had taken a toll on Liz. Between the long flight and the news I gave her, it was no wonder she was exhausted. Her beautiful blue eyes couldn't stay open.

I, on the other hand, was wide awake—and hungry. I decided a little detour wouldn't hurt. I pulled off the Van Wyck in Jamaica and drove to the only hamburger joint I knew would be open at that hour: White Castle. As I placed my order for ten tiny burgers, Liz began to stir. Always the gentleman, I asked if she was hungry. Liz declined politely, then shifted in the passenger seat and went back to sleep.

An hour later, with luggage and the remaining burgers in hand, we arrived at Liz's door. Handing her the hamburger bag, I took out my gun and began searching the place. I sensed Liz's discomfort but continued combing the rooms until I was certain we were alone. When it comes to staying alive, I'd rather listen to Liz rant about the ills of professional paranoia than have the word *careless* appear in my obituary.

After securing the apartment, I watched as she attempted to water the plants, unpack, and clean all at once.

"What are you doing? This place is spotless." I sat at her kitchen table, devouring my seventh hamburger.

"I can't help it. Things have to be perfect. You know I'm compulsive that way."

"Liz, sit down and try a burger."

"I'd rather not," she said, gingerly gathering the empty hamburger boxes as if they had been contaminated by an infectious disease. "They wreak havoc on your digestive system." She tossed all the empties into the trashcan under the sink. A spotless trashcan, I might add.

"This is worse than eating with Ron. See if I ever take you to the Castle again, lady!"

Liz began to laugh hysterically. Jet lag, exhaustion, or maybe even fear might have caused the laughing jag, but I didn't care. It was always good to see her smile. Unable to catch her breath, she collapsed in the chair next to me.

"What's the joke?"

"N-n-nothing." She continued laughing.

"You always laugh this hard at nothing?"

"Oh Jerry, it's just...I've probably been to 'the castle' more often than you."

As she wiped the tears from her eyes, I waited for an explanation. Instead, she took in a deep breath and began howling all over again. Chalking it up jet lag, I carried her down the hall to her bedroom. She was still giggling like an overtired little girl. I sat her on the edge of the bed and began undressing her. Raising her arms, I gently pulled her charcoal-grey cashmere sweater upward. As her head disappeared into the soft fabric, I paused to admire the breathtaking body that sat before me. Liz's pink camisole did little to cover her full, round breasts or conceal her enticingly erect nipples. I was mesmerized. Only her muffled laughter jolted me back to the task at hand.

Tossing her sweater aside, Liz curled her arms around my waist. I softly kissed the top of her head. She released me, falling backward on the bed. Her camisole gathered high, exposing her tight abdomen.

"Take me," she begged, drunk with exhaustion. I peeled her jeans down her perfectly curved hips and long, luscious legs.

"Don't you want me?" Her fingertips teasingly waltzed down her stomach, stopping at the top of her tiny pink panties.

"Jerry, to the victor belong...belong...oh, whatever." She began to laugh again. I took the opportunity to tuck her under the covers.

"Aren't we going to shag?" She yawned. Within a few minutes she was asleep.

I moved an armchair into the corner of the room and sat, back to the wall, legs propped up on her bed. I was entranced by her tranquil beauty. I sat surrounded by the predawn silence, wondering if we'd be laughing and making love in the days to come.

36

Sunrise came quickly. Liz and I sat at the kitchen table, drinking coffee. She looked angelic even with no makeup, in ripped jeans and my oversize blue football jersey.

"Do you mind telling me what was so funny last night?"

"Oh nothing. It really wasn't that humorous."

"Then I'd hate to see you when you find something that is."

"It was just...when you said I'd never gone to 'the castle.' A castle is what we dominas call the place we take our clients."

"I thought that was called a dungeon."

"Dungeons, playrooms, castles—it's all the same thing. You see: I *have* been to the castle more often than you."

"I may never eat at White Castle again."

Liz was pouring me another cup of coffee when the

doorbell rang. She rose to answer it.

"I'll get it," I said. "Remember our little talk? You stay away from the doors and windows."

"Yes, sir, Detective Gold," she replied.

Ignoring the mock salute she gave me, I turned the corner of the kitchen. Out of Liz's sight, I drew my gun. I didn't look through the peephole: it was too early in the day to get shot in the eye. "Yes," I said from the side of the door.

"Let me in," the voice replied.

"Ron?"

"Yes."

I unlocked the door and in the sight of my gun was my brother.

"You going to shoot me or let me in?" he asked nonchalantly, pushing my gun away as he entered.

Liz was standing in the kitchen doorway.

"You must be Ron," she said, extending her hand and staring into his face. "The resemblance is really quite amazing."

"Ron, this is Liz. Liz, my brother Ron."

I headed back to the kitchen and my coffee.

"I'm sorry we're not meeting under other circumstances."

"Yes...well...can I offer you a bit of coffee?"

"Thank you, no."

"Perhaps some herbal tea?"

"Tea would be nice."

I could tell he was impressed that a friend of mine would know what herbal tea was, let alone have any on hand. So was I.

"Were you followed?"

"No. I haven't seen our tail since you left for England."

"Good."

I continued sipping my coffee, hoping the caffeine would overpower my jet lag. Liz placed a cup of tea in front of Ron.

"Liz, has Jerry made you aware of the situation?"

"He has, although I'm quite sure you're mistaken about Judy."

"Still, you are under no obligation to..."

"I understand my obligation all too well, Ron. If I can be of any help, then I will. I couldn't live with myself knowing I was able to do something to end all this and didn't."

"I admire your courage, but there is a danger involved."

"I'm confident the Gold brothers will, as you say here in the States, cover my butt." Liz leaned over and gently squeezed both our hands.

"And isn't that a great looking butt, Ron?"

"I think we should all be going." Ron interrupted our little reverie.

"Where?"

"The safe house. We have a meeting within the hour."

"'We' meaning you and I?"

"'We' meaning all of us."

"All of us? Are you crazy?"

"I've been asking myself that question more and more often these days. I'll explain in the car. You *do* have a car? I took a cab."

"Yes, I have my car, and you better have a damn good explanation why we all have to show up."

In less than ten minutes we had Baby headed down West End Avenue. Constantly looking in my rear view mirror for our tail, I waited impatiently for Ron to explain as Liz slept in the backseat.

"Jerry, we have to set up the surveillance for Liz. We can't handle a job of this magnitude alone. We're going to need backup."

"You talked to Flaherty?"

"I did. The task force is aware of the situation."

"How much did you tell them?"

"Everything short of your personal involvement with Liz."

"And you think they're going to help?"

"I'll take help from whomever I can."

"We won't get it from them."

Turning sharply in his seat, Ron jabbed my shoulder. "Get this straight, Jerry, because I'm only going to say it once. Until now we ran this show our way. If something went wrong, it was our asses on the line."

"What's changed?"

"You involved her." Ron pointed to Liz. "The minute you left for England, you put her into play."

"We'll watch her."

"We will, and so will the NYPD. I've requested twenty-four-hour surveillance on her apartment, Corinne Moreland's place, and the Russo dungeon. Four eyes can't do all that."

I wanted to argue, but I'm stubborn, not stupid. "It's called a 'castle,'" I said, changing the subject, and turned left onto Forty-second Street.

"What?"

"*Dungeon* is passé; they call it a 'castle'."

"I stand corrected." He switched gears. "Jerry, we need the NYPD."

"It's the right move, but there aren't many people out there I trust."

243

"Even fewer than you think. The brand on my belt was a match."

I took a second to take that in, then asked, "Who else knows?"

"You, me, and Goose. I had him run the test. It's not conclusive, but..."

"It's conclusive enough for me."

"I agree. Which is another reason we need this meeting, Jerry. I want a search warrant for Russo's dungeon. I want the poker put into evidence."

"We'll tip off the killer."

"I had another poker made. The replacement has a slight imperfection. It's barely noticeable. If it's used again, we can trace it."

"I want to catch this SOB before he has a chance to use it again."

"Agreed." He paused. "There's still one thing that is bothering me."

"Only one?"

"The brass and the two of us were the only ones who knew about the branding three years ago. How did someone else find out?"

"Like Goose said, it could've leaked out."

"That means a police official could be involved."

Normally I would have thought Ron crazy. Life is cheap out on the streets. Could it be it's even cheaper to those who are sworn to protect it?

"If the leak is a cop, this might force him to do something stupid. And when he does, we'll be there." I parked in front of the safe house. "Any news on Russo?"

"As of the day before yesterday, she was in Rome. No one fitting her description has entered the country."

"How carefully could Customs be looking? They didn't even know who to look for."

"Jerry, Homeland Security would know if she entered."

"Maybe." As I reached behind me to wake Liz, I noticed a black car pulling up behind us.

"Uh oh."

"Something wrong?"

"How many times do I say 'uh-oh' before something good happens?"

Ron turned to see what I was staring at. "Uh-oh." We both reached quietly for our guns.

"My thought exactly," I said, looking at Ron's pistol resting on his lap.

"Jerry, let's take a different approach. Remember Liz."

"Good point. Shooting up the street to protect her might shake her confidence in law enforcement."

"At the very least. At the most it might get her killed."

"Ron, put your piece away and take Liz inside. Keep me between you and that car."

Ron was holding the door open for Liz. There were few people on the sidewalk. I wasn't sure if that was a good or bad. I came around the car, concealing my pistol low at my side.

The sky was overcast, and the January wind biting. The three of us started for the safe house. As we walked, I tapped my Colt lightly, ready to make the first move. We were almost to the door when Liz, oblivious to the situation, reached over for my hand. She felt the gun and froze in her tracks. The black car door opened.

"Move, Liz," I shouted. Ron pulled her sharply to the safe house door as a large, tank-shaped man barreled toward me. He looked like he was about six-foot-eight and a thousand pounds—all of it muscle. His white, clean-shaven scalp glistened.

"My boss wants to talk to you," he said as Ron and Liz entered the building.

"Is that a fact?"

"That's a fact, and he don't like to be kept waiting."

"Tell him to make an appointment." I continued toward the door.

"Mr. Westlake just did," he said, grabbing my arm.

I slid my gun into my pocket after hearing Westlake's name. After leaving Liz inside, Ron joined me. I told him it was Westlake's car.

"Go back in with Liz," I said. "I never heard of Westlake making a killing on the street unless it was Wall Street."

"And leave you alone with that gorilla?"

"You mind not upsetting the g-o-r-i-l-l-a?"

I watched as Ron unwillingly disappeared into the safe house lobby.

"After you, King Kong," I said, turning to my new escort.

As I approached the car, he opened the rear passenger's side door. Sitting in back was Alfred Westlake.

"Come in, detective," he said, looking out his window. He was wearing a dark suit and dark glasses. He looked comfortable sitting there—too comfortable.

"Once around the park, James," I said, getting in. King Kong didn't reply. He closed my door.

"I'd never picture you for a Crown Vic type guy, Mr. Westlake."

"This is a Continental," he replied, still looking out his window.

"Who would have guessed? I drive a Mustang myself."

"I didn't come here to talk cars." Reaching into his coat pocket, he removed a cigar. The cigar band read *Cohiba*. Impressive.

"I was expecting to hear from you. We agreed you would keep me informed." Westlake rolled his cigar between his fingers. "Is there something you want to say to me, detective?"

"You wouldn't happen to have another Cohiba, would you?"

Westlake stopped rolling his cigar. His facial muscles tensed. "My daughter and her oldest friend have been murdered within a few days of each other, and that's all you have to say?"

"It is for now."

"I could have your job, Gold!"

"You wouldn't want it."

"You think I'm playing with you? I can make your life a living hell."

"Too late."

"Don't push me, Gold."

"Don't push *me*, Westlake."

"I want to know who killed my daughter."

"Me too." I reached for the door.

"Tell me what you know now!" Westlake yelled grabbing my arm.

"I know your daughter's dead and all your money isn't going to change that." I peeled his fingers from my sleeve.

"You son of a bitch," he growled, throwing a sorry excuse for a left at me. I blocked it, and then King Kong threw a right at me from the front seat. He clipped my jaw. Rocking back in my seat, I shook the punch off as the gorilla awkwardly tried to lean toward me and throw another. But he was big, not agile. As he came toward me, I pivoted in my seat, nailing him with a hard left hook to his face. King Kong's head snapped backward as blood began to flow from his mouth.

"You broke my nose!"

"You got your blood on my jacket. What says we call it even?"

My suggestion didn't have the effect I was hoping for. Ape man was reaching for me. I reached for my gun.

"Enough!" Westlake shouted. His words caused King Kong to freeze. "We had an agreement, detective. I thought you were a man of integrity."

"And because I am, I know there are things you don't need to know."

"It's money you want, isn't it? Fine, I'll pay your price. Name it."

"I don't want your money."

"Tell me what I want to know, damn you." His voice softened. Please."

The desperation in his request was more than I could handle with little sleep.

"We believe your daughter was killed because of her involvement in a sadomasochistic society," I answered, regretting it instantly.

"You're lying! You bastard."

"Why would I lie? And your old friend, the honorable Vinny DiCenzio, is the one who introduced her to the scene."

Westlake was stunned.

"Vinny would never do anything to harm my daughter."

Westlake's tone became more urgent. He wanted to hear me say I was wrong. Watching him fall apart, I wished

I had been.

"Your daughter was a dominatrix," I said calmly.

"Dee wasn't a hooker."

"No, she wasn't."

"Then what?"

"From what I've learned, your daughter was a warm, caring individual who got mixed up in the wrong game."

Westlake sank back in his seat. The car fell silent. When he spoke again, it was with difficulty.

"Even so, she...she didn't deserve to die," he said, his voice cracking.

"No, she didn't."

"She was all I had." He was crying now.

I said nothing.

"I have to do something for my baby," he said softly.

"Go home," I said, massaging my jaw.

"Home?"

"Go home and grieve for her. She deserves that."

I thought about the pain and anguish Westlake would bear for the rest of his life. Tears were rolling down from under his dark glasses. I decided to let myself out. I noticed Mr. Personality in the front seat, glaring at me and holding his nose with a bloodstained handkerchief.

"This ain't over. I'm lookin' forward to meetin' up with you again," he called out.

I shut the door and left.

Another satisfied customer.

37

My adrenaline was still pumping as I made my way through the safe house. Morning brawls tend to do that to me. As I entered the conference room, I saw Ron and Liz talking to Dave Wilkins. Although Wilkins seemed like a stand-up guy, giving information to him was like giving it to his partner, Greeley, and that irritated me to no end. Noticing I had entered, Ron left Liz with Wilkins and joined me.

"Westlake sends his regards."

"I can see that," Ron said, referring to the mark on my jaw.

"This was from another admirer."

"Building up quite a little fan club, aren't you?"

"All in a day's work. Where's Flaherty?"

"Wasn't my turn to watch him. I'm watching Liz,

remember?"

"What good are you?"

"For missing persons, none. But I did find Susan Atwell's black book."

"Where?"

"According to the DD-5, Greeley had it last."

"Lieutenant By-the-Book Greeley didn't return it to the evidence locker?"

"So it seems."

"I'll be right back."

I walked the corridors looking for Greeley. I couldn't find him *or* Flaherty. Flaherty virtually lived here, and as for Greeley, even he wasn't foolish enough to miss an opportunity to meet Liz. Something was up. I just couldn't put my finger on it.

Passing an office, I heard the irritating voice of Walter Greeley through the closed door. He was shouting my name. Not one to wait on formalities, I barged in to see Greeley raving at Flaherty.

"Using my name in vain, Walt?"

"Get out of here, Gold. This is a private meeting," Greeley snapped.

"Calm down," Flaherty said firmly.

"Yeah, calm down."

"And you shut up."

"Shut up?"

"Didn't you notice the door was closed?"

"I noticed. I'm a detective."

"Did you ever hear of knocking?"

"Sure. I'm even thinking about trying it some day."

Flaherty was starting to fume. "What's going down?"

"What's going down is *I'm* in charge of this case as of

now, Gold. So if you want to remain on it, you had better be quiet and listen."

"What's he talking about, Flaherty?"

Flaherty leaned back in his chair and pointed to a paper on the corner of his desk. It was a memo from the office of Lieutenant Governor Denton requesting that Walter Greeley be given immediate command of the investigation.

"Bullshit!" I crumpled the paper.

"Are you going to let him get away with insubordination, Tom?"

Flaherty said nothing.

"You don't actually believe Greeley can handle this investigation, do you?"

"Give me a reason why not?" Flaherty said.

"I can give you a dozen reasons—starting with incompetence."

"Unfortunately, Gold, the lieutenant governor doesn't see it that way," Greeley smirked.

"The only thing the lieutenant governor sees is what's between his wife's legs."

"Watch your mouth you—"

"Shut up, both of you." Flaherty rubbed his forehead.

"You going to let him mouth off like that?" Greeley asked.

"You're starting to give me a headache," Flaherty growled.

"Come on, Flaherty, this is a mistake. Ron told you we have the woman who can lead us to the killer. I just need time."

"You're out of time. It's my case now. You're finished.

"Flaherty?" I protested.

"You ever consider making a career out of being fired?"

252

"That's enough," Flaherty said.

"It's out of your hands, Tom."

"Is it?" Flaherty asked.

"You can't cover for this guy anymore."

Flaherty leaned forward in his chair. Keeping his eyes riveted on Greeley, he reached for the ball of paper that was the lieutenant governor's memo. He unraveled it, stopped, and scrunched it up even more tightly in the palm of his hand.

"Don't do anything stupid, Tom. You have your career to think of," Greeley warned.

"How much time do you and Ron need?"

"Give me a week."

"How much?"

"Thirty-six hours." I tried to sound less desperate than I was.

"The clock's running."

"You can't, Tom."

"No?"

"You're joking, right?"

"Have you ever known me to have a sense a humor, Walt?"

"You're ending your career, Tom. Are they worth it?"

"Thirty-six hours. Now both of you get out of my sight."

"Lieutenant Governor Denton is not going to stand for this, Tom."

"Out. Now!"

Greeley left, slamming the door behind him.

"You won't regret this, chief," I said.

"I already regret it. Get out."

As I left the office, I felt the thrill of victory. I wanted to high-five somebody. Unfortunately, the only person nearby was experiencing the agony of defeat. I caught up with him in the hall.

"Greeley," I said. "I want Susan Atwell's black book."

"Go get it," he said curtly.

"According to the grapevine, you have it."

"You're mistaken."

"The DD-5 says otherwise. You were the last to have it."

"I don't know what you're talking about." .

"Don't mess with my case, Walt. Nothing would make me happier than to get you bounced for interfering with the investigation."

"I don't like you, and we might not see eye to eye, but I don't hide evidence. Now get lost."

"Touching speech, but if you don't have it where is the book?"

"I gave it to Wilkins. Go talk to him." Greeley pushed past me.

I rushed into the conference room to find Ron on the phone and Wilkins flirting with Liz. He was telling her jokes—old jokes.

"Liz, will you excuse us for a second?"

"Certainly," she smiled.

"Detective, did you hear the one—"

"No, and I don't want to, Wilkins. What I want is Atwell's black book."

"What?"

"You heard me."

"I don't know what you're talking about."

"Don't go there, Dave. You're not a good liar."

Overhearing our discussion, Ron ended his phone conversation and joined us.

"Where do you come off calling me a liar?"

"Could we lower our voices? We're all cops on the same team," Ron said.

"Our team is going to be less one player if he doesn't hand over that book."

"Don't be so quick to bark orders, Gold. Greeley has been—"

"—benched. And unless you want to be on traffic detail for the rest of your career, you should give me that book."

"I thought Greeley had it," Ron said to me.

"Greeley finked out Wilkins."

"Are you talking about the diary?" Wilkins questioned.

"Diary, book, whatever you want to call it. I want it."

"If you're referring to Susan Atwell's diary, it's over here."

We followed Wilkins to his little corner of the conference room. He opened his briefcase and handed me a burgundy leather-bound book.

"Is this what you're yelling about?" Wilkins asked.

I took the book. Thumbing through it, I saw pages of names in alphabetical order. I also noticed a few pages had been ripped out.

"It's missing pages, Wilkins."

"That's how it was when I got it."

Knowing I was unable to prove otherwise I didn't bother to answer. "Time to go, Liz," I said, sliding the book into my pocket.

"Go? Flaherty wants to talk with Liz," Ron said.

"Now is not the time. Trust me."

"Goodbye, Detective Wilkins. I enjoyed your stories."

Wilkins looked at me.

"Don't give up the day job," I added, not bothering to look back.

38

I decided to take the scenic route back to Liz's apartment and cut through Central Park on Sixty-fifth Street. I took a second to appreciate the majesty of the trees and the blue-grey tones of the afternoon sky. New York City can be beautiful in winter. While I communed with nature, Liz, still out of sorts from the trip, was resting in the backseat. Ron was perusing the Atwell Diary.

"Anything interesting?"

"Susan Atwell was a very busy lady."

"Maybe we can buy her S&M franchise."

Ron ignored me. I turned right onto West End Avenue.

"Jerry, this book reads like the Who's Who of New York City. Famous sports figures, politicians, actors..."

"Sounds like she had something for everybody."

"She did. "Fungo" Phil Brady, the major-league

ballplayer, was one of her playmates."

"Get outta town."

"Did you know he was into infantilism?"

"I must have missed that tidbit in the last *Sports Illustrated*."

"According to this, he's into diapers," Ron said, turning the page.

"Say it isn't so, Fungo Phil."

"I can see why people wouldn't want this information made public."

"Fungo has more money than God and a no-trade contract with the Clippers. It might be embarrassing if his diaper thing leaked—pardon the pun—but his people would clean it up," I laughed. "They wouldn't kill her."

"You're certain?"

"Marv Albert is back at work isn't he?"

"The public does have a short memory."

"These people, Atwell included, were part of one big play group. As long as she was alive, no one would have seen this diary. Why would she turn on them?"

"I don't know. The usual motivations don't fit. Greed is out. Her family owns Atwell Shipping Lines, the third-largest in the world. I didn't see anything in her file that would have supported a jealousy motive. Everyone thought well of her."

"Almost everyone." I made a U-turn to pull in front of Liz's apartment.

"What about these missing pages, Jerry?"

"What about them?"

"Who took them?"

"If I were writing a movie I'd say the killer."

"Wouldn't the killer have taken the entire book?"

"Good point. That's why I don't write movies. Someone on our side has those missing pages, and I'll bet my ass that person has the answers we need. What pages are missing?" I asked.

"The pages with the last of the names under the C's and the beginning of the D's."

"There's a case breaker. Now all we have to do is get the Manhattan phone book and interview everyone in the city whose last name starts with a C or D. Piece of cake."

"It's another clue, Jerry. That's what we do. We collect clues."

"Well we'd better collect them faster, or we're out of a job."

"I was wondering when you were going to tell me about your meeting with Flaherty."

"Not much to tell. Greeley got his pussy-whipped son-in-law to send Flaherty a memo to can us."

"You convinced him otherwise?"

"We have thirty-six hours."

"What do you hope to accomplish in thirty-six hours?"

I was about to say "a miracle" when my cell phone rang.

"Gold."

Ron closed the diary and slid it into his coat pocket.

"Where?"

"Where what?"

"Another body," I said.

"Where?"

Before I could answer, two patrol cars with sirens blaring came barreling around the corner and directly towards us. The commotion startled Liz.

"Where are the police going?" she asked.

"To your apartment," I said. "I think we found Corinne

Moreland."

As we made our way to the lobby, two patrol cars pulled up next to Baby and quickly emptied. Six uniforms made their way toward the building. In the lead was Sergeant Brown. He caught up to us in the lobby.

"We're in charge, Brown," I said.

Ron and I displayed our shields to the others. Brown nodded.

"I want one man here at the front door," I said.

"Right," Brown said as he turned to the patrolman to his right. "Janowski—no one goes in or out."

The cop took his post, and we kept moving toward the elevators.

"Liz, are those stairwells at either end of the hall the only exits other than the elevator?" I asked.

"I believe so," she replied. She was shaken, but I was proud of the way she was keeping it together.

"You heard the lady. Richards, Carson, each of you take a stairwell and meet us upstairs. No one enters the apartment until I get there," Brown commanded.

"Hey you," I yelled to the doorman. "Get these two elevators down here now. A short man in a grey doorman's uniform began fumbling with his keys as he ran over to the elevator control panel. "Today! I want those cars down here now," I shouted at him.

While the doorman searched for the key, Brown sent two of his men to guard the lobby's fire exits. By the time they were in place, I heard the familiar tone of an arriving elevator. Ron moved Liz to the side as Brown and I drew our guns. The elevator door slid open slowly, revealing an empty car.

"Brown and I will take this one. You grab the next one,

259

Ron. I'll meet you at the apartment."

As the elevator door closed, I flashed Liz a reassuring smile, even though I suspected Liz's uninvited guest was a corpse.

"Who called it in?" I asked as the elevator went up.

"Next door neighbor came home and heard someone in the apartment. Knew the owner was out of town. Came back later and saw the door open and the dead woman."

The elevator came to a halt. We moved down the hall. Liz's apartment door was ajar. I pushed it open slowly with my foot. Then Brown and I went in. We didn't see our perp. What we did see was worse. Hanging from the ceiling, bound by the wrists, was a nude female. A black scarf covered her eyes, and her mouth was gagged in the same manner as the other victims' had been. Her throat had been cut. Blood that just hours earlier had surged through her arteries had been sprayed across the room. A few rivulets dried on and between her breasts. Between her legs was the decorative sawhorse Liz had placed my clothes on a few nights earlier.

"Secure the other rooms," I said.

Brown headed toward the back. I didn't bother checking the body for a pulse. I approached, circled the dangling form. The victim could be Corinne Moreland, I thought. But a blindfold and gag covered a good part of her face, making a positive ID impossible. I chose not to remove them until Goose and CSU arrived. But from what I remembered of Moreland's driver's license photo and what I could see of her face, I was certain I had found our missing mistress.

I moved in closer. The killer had used an eyehook in the ceiling that had previously supported a hanging plant. I could see the woman's buttocks had been whipped in the same manner as the others. It was unclear if she had been raped or sodomized, and for now I didn't need to know. Goose would confirm all that later.

She was straddling the sawhorse. Only her toes touched the ground; her genitals endured the entire weight of her body. The thin wooden crossbeam of the horse gouged into the delicate flesh between her thighs.

As I stood there marking this indelible picture in my mind, it became all too clear: this innocent-looking sawhorse was actually some type of sadomasochistic device. My disgust built at the perversity I was examining. What sick mind could play these games—and what sicker mind would willingly acquiesce? I reminded myself that I wasn't there to judge but to solve a crime, and I turned my attention to the rest of the murder scene. Brown joined me once again.

"Everything seems normal," he said. I looked at Brown. "Everything but that." He was pointing to the corpse.

"Anyone call EMS?" I asked.

"Yeah."

"Get on the radio and tell them to save their gas."

Brown nodded as he began to speak into his radio.

"Let's get this place taped off. I want to talk to the neighbors and the doorman."

"Right," Brown said.

As he turned to leave, I heard someone approaching. Then came the cry—a mournful cry that splintered the soul of the sufferer. I turned and saw Ron holding a tearful Liz in his arms. Screams of "no" kept passing her lips. As she tried to push forward, her eyes locked with mine. My brother cradled her tightly within his arms. Ron's stare was

261

telling me I should be the one cradling Liz. I should be easing her suffering. I knew what I wanted to do. I also knew what I had to do. I stayed where I was. I had a homicide to solve.

"Why?" she cried.

"Get her out of here, Brown," I said.

Brown attempted to escort Liz from the room, but she held on to Ron.

"It's OK, Liz. You'll be alright with Officer Brown."

Reluctantly, she let go of my brother. The lost look in her eyes, combined with the reproach I sensed, was almost more than I could handle.

"What have we got, Jerry?"

"Meet Corinne Moreland."

39

I had been back at the safe house since seven o'clock listening to Commissioner Daley rant about the latest murder and how Ron and I were hired to stop the killings. He then informed me his trust in our abilities might have been misguided and that our services were no longer needed.

It was now nine o'clock and I was sitting in the safe house kitchen staring blindly into a cup of cold coffee. Closing my eyes, I watched the day's events replay on the backs of my eyelids. The movie was *The Death of Corinne Moreland*, playing in a relentless loop, only I never got to the ending. And after the meeting with Daley, I doubted I ever would.

"Any coffee left?"

I looked up to see Ron heading for the pot.

"You don't drink coffee, remember?"

"I do now."

"Were you with Liz all this time?"

"And Goose, while he examined Corinne Moreland."
Ron poured a cup of coffee.

"And?"

"He's convinced she's definitely dead."

"Goose is very thorough."

"I didn't have time to wait for the details. I received a
message to report here."

"Then you heard the news?" I asked.

"Which news? That Greeley's heading the
investigation?"

"Nooo..."

"That we've been relieved of duty?"

"*That's* the news. Only Daley didn't say I was relieved.
He told me I was 'fucking fired.'"

"I just left him. You're still 'fucking fired.'"

"Did they take your gun?"

Ron lifted the left side of his jacket revealing an empty
holster.

"At least they let you keep your holster." I opened my
jacket revealing just a shirt. "How's Liz?"

"As well as can be expected."

"Who's watching her?"

"A female cop out of the four-three. I left her at a safe
house in the Bronx with around-the-clock protection."

"Was she doing anything when you left?"

"Cleaning."

"She's compulsive that way. She eat anything?" I asked,
avoiding the question that was really on my mind.

"I tried surprising her with a few of your favorite

264

burgers from the White Castle."

"And?"

"She threw them out. I hate to admit this, but she's one of the few women you've been involved with who exhibits impeccably good taste—in everything except men."

Ron's response didn't bolster my courage, but I asked the question anyway.

"Did she ask for me?"

"You expected her to?"

"I'm not sure what I expected."

"Well let me tell you what Liz expected. She expected her lover to come to her rescue, not Jerry Gold, New York City Detective."

"That's what I am."

"I know what you are, and I accept it. But I'm not your lover. Something I may share in common with Liz unless you get your act together."

"You don't think I wanted to hold her, to comfort her?"

"Why didn't you?"

If I would have been there for Liz, who would have been there for Corinne Moreland?"

"Like you always tell me, stop trying to save the world."

Save the world? I couldn't even save our jobs. Three women dead, one in hiding, and we're fired. Again. Can things get any worse?

A grinning Walter Greeley entered the kitchen, interrupting my thoughts.

"There's your answer," Ron mumbled.

"If it isn't New York City's former ace detectives. You two guys amaze me. I knew sooner or later you'd screw up and I'd get the pleasure of watching you get canned, but even I didn't think you could work this fast."

265

"Jerry tends to be an overachiever."

"Look at all he's achieved. Another dead woman and a lady in hiding, thanks to your great surveillance."

I contemplated taking a swing at him.

"Would you mind excusing us, lieutenant? Jerry and I have matters to discuss."

"Not here you don't. This area is for police personnel only. Pack your things and get out. I can phone for a few uniforms to give you a hand...."

"Do you think you can master the phone by yourself, Walt?" I said.

"Well, I have the entire NYPD to help me. What have you got?"

"A great right hook."

"You want a piece of me, punk?"

"Everybody calm down," Ron said, stepping between us.

"You need your brother to protect you, Gold? Come on, come at me!"

The absurdity of this white-haired relic goading me on, ready to rumble, made me start laughing. The harder I laughed, the hotter Greeley got. He was about to lunge at me when we were interrupted by the ring of his cell phone.

"Stand back, Ron. It's his two-minute warning. He's going to explode."

"Screw both of you." Greeley looked down at his phone and then went for the door.

"If I knew that's all it took to get rid of him, I would have called him myself," I said.

"Where do you think he's going in such a hurry?"

"Either Manhattan is under siege, or dinner. The smart money says it's prime rib night somewhere."

"It seemed urgent," Ron said, heading for the door.

"Where you going?"

"To pack my things."

"You're not thinking of quitting?"

"In their infinite wisdom, the NYPD has saved me that difficult decision, Jerry."

"I'm not quitting."

"News Flash. The powers that be took that into consideration when they fired you."

"I'm sticking with the case."

"Then you have quite a little dilemma. Without your shield, this case will be tough."

"It hasn't been so easy with it. Ron, we're close; I know it."

"You're obsessed."

"This case—"

"—will go on without the great Jerry Gold."

"Maybe longer than it has to."

"It's a dangerous thing when a cop begins to believe he's indispensable."

"What are you getting mad about, Ron? This is your chance if you want out."

"We *are* out. Read my lips. We've been released, fired, canned, ousted!"

"We'll work on our own."

"It's illegal for civilians to get involved in an active police investigation. I could be disbarred."

"I could think of worse things than one less lawyer."

"Like what?"

"A mass murderer on the loose."

"The NYPD is one of the best-equipped law enforcement organizations in the world. They don't want our help—they never did. They brought us on to do just what they did:

throw us to the wolves when the going got tough."

"I don't care what they needed; it's what I need."

"And what exactly is that?" Ron asked.

"To stop a maniac."

"Jerry, we can't use Goose, or the labs, or the crime teams. Who are we going to work with? All that's left is 1-800-P-S-Y-C-H-I-C."

Frustrated, I closed my eyes and began drifting back to the matinee in my head. Something Ron said had hit a nerve. I was on autopilot, searching beyond Corinne Moreland to the beginning of all this madness. But I still didn't know what I was looking for. I did know calling a psychic wasn't the answer. Or was it?

"Are you listening to me, Jerry?" I heard a voice say. I didn't answer it. "If you're going to ignore me, I'm going home to Emily to be ignored."

"Call 1-800-PSYCHIC," I said, almost inaudibly.

"Call 1-800-BELLEVUE. You don't need a psychic, Jerry, you need a shrink."

"A shrink?" I echoed unconsciously.

"The pressure has finally gotten to you. You sound like a broken record."

"Broken record? How about a broken CD?"

"Jerry, don't weird out on me."

"Ron, do you have the printout from Westlake's CD?"

"In my briefcase."

"Get it," I said, dragging him toward the door.

"You're going to try to crack that code *now*?"

"Don't have to. You did."

"And I did that how?"

"Go," I said, pushing Ron out of the kitchen.

As I followed him into the empty conference room I

pictured getting reinstated—and the look on Greeley's face when he discovered we had solved what he couldn't. I felt my adrenaline surging.

Ron opened his brief case and handed me the printout. Taking a pen and pad from my pocket, I began with the first line on the page.

"Do you mind telling me what we're looking for?"

"You see this fourth column on the printout containing the jumbled numbers we've attempted to decipher?"

"I've seen it in my dreams for the last few weeks."

"Well, we've been going on the premise that column was corrupted when you did the conversion."

"The file was probably encrypted, not necessarily corrupted. Get to the point."

"Patience," I said, taking my cell phone from my pocket. "What if this file wasn't corrupted or encrypted? What if we overlooked the obvious, and these numbers are as they should be?"

"You don't think I considered it might be a code?"

"What if the numbers stood for letters?"

"Been there, done that. Look here," he said pointing to a line displaying the digits 9 and 4. "There are only twenty-six letters in *my* alphabet. What does ninety-four stand for?"

"1-800-BELLEVUE."

"Who's on first?" Ron replied. "I don't want to play Abbott and Costello." He got up to leave.

"What if the numbers stand for letters? Letters on a telephone," I said, holding my cell phone in the air.

Ron stopped in his tracks.

"Numbers on a phone pad." Ron moved in next to me. "What made you think of it?"

"When you said 1-800-PSYCHIC, the old cabbie who first took me to Liz's apartment came to mind. I wasn't sure why until you said I sounded like a broken record. Then it hit me. Ben Alright said if ever I needed a cab to call him at Murray Hill 2-2232. Murray Hill once stood for MU2-2232, or 682-2232."

"Could be."

"It is," I said. I chose a line close to the top of a page. "The first number on this line is 3, which stands for the third button on the key pad, which has three letters printed above it: *D*, *E*, and *F*. The second number on the line is—"

"—One," Ron interrupted. "Which stands for the first letter on the third button or the letter—"

"—*D*," we both blurted out.

I watched as Ron worked through the next set of numbers. Slowly, the numbers 2273213193 transformed into B-R-A-D-Y. And 71424353 converted to P-H-I-L.

"Phil Brady," I said. "*She* was playing with Fungo Phil too? He's one busy ball player."

"Seems like old Fungo Phil made it around more than just the bases," Ron smirked. He gave me a high five.

"Give me part of the list. If it's in alphabetical order, our killer is going to be somewhere around Brady's name, in the *C*'s or *D*'s."

"Assuming our missing-page theory's correct," Ron added.

I smiled smugly and started working. In less than a half hour Ron and I had decoded nearly forty names, many of which were as famous as Brady's. And some of those people were quite powerful.

"Ron, if we were blackmailers, I'd say we'd hit pay dirt."

"What do you say if we're just unemployed detectives?"

"I'd say we hit pay dirt."

"Me too, but I don't see the name of any person here who would have a motive to kill these ladies."

"We're going to have to check them all out," I said. Unless..."

"What? You found something?"

"Big time."

"Who?"

"Patrick Denton."

"Lieutenant Governor Patrick Denton?"

"Yes."

"Greeley's son-in-law, Lieutenant Governor Patrick Denton?"

"One and the same," I said.

"You're sure?"

"Ron, I know how to read. It says right here: 3132628...

"Cute."

"Wouldn't this little tidbit put a permanent kink in his political career? Denton into hardcore S&M. Greeley would turn over in his grave," I laughed.

"He's not dead."

"Yet. This could do it."

"Denton could be our killer."

"I don't think so," I said, as I kept deciphering.

"You want to share your reasoning?"

"He's been stuck in Albany for the last month and a half with the budget crisis. I don't think he's had time to be anywhere near the city. We'll check it out, but I wouldn't bet on..."

"Whose name did you find this time, Big Bird's?"

"Bigger," I said, pushing my paper work in front of Ron. I knew he saw what I had seen when his jaw fell open.

271

"It makes sense," he said quietly.

I nodded.

"It explains how he knew that the victims had been branded. He had access to all the files, both old and new. It also explains why our tail never followed us into Jersey. He knew we were done for the night."

I nodded again.

"What do we do?"

I shrugged.

"Jerry, he knows everything, including—"

"—where Liz is," we said in unison.

"Call her," I shouted.

Ron grabbed my cell phone. I ran to Jeanne MacDonald's desk.

"Where's Flaherty?" I barked.

"He's at the mayor's charity gala."

"Get him on the phone."

"He's doesn't want to be disturbed."

"And I didn't want to be born good looking. Get him on the phone now," I demanded, handing her the receiver. Jeanne's face tightened. "Please."

She took the phone from my hand and punched in Flaherty's pager number, followed by 911.

"Thanks," I said, waiting impatiently for the return call.

"This better be important. I had hopes of making the police force my life's work."

"Me too," I replied.

"I don't find that very comforting."

I saw her point and was about to comment when her phone rang. I took the phone from Jeanne.

"Flaherty, we got the answer; we broke the case," I said into the phone. He began to ask rapid-fire questions. I cut him short. I had plenty of my own questions; it was answers I wanted. Then Ron barged in.

"No answer at Liz's."

I hung up on Flaherty. "Line dead?"

"No, they're just not answering."

"Or they can't answer. Jeanne, reach out to Sergeant Brown and get his squad car over to the Bronx safe house," I ordered as Ron and I headed for the door.

"Yes, sir."

We were just about at the elevator when my cell phone rang. It was Flaherty, picking up our discussion where I'd cut him off. "Chief, Ron and I are on our way to the Bronx." My cell phone signal was beginning to break up. "Where is Commissioner Daley?"

"He should be meeting me here," Flaherty replied through heavy line interference.

"He hasn't arrived?"

There was no response, just static. I was about to throw the phone against the wall when I heard the chief's voice crackle through.

"If you've found the perp, the commissioner will have to be informed...."

"Damn it, the line's dead!" I shouted loud enough so Flaherty could hear it across town.

"Technology: a wonderful thing," Ron said.

As we rode the elevator down to the lobby, all I could think about was Flaherty's voice telling me, "The commissioner will have to be informed."

Hell, he's already informed, I thought. He's our man.

273

40

I stomped on Baby's gas pedal and drove diagonally across Fifth Avenue, making a sharp left onto Thirty-eighth Street. I was racing east for the FDR Drive knowing, unlike the Rolling Stones, that time was not on our side.

"Try the number again."

"What do you think I've been doing?" Ron pressed a button on his cell, and out from the speaker poured the unanswered rings of Liz's phone.

"Damn it!" I slammed the steering wheel.

"Watch out!" Ron yelled.

I looked up and hit the brakes in time to avoid the unmoving cars lined up in front of us. I threw Baby into reverse and was about to back her up, but there were cars behind us as well.

"Hit the siren," I said, as I laid on the horn.

"There's nowhere for them to go."

I was desperate. "Hold on."

"What are you doing?"

I turned baby's wheels hard to the right and gave her the gas. We flew into the only empty space Thirty-eighth Street afforded: the sidewalk.

"Are you crazy?" Ron yelled.

"You want to get to the Bronx?"

"Yes. But I want to get there alive."

I continued up the sidewalk, hoping to catch a break. Kiss that thought good bye. A Con Edison utility crew had set up a work tent on the next block. I couldn't go left, and I couldn't go forward, so I went the only direction I could, right. Which as it turns out was wrong. Third Avenue ran in the opposite direction.

"This is a one-way street," Ron screamed.

"I'm only going one way."

"Then go fast before you get us killed."

Without sparing any horsepower I raced to the first empty side street going in the right direction. Within minutes we were across town and on our way to the Bronx.

We pulled up in front of the safe house. Without exchanging a word, I banged my fist on the dashboard. The glove compartment opened, revealing two snub-nose .38 caliber police specials tucked into ankle holsters.

"They're not much, but they're all I got," I said, handing one to my brother. We both checked the weapons with a quick spin of the chambers. Flipping them closed, we ran for the building.

"She's on the third floor, middle apartment," Ron said, running up the stairs behind me.

Arriving at the floor, I saw an open door.

"Looks empty, Jerry. Could be a set up. Stick to procedure."

I responded by diving low into the apartment, ready to blow away anything that didn't resemble Liz or a cop. I saw neither: just a large, empty living room. I scanned the kitchen to my left and the hallway beyond. Still nothing.

"What happened to procedure?" Ron asked, falling in behind me.

"The hell with procedure; where's Liz?"

"Check the bathroom, and I'll take the bedroom."

I found the bathroom door partially open; the light pouring out from behind it cut the dark hallway in half. The only sound I heard was the hum of the ventilation fan. Staying tight to the wall, I pushed the door. It moved slightly, no further. Something was blocking it. Looking down I saw that the door was pressing against a female foot. A bare female foot drenched in red.

Not Liz. Please not Liz.

I forced my way in. There, lying in a pool of blood, was the body of a woman.

It was not Liz's body.

A wave of relief rolled through me, but it only lasted an instant. I knelt down to check the victim's neck for a pulse. There wasn't one. Her ID tag read Detective Maria Gonzales. She was still warm to the touch. I reached for my cell phone called 911 and said, "officer down" twice, then gave the operator the address.

"Jerry!"

I ran for the bedroom. There laid out on the floor was Walter Greeley. Ron was kneeling beside him.

"Dead?"

"He'll live. Has an ugly gash on his head."

"Ask him about Liz," I said.

"He's unconscious. We're not going to get anything from him."

"Bring him around. He knows where Daley took her."

"I've called EMS. He's out, Jerry."

"And so are we without him. She could be anywhere in the city."

"We'll find her."

"You're damn right and after I do I'm going to rip Daley's fucking heart out." I punched the wall.

"What have we got here?" a voice said from behind.

"A complete fuckup," I said.

I watched Officer Brown approach.

"One dead, one injured," Ron said, exiting the bathroom. "EMS and backup's been called. Jerry, did you notice anything about the detective in the bathroom?"

"She took a .22 in the back of the head."

"What?"

"You heard me. He shot her."

"A .22 is not his MO."

"Definitely not," Ron said. "I think the commissioner planned to play with Liz right here, so he did Gonzales fast with a .22."

"Like the one that sprayed Flaherty's car and the one from his study that won him all the awards."

"Gonzales must have threatened him. Daley wasn't used to dealing with women who could defend themselves."

"Then he goes to play with Liz, but he's interrupted by Greeley."

"Right, so he takes Greeley out."

"And takes Liz somewhere he can torture her and won't be interrupted."

"That's my guess, too. If he wanted her dead, she'd be on the floor next to Gonzales," Ron said. "He couldn't have left long ago. We have some time."

"We could have all the time in the world and still never find her."

Ron didn't answer. He didn't have to. I was right. The odds of finding her in time in a city the size of New York were slim.

"Let's put out an APB on Daley."

"What cop in his right mind is going to nail the commissioner of police?""You have a better idea?" Ron asked me.

I didn't, but I was trying hard to think of one. And that's when I saw it. There, in the kitchen, on the immaculately clean floor, was an empty container.

"What's that?" Brown asked as I knelt down.

"A ripped container. A White Castle hamburger container."

"Probably fell out of the trash," Brown said.

"Maybe." I went over to the trashcan and lifted the lid. There were other hamburger containers in there, hamburgers intact. "How did it get on the floor?"

"Maybe it fell out during a struggle," Brown replied.

"What struggle? Do you see anything here disturbed other than my partner?" Ron said.

"What was Liz doing when you left her earlier, Ron?"

"Cleaning."

"That's it."

"What's it?" Brown questioned.

"When Liz is upset, she cleans. She wouldn't leave anything on the floor unless she wanted us to see it."

"Why not? My wife leaves more than that when she

cleans. If you can call what she does cleaning," Brown said.

"This woman is compulsive. She wouldn't do that," Ron replied. "Besides, I don't think she'd ever go to a White Castle, let alone pick through the trash for one of their containers."

"You're right. I know where they took her," I called out as I started for the door. "Brown, hang out here for the backup."

"Where are we going?" Ron asked, following me.

I flipped Ron the empty container as we headed down the stairs. "She's telling us he took her there."

"To White Castle?"

"To *the* castle. Look again. What do you see?"

"A ripped carton. Liz didn't even eat fast food. I was there when she threw the burgers away."

"She would. But did she take any of the burgers out of their container?"

"No, why would she?"

"She wouldn't. But this container is burger-less—and ripped. Read the carton."

"*Castle*. It reads *Castle*." The word *White* had been torn away.

"You've got it. And we've got him!"

41

"She tore away the other words on the carton to tell us she was being taken to a castle?" Ron asked.

"What could be simpler?" I kicked Baby into first.

"Nothing, if you're in Scotland."

We shot down Bruckner Boulevard toward the Triborough Bridge. As we drove, I explained what Liz had taught me: that 'the castle' was a euphemism for an S&M playroom or dungeon.

"Judy Russo's dungeon was Commissioner Daley's playroom of choice," I said, taking the corner of East Seventy-eighth Street on two wheels. Slamming on the breaks, Baby came to a screeching halt in front of 'the castle'.

"It looks quiet, Jerry. Maybe he didn't bring her here."

We approached the back door.

"He's here all right. I can feel him."

Frozen rain started to fall.

"God, I hate the cold," I said, heading for the building.

"Let's wait for backup, Jerry."

"He's got Liz; I'm not waiting."

I kicked in the door, and we burst in. Ron went right and I went left, our guns in front of us. In the foyer, everything was still. As my eyes adjusted to the darkness, I noticed the curtains that led down to the dungeon. I peeled them back, and a dim light bathed the room. In the soft light, I saw the mannequin that had once held the executioner's suit. It was bare.

"Down in the dungeon," I whispered. *Don't let us be too late.*

Ron stood at the head of the stairs, covering me as I rushed down. The playroom was quiet. I cased the room— no sign of Liz. The mirrored walls and the dim lights were making me jumpy. Ron moved in behind me as we weaved among the whipping posts, stocks, and Saint Andrew's crosses. Midway through the room, Ron motioned to the mock doctor's office. The door was shut.

"He's got her in the back room?" I mouthed, unsure. Ron nodded.

"I'm going in."

"That office has only one way in or out. You move now you'll be cornering a desperate man."

I nodded. I positioned myself behind a large, black iron figure adjacent to the room. The iron maiden, with its massive girth, made excellent cover. I listened hard, hoping to hear any movements in the office. It must have been sound-proofed—or empty. I kept an eye on the door, hoping Daley might make an appearance so I could take him out with a clean shot. No such luck.

"Jerry!" Ron stepped back from the iron figure and pointed toward its base. A pool of blood was spreading. "We're not alone."

Oh God, Liz. I felt my hand tremble as I tucked my .38 into my belt. *Don't let it end like this. Don't let it be her.*

I pried apart the two iron halves making up the vicious maiden. Blood funneled downward into two red tributaries that gathered in a pool by our feet. With one fast tug I opened the iron device. Spikes lined the cavity and impaled a figure within. It took a second for what I saw to register.

"Jerry—it's Commissioner Daley."

The commissioner was being held in place by iron spikes that pierced many different parts of his body. His eyes had been gouged out, and on the middle of the forehead was a small branded *R*. Ron and I looked at each other.

"If he's here, then who's in there?" Ron whispered.

"Good question. I'll let you know."

I pulled my .38 from my belt, turned, and kicked in the door. The wood around the lock splintered. I jumped into the room before the door swung closed behind me.

I saw Liz suspended by her wrists from chains attached to a beam overhead. She was stripped naked; her lean body swayed in the air. Her long blonde hair was entwined in the left hand of her captor: the Executioner.

The maniac grabbed Liz and positioned her between us. I didn't dare attempt a shot. Staring at me, the Executioner pulled hard on Liz's hair, jerking her head back and exposing her smooth, soft, white neck. The Executioner's right hand rose, bringing with it a razor-sharp scalpel. Feeling the blade press against her throat, Liz tried to call out, but the red latex ball lodged in her mouth made it impossible.

"It's over. Put the knife down and step away."

As I moved closer, the Executioner released Liz's hair and spun her around. I could see she had been beaten like all the others.

"The whore must die," a voice said, pressing the scalpel closer to Liz's throat. "Drop your gun and kick it away."

I gripped my pistol tighter.

"My patient would also like you to comply," the Executioner said, methodically dragging the flat side of the scalpel across Liz's delicate throat. "You're making her nervous, Detective Gold."

"You know my name?"

"Yes," the Executioner said, turning Liz to face me once more. "Now drop your weapon, or I dispatch her now."

The sharp steel at Liz's throat began to draw blood. I dropped my pistol.

"Kick it away," the voice said. I complied.

"Now what?" I asked, listening hard, trying to recognize the voice, to identify who was under the mask. I had to keep him talking. I was sure Ron was out there somewhere, vying for a position to take his shot.

"You know the difference between right and wrong, detective? You know she chose to do wrong. Her vocation is the devil's work. She must be punished."

"She's suffered enough."

"What about the suffering she's caused?" The Executioner smacked Liz's bruised bottom. Her body lurched forward, causing the blade beneath her neck to draw more blood.

"What suffering could she or any of those women have

caused that would justify taking their lives?"

"They played in manners that were unholy. They involved themselves with others."

"Others?" I repeated, trying to keep the voice talking. It was familiar. "They were not the only ones playing. Why single them out?"

Who the hell was it? I knew I'd heard that voice before—but where?

"They played with what didn't belong to them. You're supposed to be a man of justice, but you know precious little about the wrongs they've committed."

"Then explain."

"There's nothing to explain. Only to punish."

"Is that your idea of justice?" I pointed to Liz.

"For stealing, yes. 'Thou shalt bruise them with a rod,' the Bible says. Spare the rod and..." the maniac said smugly, removing the blade from Liz's neck.

I saw my chance and rushed forward. I was wrong. From out of the black robe came a .22 caliber gun. It was pointed at me. I stopped well short of my target.

"Eager to die, detective?"

Where the hell was Ron? Why hadn't he tried a shot? I peered at the closed door behind me. He couldn't shoot what he couldn't see.

"This isn't a game."

"It's all a game, detective."

My eyes shifted around the room, looking for a weapon. A few feet to my right was a table holding a tray of scalpels. A sharp scalpel could make a great weapon, but a gun would make a better one. Alongside the tray, on the corner of the table, was an open bottle of alcohol—useful if I could get close enough to throw it in his eyes, but still not better

284

than a gun.

"You enjoy games, detective?"

"I dabble in checkers," I said from where I stood. "You want to give me the weapon and we'll play best of three?" I observed an iron bucket holding two branding irons resting in hot coals. The bucket sat next to the table.

"No checkers."

"Don't play anything else." I moved slowly toward the irons.

"A shame you can't appreciate this game, because it's about to crescendo to its climax."

Crescendo. Crescendo. The word echoed in my head. An odd choice of words—and that voice...

"Say good-bye to your friend, detective."

The Executioner raised the gun to Liz's temple. As the trigger drew back, I knew whom I was talking to.

"Brava," I shouted. "Brava!"

The Executioner lowered the gun slightly.

"You do retain what you're taught. Bravo, detective."

Our eyes locked as my lips framed a name. Then came a stunned silence.

Slowly, carefully, the Executioner removed the hood, confirming what I already knew. The face of Rose Daley, the commissioner's wife, appeared.

"Don't. You've caused enough pain," I said gently. "It's time to stop. She's suffered enough. You've suffered enough...."

"What do you know about my suffering?"

"I know this won't ease it. Give me the gun."

I put my hand out.

"It's too late for that."

"Rose..."

"I refused to sit and watch as they tore him away. Those bitches! Tempting him into unholy trysts. He was a leader, a man of strength, a protector of the law. They perverted him."

"Even protectors stray." I crept cautiously toward the irons.

"I gave him everything: wealth, power, love. In return, after he took it all, he didn't have need for his—"

"—wife?"

"Yes, his wife."

I egged her on.

"I said we would meet again, detective. Where is your partner?"

Good question. Where *was* my partner? "I'm alone."

"You wouldn't lie to your employer's wife, would you?"

"I'm not with the NYPD anymore."

"Neither is your employer," she pointed toward the Iron Maiden and laughed a long, cold laugh.

"Rose, it doesn't have to end this way. I can get you help. Give me the gun." I stepped toward her.

"I'm quite good with this," she warned. I heard the hammer of the gun click. "I suggest you stay where you are."

Damn good suggestion. Looking down the barrel of the gun convinced me that further movement would not be in my best interest. I stood still, feeling the surgical table press against my side. "The study? Those trophies were—"

"—mine."

"The picture... The commissioner was handing you the trophy."

"Surprised? The commissioner and I shared many interests."

"Like S&M?"

"Filth. Don't include me in that filth. It was not my perversion."

"That's just your evening wear?"

"My costume. Part of the game. One must always dress for the part."

"Why the masquerade, Rose? The Madam Murderer impersonation? All the death and suffering? For what? Jealousy?"

"Retribution. We were fine until he came back into our lives," she spat.

"Senator DiCenzio?"

"That pimp, DiCenzio. He introduced my Raymond to this world of sin. Because of him I had to learn these games to please him. I defiled myself and even then, even then—"

"—he preferred these other women."

"Not women. Whores!" she cried. "He made me play their sick games, and when I no longer would, he went to them. He shut me out."

"But why copy the Madam Murderer?"

"It was easy enough to gain access to my husband's private files. We shared the study. The Madam Murderer was his most cherished case. He said he had characteristics of Jack the Ripper. Raymond loved playing games. He insisted I play. I insisted he play one of mine. In the end," she laughed, "I won, retrieved him from the obscenity he loved, and dispatched him to God—as I will now dispatch her to hell."

Rose Daley backed up cautiously toward the hot irons, keeping her gun aimed at me the entire time.

"I think you may have an iron deficiency. Perhaps you haven't had some today young lady?" Rose said, grinning at

Liz, who hung their, terrified. "The doctor has just the treatment."

Rose reached behind for one of the hot pokers. Hearing the iron rustle among the coals, Liz twisted her body toward her captor. The sudden movement stole Rose's attention.

Seeing a chance, I pushed my hip hard into the table. The scalpels scattered, and the open bottle of rubbing alcohol fell into the hot coals and burst into flames. The fire caught hold of Rose's sleeve, engulfing her hand. As she tried frantically to remove the black cloak, I lunged forward and kicked her gun away. I was about to knock her lights out when she took hold of the hot iron and jabbed it deep into my left shoulder.

I yelled. The pain was instantaneous and intense, and I could smell my burning flesh. She was trying to cram that hot poker right through me. I faded back, giving myself enough room to reach around and clock her with a weak right. She dropped the iron and we both went sprawling to the floor just as Ron entered the room.

"Take the shot!" I screamed as Rose and I rolled toward her gun.

"You're in the way."

I landed on top of Rose as she got hold of her gun. She fired at Ron. He dove for cover behind the examining table. I reached for her weapon, but she punched my wounded shoulder. I yelled as the pain shot through my body.

What happened next is a blur—Ron filled in the details for me later. Rolling backward, she took aim at Liz.

"You stupid bitch," I spit.

I mustered up what strength I had left to lunge at her. I hit her with another right to the jaw just as she turned to release another round into my already wounded shoulder.

Rose's head snapped back, and she landed hard on the floor. Ron was over her, gun drawn, but she was out.

Light-headed, I placed my hand gently over my wound. When I withdrew it, it was covered in blood—my blood. After cuffing Rose Daley, Ron placed a towel over my shoulder and told me to put as much pressure on the wound as I could.

"Help Liz," I insisted. I leaned against the table as Ron released her and then removed his coat to drape over her bare body. Barely standing, she came to me. I kissed her tear-stained face as we embraced.

"You're safe now," I uttered hoarsely. She began to cry quietly. Despite the pain in my shoulder, I held her closer. I looked over at Ron. "Nice shooting, partner."

"I wasn't going to risk hitting you. I didn't have a shot."

"What if she had killed me?"

"Then I would have had a great shot." Ron moved toward a waking Rose Daley. "Rose Daley, you have the right to remain silent," Ron intoned. "Anything you say..."

We were arresting one of the most vicious killers the city had seen since Son of Sam. Looking at her now, all I saw was a sad woman pushed over the edge by a sick senator and a depraved husband.

It should have been Vinny DiCenzio and the commissioner hearing their Miranda rights. But they already had paid a higher price.

42

"Where are they?" I asked impatiently

"The lady's being attended to inside. You're a lucky man, detective," the medic said as she took care of my shoulder.

"I don't feel lucky."

"A few inches lower and you wouldn't feel anything at all—ever."

"Just finish bandaging me, Florence Nightingale."

Cold and tired, I sat on the back bumper of the ambulance looking out into the dark. Sometime during the night the sleet had changed to snow: a soft, gentle snow. I watched as the drifting white flakes assumed the colors of the flashing lights of the ambulance and patrol cars.

"How are you feeling?"

I turned my head and saw Flaherty.

"I hate winter."

"The crime unit is about finished."

I didn't answer. I watched as to two female detectives escorted Rose Daley out of the castle and into a waiting unmarked car.

"What will happen to her?"

"That's up to the DA," Flaherty said. "My guess, she'll see the inside of an exclusive psychiatric hospital for the next few years."

"A few years? She murdered five people."

"The family is old money. If you have political aspirations, the van de Meer name matters."

I stood and slowly tried to get my jacket over my shoulder.

"You shouldn't be up," Ms. EMS informed me. "You're going to start bleeding again."

"I've heard Elizabeth Drake's account of what went on in there. How did you know it was Daley?"

"Dumb luck."

"I'm listening."

"*Crescendo*. She used the word *crescendo*. I thought it was odd."

"It is."

"Not for a music professor. It started me thinking."

"Whatever it started, it finished. You and Ron did the job proud."

"Sure."

Flaherty headed back into the building.

I watched as the car holding Rose Daley headed down the street. I didn't know if what the law had in mind for Rose was right or wrong. I only knew it wasn't my decision. I'd made enough decisions tonight.

Making my way slowly towards the castle, I saw two paramedics coming down the steps with a stretcher. Walking alongside was Ron, holding Liz's hand. I moved through the crowd to meet them.

"They just gave her something to help her sleep," Ron said, placing Liz's soft hand into mine. I could see bruises around her delicate wrists where the chains had bound her. Looking deep into Liz's eyes, I could see the pain she was in. I leaned over and kissed her gently on the forehead. I didn't ask her if she was alright, though I wanted to hear her say she was. It was going to take a long time for her to move beyond what had gone down here tonight.

"You look wonderful," I smiled. Liz motioned for me to come closer.

"Thank you," she whispered.

"Hey, 'serve and protect,'" I said, softly combing her hair with my fingers.

"You're hurt."

I winced as she touched my bandage.

"I still get to you, detective." She smiled faintly. "God help me, I think I love you, Jerry Gold."

I don't know why I couldn't repeat the words that had fallen so easily from Liz's lips. It wasn't that I didn't want to. I just didn't know how.

As they moved her toward the waiting ambulance, her eyes began to close, and another smile came to her lips. I knew she understood.

"Hey you! Detective." Ms. EMS called out.

Ron and I turned.

"The one with the hole in his shoulder bleeding on the street. You ready to get in the ambulance, or should I call a hearse?"

292

I looked down at my shoulder. Blood was beginning to seep through the bandage. I started for the ambulance when a black Ford with tinted windows pulled up. Detective David Wilkins appeared from behind the wheel. Exiting from the passenger's side was none other than Deputy Police Commissioner Edward Sanchez.

"Fine job, detectives," Sanchez bellowed while extending his hand.

"We're not detectives; we were terminated," Ron reminded him. We both ignored his hand.

He put his hand back at his side. "An oversight. My new aide will see to that." He nodded toward Wilkins.

"In case you're interested, Dave, your previous partner survived the attack," Ron said.

Wilkins couldn't have cared less. I tried to laugh but it hurt too much.

"Something strike you as particularly funny, detective?"

"Pathetic, not funny."

"You obviously have something to say. Say it."

"You used us, Sanchez."

"How's that?"

"You knew from the minute you brought us on there was no Evanston—no Madam Murderer."

"So did you," Wilkins said. "You saw the medical examiner's reports. He said Crisco had been used, not Vaseline. Evanston used Vaseline."

"Goose never put that into his report," Ron said, confronting Sanchez. "Did you know Wilkins was breaking and entering, deputy commissioner? Or is it just 'commissioner' now?"

Sanchez remained silent.

"You knew Commissioner Daley was involved," I said.

"Wilkins gave you Susan Atwell's diary." I turned toward Wilkins. "Didn't you, bozo? Didn't think we'd track that down, Dave?"

I turned back to Sanchez. "Did you know Wilkins removed a few key pages? Was that on your orders, or did Dave get the idea himself? A little blackmail, huh Dave?"

"Call it insurance."

"Quiet, Wilkins," Sanchez said sharply. "That's an interesting story, Gold. But that's all it is. Can you substantiate those allegations?"

"You politicians amaze me. You're more concerned with what I can prove than what you did. You wanted to be commissioner so badly you found a way to embarrass Commissioner Daley and you jumped at it. You didn't have the balls to call him out yourself. You used us as your hired guns."

"I have something to offer this city. I can do good things for the people," Sanchez roared.

"Save that for the press."

"Then let's talk straight, Gold," Sanchez grinned. "You're going to forget this conversation after tonight."

"Am I?"

"Because I have what you need."

He nodded toward Wilkins. Reaching into his overcoat, Wilkins withdrew two gold shields. Our gold shields.

"Do the right thing and you'll not only be heroes, you'll be back on the job with the gratitude of the next commissioner of police."

"We'll be on the same team again," Wilkins said smugly as he tossed me my shield.

I watched as everything I had ever wanted drifted through the air. I made no attempt to catch it. The shield landed at my feet. As the snow began to cover it, I stepped to the side and headed toward where I had parked Baby. Ron gave me a hand.

"Take me to the hospital. I want to see Liz."

"Where do you think you're going?" Wilkins yelled.

"Let them go," Sanchez replied calmly. "They'll be back."

"Don't hold your breath."

"Do you know what you're saying, Jerry?" Ron asked.

"No, but it feels right."

Ron pulled Baby onto the street. I could hear ice being crushed beneath her wheels. The windshield wipers rhythmically brushed back and forth while I watched the gently falling snow. I had always preferred the warmth of the other seasons. But the snow now coated the city with a purity I hadn't felt in some time.

I began to feel a chill. I looked down: shirt, jacket, and overcoat were all soaked with blood. I closed my eyes, unconcerned, content in knowing that the one person I trusted most was bringing me closer every moment to the woman I loved. Suddenly I didn't feel so cold.

Acknowledgements

This work could not have been possible if not for the assistance and support of the following people:

Sandy and Bill Feldman who stopped me from destroying the first draft with words of encouragement. If you're dissatisfied with this work talk to them.

Detective Douglas Lang (NYPD, Retired). Doug's insight to the life of a detective was invaluable. His willingness to inform and his offbeat humor helped to breathe life into the brothers.

Joyce Segal Goldin whose understanding of the English language and initiall editing helped to make me look literate.

Rob Wolf for his technical genius.

Michael Lopez and Claire McNulty for all their input.

The best family and friends anyone could ask for. I would need another book to thank them all, but you know who you are.

To the writer's circle of West 66th Street. A place to perfect my stories.

Most of all to Ann Loring for teaching us what we never thought we could learn. Her patience, talent, and advice helped many working in the art of screenwriting, plays, and novels. We count ourselves fortunate to have been among them.

Made in the USA
Lexington, KY
31 October 2016